Falling

*01

Yu Cheng
Author

Via Lactea

Falling

An imprint of Via Lactea Ltd.

Author: Yu Cheng
Translators: Arien; Yun; Hobbitsflower
Editor: Moca
Proofreader: OWL
Layout Designer: Ayan

CONTACT:
Customer Support: info@vialactea.ca
Wholesale & Distribution: market@vialactea.ca
Other Cooperation: https://vialactea.ca/pages/cooperation
Discord Channel: https://discord.gg/vialactea

Follow us on X/Instagram/Facebook: @ViaLactea_Ltd
Official Website: www.vialactea.ca

ISBN 978-1-77408-520-2 (pbk)
Printed in Canada

LOCATION:
Shops At Waterloo Town Square
#27, 75 King Street South, Waterloo, ON
Canada
N2J 1P2

"*Good night,*

my darling."

CONTENT

Volume 01

Falling

CHAPTER 01

"LOOK. That's him."

Sitting in a corner shop, Ye Qin had just taken a gulp of water when Zhou Feng suddenly elbowed him.

Through the store window, Ye Qin squinted at a tall teenage boy in a white T-shirt and black trousers. He was unloading boxes of bottled water from a delivery van. And it was a piece of cake for him, it seemed—he piled three boxes into a stack and walked towards the shop.

Ye Qin licked the tiny drops of water lingering on his upper lip, and absently asked, "Sun Yiran... She'd rather sit in a van with a guy like that?"

It took Zhou Feng a few seconds to digest those words before he banged on the table. "How can that be?! That guy's from the other class; now he's working part-time here. He's not a real delivery man."

Ye Qin's eyes chased after the boy, observing how he set those three heavy boxes on the ground, adeptly opened them, and grabbed two bottles in each hand before putting them all neatly aligned on the shelves. The midday sun was burning hot, yet there wasn't a sign of perspiration on him—unlike other schoolboys who usually sweat like pigs after only a stroll across the recreational yard, their soaked clothes sticking to filthy flesh.

Finishing another gulp, Ye Qin smacked his lips and frowned. "He studies here; at our school?"

"Yes. Weren't you listening to me? He transferred from the university's affiliated high school to ours when the semester began. Straight-A student with a scholarship. I heard that the school promised him a six-digit bonus once he's admitted to a top university, like Tsinghua or Beida." Zhou Feng spat at the thought and continued, "See how the school board kisses his ass just because he can help build them a better reputation? Last month, he got reported *again* for doing part-time jobs outside school. Guess how the teachers handled it? They just said that his jobs didn't impact his attendance. And that was it! I see how it is now—regulations and rules mean jack shit when it comes to the top students."

Zhou Feng was so furious with this guy for one simple reason: Sun Yiran, the girl he'd been pursuing recently, had just friend-zoned him. After enjoying being brought breakfast by him for nearly two months, she told him with wringing hands, "Sorry, I'm actually...into someone else."

Zhou Feng had instantly felt the adrenaline coursing through his veins. He managed to make Sun Yiran tell him who the "someone else" was, and then he immediately dragged his buddy, Ye Qin, to this place, in order to teach the boy a lesson he would never forget.

Ye Qin was far from getting as wound-up as his friend. He gracefully drank his water, and knocked on the table with the empty bottle. "Tell me, have they started dating yet?"

Shaking his head, Zhou Feng answered, "No."

"Then what am I here for?"

Zhou Feng had really gone so haywire that he'd just dragged

Ye Qin all the way down here. But now he was no less confused than Ye Qin was, having totally forgotten why he needed the latter to come.

Such low-level EQ...Ye Qin surrendered to his muddle-headed friend. Pursing his lips, he concluded, "So, Sun Yiran likes him. You like Sun Yiran. But none of you are actually in a relationship. That means you still have a chance."

"But..." Zhou Feng went tongue-tied.

Ye Qin tapped Zhou Feng on the head with the bottle. "But what? You got two ways out. You can either try to win her back, or back off and chase someone else. Need me to flip a coin for you?"

Saying this, Ye Qin reached into his pocket, only to have his hand pressed down by Zhou Feng.

"Wait, I got this... I can do it myself," Zhou Feng said coyly.

Ye Qin tossed the bottle into the bin, rose to his feet, and was about to leave. "Fine. I'm off. Cover for me this afternoon, in Mr. Sun's class."

Zhou Feng immediately jumped to his feet. "Where are you going? I don't dare lie to Mr. Sun anymore. Last time he was *this* close to calling my parents."

Ye Qin pulled the car keys from his pocket and juggled them in his hand. "I forgot who it was that wanted to borrow my car yesterday. Was it Liu Yangfan, or Zhao Yue...?"

Upon hearing this, Zhou Feng raised his hands at once, giving Ye Qin a very bitter look as he compromised. "Fine. It was me. I asked Sun Yiran to hang out with me on the outskirts of Beijing next week. I'll keep you out of trouble; not just once, but a million times. Is that enough?"

Ye Qin was satisfied. He balled the keys together in his fist and swung it into Zhou Feng's shoulder, trying to comfort him. "Here's what I think. Sun Yiran said yes to your invite, so there's still a chance for you two. Try harder. Don't give up so easily."

The water they'd bought here tasted weird, and Ye Qin was still feeling odd when he exited the small shop. He turned on his heel and was about to sneak out through the school's back gate, when he inadvertently glanced through the shop window and saw Zhou Feng's "love rival" was still carrying stuff around.

Ye Qin's good eyesight allowed him to make out the biceps under the guy's short sleeves, which were firm and sleek even seen from afar. A girl was talking to him, so he slightly angled his head toward her, revealing a Roman nose and a pair of thin, naturally curved lips.

Ye Qin rested his gaze on the guy's profile for a second. This one looked nothing like a typical model student, he thought.

Only a small side entrance by the back gate was open during the lunch break, which allowed one person to pass at a time. The elderly gatekeeper was drowsing in his booth. Ye Qin strode out the gate in an experienced manner and met a real model student head-on: Liao Yifang happened to be parking his bicycle there.

The school Ye Qin attended was High School No. 6; barely good enough to be counted as a key school at the district level. In order to "promote inclusive education with an emphasis on cultivating high-caliber talent" as the national authorities required, this high school welcomed qualified students, unqualified students who were willing to pay extra fees, and outstanding students who were invited to enroll with scholarships. The brilliant students in the third group, such as Liao Yifang, constituted the pillars of the school's reputation. They were expected to pass the National College Entrance Examination with flying colors and receive offers from the country's top universities, so that their names could appear on red banners reading "Congratulations to Our Student xxx for Their Admission to xx University" above the school's front gate.

Most students, along with their parents, chose this school for fortune or for fame. Ye Qin, however, was never one of their number. The reason he chose this school was due to its proximity to his home. It was way more convenient for him than some boring international school.

For instance, he could walk home right now in a mere fifteen minutes. Every day, he could have all three meals at home and more time for sleep, sometimes even taking a nap after lunch. Moreover, the school wasn't too strict with students, so he could study and live at a slow and comfortable pace. When he was about to enter high school, Ye Qin tried his best to reason with his parents, even going as far as crying and nagging at his dad, so he could attend this school in particular. He doubted there could ever be a better fit for him.

Yet, even the paradise was be perfect. Having Liao Yifang as his class monitor, who was much more responsible and serious than his head teacher, was not good news for Ye Qin. Liao Yifang was dubbed "Liao Baoyuan" (meaning he was a *very* good Samaritan) because not only did he work hard himself and help the teachers encourage other students, but he also spent all his spare time and energy caring for the daily lives of his classmates. He even knew when each girl in the class was on her period and would ask for a break for her in P.E. classes. Completely a giver, he was.

But his kindness could be quite annoying for the rebellious seventeen- to eighteen-year-olds—for example, it was at this very moment.

With his bike locked, Liao Yifang ran towards Ye Qin, several books in hand. "Hey, where are you heading? You're supposed to be preparing for the next class. There's only three minutes to go."

The road near the back gate was quite narrow, so it was

impossible to get away from Liao Yifang. Ye Qin therefore chose to answer him with a lie. "I'm going home to grab a book for an afternoon class."

Liao Yifang turned even more serious. "Which book? Physics or biology? I can borrow one from the next class for you."

Ye Qin barely resisted rolling his eyes, but he still managed to smile. "Both. It's okay. Don't bother. I also borrowed Sun Yiran's notebook yesterday and left it at home as well. If I don't return it this afternoon, she may very well kill me."

Liao Yifang pushed up his glasses. "I see. Then hurry up! I'm going to borrow Chemistry notes from Cheng-tongxue in the next class; I'll get a copy for you, too. Your class ranking dropped by five places last week."

Ye Qin had never heard of any "Cheng" in the next class. But right now, he just wanted to brush the class monitor off and leave as soon as he could. So he thanked him with a big grin, and then ran away.

Ye Qin had gotten hung up because of Zhou Feng's love issue, and he also happened to leave his car at home today. Luckily, he ran fast enough to pick up the flowers and cake he had ordered on the way.

When he got home, his mother Luo Qiuling was about to lie down for a nap. Catching sight of her son, however, she put her housecoat back on and told the maid to set out the jelly milk cubes that had just been put into the fridge. She then led her dear son to the table.

"They've been ready the whole morning, but you got home so late. Eat. They're not as fresh anymore."

Luo Qiuling's voice was as gentle as a subtle breeze, making Ye Qin less fretful about the fact that his dad wasn't home. He nibbled at the dainty cubes while praising them. "This is good."

Luo Qiuling gave him a very tender smile. "You don't need to be in such a hurry. It's okay if you only come home in the evening."

Ye Qin patted the cake box. "If I wait till evening, the flowers and the cake won't be as fresh."

Ye Qin didn't choose numbered birthday cake candles. It would be hard for a stranger to tell by appearance that Luo Qiuling was over 40. She held her hands together and rested her chin on them. The sunlight cast a soft golden glow as she made her birthday wish, as if forming a celestial halo around her.

Ye Qin's eyes narrowed slightly. He could almost see time flashing backward—this woman in her white dress returning to the maiden in the old pictures; innocent and carefree. Yet her beautiful eyes remained unchanged: they were forever lit by her gentleness.

With Zhou Feng there to cover for him, of course Ye Qin wouldn't go back to school now.

However, he still didn't take his car. Instead, he casually wiped off his dusty bicycle and set out on it.

The cellphone in his pocket was giving him directions through his earphones. He made a number of turns as he was told, and slowed down when he saw a sign saying "Yulin Compound."

He had never been here before. Even when he drove by this place in the past, he never really looked at it. Several unkempt five-story buildings were jostling each other. There had to have been at least 300 households living here, but the whole compound was no bigger than half of the suburban villa that belonged to the Ye Family.

Ye Qin sneered at the thought that his father was hiding his young lover in such an awful place. Well done for the old man.

Since the gate of the compound was unguarded, Ye Qin entered the place very easily. The building numbers on the

weather-stained exterior walls had long been worn away. Ye Qin asked an elderly man strolling around the open area before realizing that he was standing right in front of building #3.

He looked up, but only saw clothing of various colors hung from balconies. Nothing else in particular.

The summer heat hadn't yet subsided, though the autumn was already coming. The old man tilted his head back just like Ye Qin did while fanning himself. "Which one are you looking at?"

Ye Qin caught a whiff of rancid food waste from the wide-open rubbish bins at the foot of the building. He frowned and shook his head. "None of them." Then he turned his bike around and looped back toward the gate.

Before he'd pedaled twenty meters, he turned his bike around and looped back. With one foot balancing the bike, he slightly lifted his chin to hide his anxiety with arrogance. He asked of the old man who was still standing there, "Excuse me, is there a woman whose family name is Cheng living in this building?"

Ye Qin had intended to skip the self-study session in the evening, but Zhou Feng kept calling him every fifteen minutes. Unable to get through to him, Zhou Feng started bombarding him with text messages.

"Mr. Sun's here!"

"He's back 2 hand out chemistry exam papers!"

"Roll calling! I said u'r in the restroom."

"Yiran's also asking about ur whereabouts. Is she gonna tell her dad?"

"Liao Baoyuan's on the way to the restroom to find u!"

"COME BACK plz!!!! I really can't do it anymore."

Ye Qin couldn't stand his pestering, so he turned off his phone and continued resting on the massage chair.

After a while, his friends woke him up. "A-Qin, Lao-Zhou's looking for you. He wants you to turn on your phone."

Zhou Feng and Ye Qin usually hung out with the same group of people. When you couldn't reach Ye Qin, just reach out to this crew, and you could definitely get through to him.

With his eyes still closed, Ye Qin turned on his phone and accepted the incoming call from Zhou Feng. Zhou Feng's voice boomed through the phone.

"Come back *now*! The class monitor is going to Mr. Sun's office with the attendance record!"

"Make him stay. I'll be there in a minute." Ye Qin felt dizzy, and also had a headache. He put Ye Qin on speaker, set the phone aside, and slowly pulled himself up to get dressed.

"It's impossible! Fuck!" Zhou Feng shouted. A burst of chaotic noise filtered through the phone, and Zhou Feng's voice seemed to be dragged away. "You look so skinny. Where does all that strength come from?!"

Fresh out of the bath, Ye Qin felt exhausted, so he asked an attendant to call him a cab. He meant to take his bike with him, but the trunk of the taxi wasn't big enough, so he just left it behind in the hall of the club.

With his head tilted to the side, he kept drowsing all the way back to school. When he got out of the car, he finally felt like himself again after a good stretch. He picked up the drink he'd brought from the club, and swaggered toward the teaching building.

Upon his arrival in the classroom, Ye Qin heard the bell ring, reminding students to get ready for the evening's self-study session. The sight of him made Zhou Feng so thrilled it was as if God himself had come. Zhou Feng couldn't help but hug Ye Qin while pitifully narrating how he'd tried his best to cover for him in front of Mr. Sun, and how he'd stopped the class monitor

from leaving the classroom with a stroke of genius.

"I saw Mr. Sun coming from the far end of the corridor. And the class monitor was about to leave his seat. But before you even knew it—I pushed him up against the wall, and immediately covered his mouth with my free hand..."

Ye Qin conjured up that image and felt a shudder go down his spine. "Okay, okay. I can't thank you enough. If I get a perfect attendance record at the end of the month, I'll buy you a meal. You name the place."

Zhou Feng put on an obsequious grin. "I don't need a meal. I'd prefer another chance at using your car. Yiran's birthday is next month."

In their friend circle, Ye Qin was the first one to turn old enough to get a driver's license, and he'd already gotten one. As for the car, his father had given it to him as an early birthday gift. As the only one legally in possession of a car, Ye Qin was always asked by the other teens to lend it out. He had always been generous, and he didn't care too much about cars, so he was willing to lend it to them as long as there was a good reason.

Having gotten Ye Qin's approval, Zhou Feng eagerly grabbed his phone and texted someone. Then he craned his neck towards the front rows. But Sun Yiran just sat still, a book in her hand. After waiting for a while, Zhou Feng got so bored that he elbowed Ye Qin, who was dozing with a book upside-down in his hand.

"Hey, how's that thing going?"

Ye Qin was totally at a loss. "What thing?"

The two boys sat close to the window that teachers passed from time to time. To avoid being overheard, Zhou Feng leaned closer and said in a lowered voice, "I'm talking about that private detective that you asked Liu Yangfan to introduce to you. Is he good? If so, give me his number. I wanna look into the back-

ground of that straight-A student from the next class."

Probably because he happened to hear the word "straight-A student," Liao Yifang turned around. He pushed up his glasses, eyeing Zhou Feng warily from the front seat.

"We're not talking 'bout you." Zhou Feng shoved his shoulder, turning him back. "Keep studying. It's none of your business."

Ye Qin was still hiding behind the book, revealing a small portion of his face with one of his eyes half-closed. He murmured slowly, "You don't need a private detective for that kind of crap. Why don't you just ask around in the next class?"

Zhou Feng gnashed his teeth. "I need every last piece of information about him. His birthday and birth time to the minute, his whole family tree, and every bit of gossip about him..."

"What are you gonna do to him? Secretly curse him with a voodoo doll? Why do you keep fixating on this? I've totally wasted my time talking to you this afternoon," Ye Qin interrupted him. He continued in a lazy way, "Why are you spending so much energy on that poor schmuck? Next month, on Sun Yiran's birthday, just give her a handbag, put a bottle of perfume inside, and you definitely got it. He's just a wage slave; what kind of treasures could he ever get for her? And Sun Yiran's such a picky girl; how could she possibly bear that kind of treatment?"

Zhou Feng thought for a while and agreed, so he changed the subject to Ye Qin. "Then are you investigating a love rival too? Have you been absent from school to scout for info about him?"

Ye Qin scowled at him. "I was just checking things out."

Zhou Feng became even more interested. "Where did you go? Next time, take me with you. I can be there for you, just in case."

Ye Qin thought of the investigation report. It had said the mistress was in poor health, and seldom left the house. He

couldn't help jeering at his dad for such a weird choice of woman. "Nothing can go wrong."

Having failed to actually get Ye Qin talking despite all the effort, Zhou Feng lost interest and put his book up as well, fiddling with his PSV.

After the first session, Liao Yifang entered the classroom with a pile of A4 paper in his hands, which he asked the other students in the classroom to help staple together. Ye Qin was still feeling a bit groggy, so he just punched the stapler with his eyes closed.

Liao Yifang shouted, "Ye-tongxue! Mind the margin! You've stapled the words together."

Ye Qin reluctantly lifted his eyelids a little bit and saw the neat and nice handwriting on the paper. When he pressed down on the stapler again, he did it with more caution. He then turned to the first page and read the name on it.

"Cheng...Fei...Chi?"

The surname already irritated him; the surname of his father's mistress was also Cheng. Though it was—to some extent—a common surname, Ye Qin still felt quite uncomfortable.

"That's right. That's the 'Cheng' I mentioned earlier today. He was originally studying at the high school affiliated with Normal University, but recently got transferred to the class next door." Liao Yifang started to introduce the owner of these notes. "He won first prize in last year's China Physics Olympiad. I first made his acquaintance at that very contest. Otherwise, he wouldn't have let me copy his notes."

"Aren't these notes for Chemistry class?" asked a classmate nearby.

Liao Yifang seemed so awfully proud of his friend. "He's very good at Chemistry as well. A master of all trades!"

Ye Qin pursed his lips, but thinking of how the class monitor had cut him slack today, he thought he'd better play along with him. "Our class monitor's got a lot of outstanding friends."

Zhou Feng, who didn't take naps until class was over, was suddenly triggered by some word. He asked, jerking his head up, "Cheng Feichi? Are you talking about that straight-A student in the next class?"

He caught the notebook that Ye Qin tossed to him and recognized the name on its cover. Jumping to his feet, Zhou Feng was about to rush to the next class. Rolling his sleeves up, he let out a low roar, "How dare he come into *my* class and try to kiss everyone's asses?!"

Afraid that Zhou Feng would get himself into trouble, Liao Yifang kept a grip on Zhou Feng's arm. Having heard the commotion, Sun Yiran came down from the front row and, surprisingly, snatched up Cheng Feichi's notebook.

"I'm gonna return this for you!" she exclaimed in delight before hurrying out of the room.

Zhou Feng kicked Liao Yifang away with mighty force and dashed after Sun Yiran. Once he was facing down the girl, his outraged expression switched to a flattering smile. To get the notebook back from her, he tried appealing to her with sweet nicknames like "sweetheart" and "Your Highness."

It devolved into chaos, which Ye Qin couldn't bear anymore. He first helped Liao Yifang up, who was suffering from calf pain, and then he snatched the book from Sun Yiran, who was holding it high. He stared at them with a resigned look.

"You guys just sit tight. I'm gonna return this."

Though Class No. 1 (which Cheng Feichi was in) was habitually referred to as the "next class" by Class No. 2 (which Ye Qin and the others were in), their classrooms were actually

very far apart; they weren't even in the same building. Ye Qin had to walk across one men's bathroom, two flights of stairs, and a corridor connecting the two buildings that was more than ten meters long, before he arrived at the classroom of Class No. 1.

Completely composed of top students in science studies, Class No. 1 had an atmosphere that was totally different from any other class in the school. There was no horseplay, and no noise aside from barely audible page-turning sounds. Here, even the summer wind slowed down to silent breeze.

Ye Qin tapped the window while holding a lollipop in his mouth. A few students lifted their heads, only to find it was someone they didn't know, so they just returned to their studies.

Ye Qin tucked the notebook in the slit of a window, murmuring, "This is to be returned to Cheng...Cheng..."

He wasn't good at memorizing names, especially those of people whom he'd never met. The girl sitting by the window quickly responded, "Cheng Feichi?"

Ye Qin nodded. "Yes. Please pass it over to him."

His arrival didn't stir up any change in the solemn vibe in the classroom. The students passed the book quietly along the diagonal direction towards the southwest of the room, which effectively shortened the distance and the time needed.

When the notebook finally reached its owner, Ye Qin was still standing by the window. He was a little curious about the straight-A student's physical appearance. Zhou Feng had already been overshadowed by his love rival in terms of academic achievement, so the only match left undecided was a comparison of their looks.

However, the last thing Ye Qin would expect happened— Cheng Feichi was sleeping on his desk with his face fully covered by his arms. When his deskmate touched him on the arm to

hand him the notebook, he simply took it and stuffed it inside the drawer, adjusting to a more comfortable posture before continuing his slumber.

His physical figure confirmed that this Cheng Feichi was indeed the laborer Ye Qin had seen at noon. He was extremely tall, with his long legs squeezed into the space under the desk, unable to stretch out, and he was still wearing the same T-shirt, revealing his arms in the cool night air. It seemed that the cold didn't bother him at all.

Ye Qin didn't get to see his face even after he finished his lollipop. The cool wind sent uncomfortable coldness through his limbs. Disappointed, he strolled back with his neck tucked in, and received a call from his father at the staircase.

"Still at your night study session?" Ye Jinxiang asked very directly.

Ye Qin spat the lollipop stick out of his mouth, which went right into the trash bin in front of him, and then started talking. "Yeah, I'm actually doing the warm-up exercises."

Ye Jinxiang seemed quite used to his son being ridiculous, so instead of giving him a lecture, he said, "Today is your mom's birthday. Come home early after your session."

"It ends at 9:30. Of course I can't leave early, can I?" Ye Qin replied with a sneer. How could a father not know when his son could leave his school?

Their conversation was punctuated by a short uncomfortable silence. When Ye Jinxiang resumed talking, his usual awe-inspiring tone turned, unexpectedly, into a slightly softer one. "If you've got the time, just spend more of it with your mom. If you want anything, just tell me and I'll get it for you."

That very comment made Ye Qin clench his teeth through the rest of the session. Even his jaw went numb with the strength

of it.

He had planned to make an issue of his father's ignorance and vent his feelings, but now he felt like he'd just thrown a punch at cotton. All his anger and frustration had nowhere to go, and got congested inside his stomach.

When he got home, Luo Qiuling was still up. Seeing the pale look on her son's face, she went to the kitchen and heated up a bowl of papaya and pork rib soup.

Ye Qin had no appetite, so he just feebly stirred the soup with his spoon. Luo Qiuling knew that he had a sweet tooth, and the soup might be too bland for him. She tried to persuade him. "Your digestion has never been good, ever since you were young. Just drink the soup. It might be a little bland, but it's good for you. If you get sick, my heart will hurt."

This is how any caring parent should behave. Ye Qin didn't want to make his mom worry, so he had a few spoonfuls of soup and accompanied her upstairs to her bedroom—and then he saw the two tacky flower bouquets displayed in a prominent position there. It really took him a lot of effort to resist the impulse to throw them out. His father was still so bad at pleasing his mother—she never liked bright and cheery flowers.

Lying on the bed, Ye Qin had been tossing and turning for quite a while. He couldn't get the images out of his head—the clothes hung outside that dilapidated building, and the honest look his dad put on when he left the house for an alleged one-week business trip.

He regretted not having gone upstairs to confront that mistress face-to-face. Though the elderly man hadn't known which apartment the woman lived in, he could've still tried his luck. He had always been a lucky boy, so maybe he could've bumped into Ye Jinxiang on the staircase.

But what was he gonna do after encountering his dad?

Curse him, or even throw a punch at him?

What about his mom? What would happen if she knew about it?

His phone beside the bed suddenly started to buzz, dragging Ye Qin from his wandering thoughts.

He picked up the phone. A short message from an unknown number popped up. "Room 304. Owner: Cheng Xin. She has a son."

His heart thundered uncontrollably in his chest. Before the throbbing abated, he had started typing swiftly. "Name? Grade?"

He got a very quick response. His correspondent seemed well-prepared, even answering questions Ye Qin didn't put forward. "Cheng Feichi, an eighteen-year-old in Class No. 1 of Grade 11 at High School No. 6."

"What are you looking at?"

In P.E. class, Zhou Feng waved his hand in front of Ye Qin's staring eyes but failed to get his attention, so he turned to look where Ye Qin was gazing.

There was only one large recreational yard in the school. Consequently, it was normally occupied by several classes at the same time. Zhou Feng stared at the students in the recreational yard and gradually became agitated. "Fuck. Class No. 1 is here. No wonder Yiran was putting on makeup. I thought she was getting ready to hang out with me."

Ye Qin answered slowly, without paying much attention. "She's not going anywhere alone with you. There's nothing to get excited about."

Zhou Feng was hurt by Ye Qin's words, looking sad for quite a while, but became normal after walking a lap around the track. Seeming not bothered at all, he asked Ye Qin, "Tonight, are you coming or not? All of our friends will be there."

Ye Qin turned his eyes away from the recreational yard. His foot jittering fretfully on the lawn, he took out his car keys, tossing them to Zhou Feng as he said, "No. You guys have fun."

During the break in the afternoon, Sun Yiran noticed Ye Qin's weary look when she came to the back row, so she gave him a bottle of yogurt.

"You've decided not to come with us? I heard Liu Yangfan got two bottles of really good wine especially for you."

Ye Qin wasn't interested. He held his head with one hand, and tried to open the bottle with the other. "We're at school right now. Aren't you afraid of letting Mr. Sun hear that?"

Sun Yiran startled, looking around anxiously, and then turned back and patted Ye Qin on his shoulder to blame him for the shock. "You really got me."

This group of youngsters had been friends since middle school, and therefore they'd witnessed each other's growth. Having different personalities and life paths, they were never perfect fits for each other and had gone through many quarrels. It was a certain kind of fateful magic that they could be friends for such a long time.

As the only girl in their friend group, Sun Yiran was always treated with forbearance by everyone. Though Ye Qin didn't like being close to people, he didn't seem annoyed by her intimate act. However, he did lean away and into a slouch in his chair.

"Well, what about that straight-A student? Is he your boyfriend now?"

Sun Yiran immediately blushed, looking so shy that she completely lost her usual poise. "Not yet. We're not even close to that stage."

"Ask him to come over. You can introduce him to everyone."

Ye Qin regretted it the moment he uttered those words.

Why was he inviting Cheng Feichi to their gathering? What if someone among his friend group didn't know about his family scandal?

Fortunately, Sun Yiran turned down his offer with a bashful smile. "He's usually busy in the evening. He can't make time for any lengthy gatherings."

Sun Yiran was just as sharp-tongued as her Chemistry teacher father. She was straightforward and quite good at mocking others. They didn't have night sessions on Fridays, so Zhou Feng got into the driver's seat and was about to show off his driving skills, but Sun Yiran soon pushed him out of the car.

"You don't even have a driver's license! Are you trying to get us all killed?"

The car was parked near the median strip, close to the turn at the front of the school. Ye Qin was about to leave as soon as the boys took his car, but Liao Yifang happened to be passing by on his bike and overheard their fight. He immediately halted his bike and tried to talk Zhou Feng out of driving.

"Zhou, you haven't turned eighteen. You're not allowed to drive yet."

Zhou Feng was extremely annoyed by him. "I'm not at school right now. Piss off and mind your own business."

Liao Yifang stopped. He took out his cellphone and started dialing. Zhou Feng asked him flippantly, with a cigarette in his mouth, about whether he was going to report him to the teacher again. Liao Yifang put the phone near his ear and replied loud and clear, "I'm calling the police."

For three generations, Zhou Feng's family had served in the army, resulting in him being strictly disciplined. He was thus the most rebellious boy among them, but he was at the same time very intimidated by his parents. His parents would beat the shit

out of him if they found out that he dared to break the law.

The class monitor just never gave him any kind of good news. Zhou Feng became uncontrollably angry, and was even ready to climb the fence and knock Liao Yifang down. At Sun Yiran's pleading, Ye Qin was left with no option but to drive his friends to Liu Yangfan's club. Then he was dragged inside by several friends to join the party, albeit unreluctantly.

He used to enjoy their noisy gatherings. Just as Sun Yiran had once said, since they were going to waste their time anyway, it was better to have fun together than to stay at home alone.

But today was different. More specifically speaking, it had been different for quite a while recently. Having so much on his mind, Ye Qin seemed to be on pins and needles. He didn't pay much attention when Zhou Feng and some other guys asked him to open a wine bottle. When the cork was carelessly pulled out, the wine spilled on Liu Yangfan, who was sitting right next to Ye Qin. Yet, not a bit annoyed, Liu Yangfan just took off his shirt on the spot, continuing chatting with only a singlet on. The stained shirt got rolled into a ball and went into the trash bin.

Sun Yiran asked him why he didn't take the dirty shirt home to get it cleaned up, and he replied with contempt, "My step-mom bought it. I only wear it to spare my dad's feelings. Now it's dirty, and now it's complete shit. Why should I keep it?"

The Liu Family had acquired its wealth in the real estate industry. Liu Yangfan's branch of the family had a flourishing population and complicated relationships. Though they appeared to be happy and harmonious from the outside, they just kept their numerous scandals hidden amongst themselves. But Liu Yangfan didn't seem to care about hiding those "secrets," and his friends surely didn't mind listening.

This sent their conversational topic off its original course. Zhou Feng's father was a kind man, and he himself was an

obedient son, so he was quite curious about the scandals and rumors. He and Sun Yiran kept asking Liu Yangfan all kinds of questions, such as "Is that woman pretty?", or "I heard that you had a younger brother," or "Are you afraid that he's going to take everything from you?"

Before, these questions were merely interesting gossip to Ye Qin. But now he couldn't stand by anymore.

He couldn't help but think of his mom, Luo Qiuling. Ever since he could remember, she was never away from home. She always cooked, watered the flowers, did all the household chores, and welcomed him and his dad at the door with a smile. She was the typical and perfect wife and mother.

If she was just some trophy wife who only knew how to be pretty and do basic housework, the fact that Ye Jinxiang was having an affair might be a bit more understandable. But it was widely known that "his" company originally belonged to the Luos. Ye Qin's maternal grandfather had built his business empire on Chinese herbs, and having no son of his own, he passed all expertise and experience down to his son-in-law. However, he wasn't lucky enough to enjoy a relaxing retirement. He developed cancer after turning 50, and died of it after two years of suffering. His dear son-in-law rechristened the company right after his death.

For most of the achievements that Ye Jinxiang now had, the credit should go to his father-in-law. It made Ye Qin feel ashamed, and even indignant at his mother for being too meek and mild.

Probably only Ye Jinxiang could still feel proud of his success—he ignored all the ugly rumors, and was so barefaced that he had a bastard son even older than Ye Qin with a damn mistress.

A beer can was crushed in Ye Qin's hand. Zhou Feng noticed it and thought Ye Qin was unhappy at being left out, so he poured

him a glass of wine. "A-Qin's birthday is also next month, right? How about we throw a party for you? Yangfan can bring more good wine then..."

Ye Qin didn't catch his words after that. His thoughts were as uncontrollable as tidal waves that could never be held back. He was the oldest of them all on paper, but his actual birthday was one year later than the date on his ID card. Ye Jinxiang used to explain that this was done so Ye Qin could start elementary school earlier, so he wouldn't cause trouble at home.

Ye Qin had not understood the point of such efforts before, but now he was forced into enlightenment. What a disgusting joke would it be if the bastard son was older than the legitimate one?

He tossed the Bordeaux glass down on the table with such force that the stem of the glass was smashed to smithereens.

He had always been spoiled in the ocean of wealth and treasure. He knew nothing about wine, and cared even less about it. The exclamation from Zhou Feng and Sun Yiran didn't stir up any feeling in his heart.

It was not yet 10 o'clock at night. The boys first escorted Sun Yiran home, where she was expected, and then Liu Yangfan suggested going to Zhao Yue's home to play video games. Ye Qin had cooled off by this point, after his emotional outburst. Holding the steering wheel and calmly looking ahead, he kept the car running smoothly on the road.

Liu Yangfan and Zhao Yue both attended the international school, and both lived in the eastern part of the city. When they reached Yulin Road, Zhou Feng saw a 24-hour convenience store and patted the back of the driver's seat. "Ye Qin, stop here. Let's buy some snacks. How can we make it through the night without any food?"

Hearing this, Ye Qin pulled over. The three drunken boys

had made the car smell really foul, so he also got out. He was going to buy some sweets to cheer himself up, and get some fresh air.

On the outside, he seemed a carefree and straightforward person, but actually he had been hesitating and pondering for a whole week. He had been secretly comforting himself with the fact that, in such a megacity, it'd be impossible to encounter a guy that he hadn't easily run into even in the small Middle School No. 6. At least he'd never run into him before he'd prepared himself.

However, at 11 o'clock this evening, with just an hour to midnight, Ye Qin was surprisingly fated to meet Cheng Feichi head-on.

Zhou Feng was the first to recognize him. He was holding several bottles of beer when he popped his head out to ask the cashier, "Would you please show me where the shopping baskets are?"

Before the cashier answered him, Zhou Feng hid back behind the shelves with a low curse. "What a fucking small world!"

Ye Qin was looking at the pastries and sweets on the shelf near the check-out counter. The store only had a limited selection of food, and none of the foreign snacks he preferred. After hemming and hawing for a while, he realized that he had to make do with a bag of fruit jam gummies.

Zhou Feng had always been a talkative person, so Ye Qin didn't pay much attention to his curse at first. It wasn't until Zhou Feng specifically asked him to turn back and look at the cashier that he realized who the person was.

"I was planning on giving him a hard time, and now there he is!" There was eagerness and excitement in Zhou Feng's voice. "He can only blame it on destiny! I wasn't the one who put him here."

Zhao Yue was always full of wicked ideas. His glorious history of dancing on the edge of breaking school regulations with his gang of hotheads could be traced back to middle school days. It was a real miracle that he was still alive today. Knowing that this young cashier was Zhou Feng's love rival—the guy who refused to admit that Sun Yiran was his girlfriend, even after making her totally infatuated with him—he quickly came up with a plan to avenge his buddy.

Ye Qin wasn't listening closely to the details of their plan. He told himself that this was none of his business, but he couldn't help looking through several shelves at the young lad standing behind the counter.

Looking from such a short distance, Ye Qin discovered that Cheng Feichi was even taller than he'd imagined. The top of his head could almost reach the highest row of shelves, making it easy for him to get anything without standing on tiptoe or raising his arms. Besides his height, his face was another thing that differentiated him from his peers, who were still trapped between childish naivete and awkward adult vibes. His features were strong and defined, as if molded from granite. Beautifully shaped eyebrows and a straight nose cast deep shadows on his face, with clearly defined thin lips—it was definitely the kind of face that would make Sun Yiran's heart flip.

Few people would still be on the street at night. Cheng Feichi was standing straight with good posture, with only his neck slightly bending to focus on something behind the counter. He was so focused that the noise the boys made didn't bother him at all. Only when he moved his fingers to turn the page did Ye Qin realize that he was reading a book.

Sleeping through night sessions, yet studying when doing part-time jobs—of course model students were experts of time management.

When Ye Qin was done with his observations, the other three boys were just concluding their discussion with their final strategy. Zhao Yue took the lead. He waddled his way behind the cash register and bent down to look at the cigarettes displayed beneath the glass. Zhou Feng and Liu Yangfan stood in front of the cashier, one of them tapping at the counter while the other said, "Do you have Yellow Crane Tower?"

Cheng Feichi turned his eyes from his book to the two boys and quickly put his game face on. He uttered a polite answer, "Sorry, we don't."

"What about Suyan? Platinum Crystal or Agarwood are fine, too." Liu Yangfan's father was a heavy smoker, so he'd also become very familiar with these high-end cigarette brands from an early age.

Cheng Feichi replied, "Still, we have none of them."

He spoke in a calm, cool, and toneless voice that somehow reminded Ye Qin of the low-frequency vibration that usually came after tapping against metal. Even when he was talking about these trivial things, he sounded confident and powerful. Looking at him from the back of the group, Ye Qin was suddenly struck by a strange thought that this young guy didn't belong here.

Zhou Feng tapped his fingers again on the glass display counter, a frown on his face. "Then what on earth *do* you have here?"

Other people might not be able to read Zhou Feng's mind, but Ye Qin had been close friends with him since their childhood. They stuck together 300 days out of the year. He could tell that Zhou Feng was feeling nervous and guilty even from a slight glimpse. Glancing at what was going on in the space behind the counter, Ye Qin saw Zhao Yue adjust his position, raise his arm a little bit, and artfully sneak something into the pocket of Cheng

Feichi's track pants.

Cheng Feichi didn't notice anything wrong. He took a glimpse at the counter and said, "Chunghwa Soft. 68 per pack."

That was the cigarette product with the highest retail price in this small store.

Having successfully performed his trick, Zhao Yue stood up and went around the counter with both hands stuffed in his pockets, looking quite impatient. "Chunghwa Soft, then. Two packs."

After checking out, the four boys left the store, but rushed back in less than five minutes.

They searched throughout the store without any success. Zhou Feng was the first to question the one behind the cashier. "Hey, did you see my buddy's watch?"

The police arrived in twenty minutes, when the two sides were still standing in confrontation with each other.

Cheng Feichi was alone, but not even the slightest sign of panic was visible on his face. He presented the policemen with his ID card and started describing what had happened.

"These four customers came into the store around 11:15 p.m. Three lingered in front of the shelves that were farthest from the counter for approximately seven to eight minutes, and then went toward the counter together. At that time, this young man," Cheng Feichi pointed at Liu Yangfan, "went behind the counter to look at the products. He was about a half meter away from me, while the other two people were standing over there talking to me face-to-face. The whole interaction lasted for no more than two minutes. And during the whole process I never left the counter. In the end, the one standing closest to me decided to have two packs of Chunghwa Soft, and the four of them left together after checking out. Five minutes later, they came back

and said that they lost a watch."

Zhou Feng was irritated by his narration. "Nonsense! You're accusing us of framing you?"

Almost speechless after hearing Zhou Feng's stupid response, Liu Yangfan interjected, "You're dodging the most important thing. If you're really so innocent, then why was my buddy's watch in your pocket?"

Cheng Feichi took a look at the two boys and then turned back to the police. "The whole incident must have been captured on CCTV. If you watch it, you can tell that I'm not lying."

The store owner arrived after receiving a call from the police. Seeing the policemen and four posh-looking teens, the middle-aged woman began apologizing before even learning the facts. "I'm deeply sorry for the trouble that we caused. Xiao-Cheng just started working here. If he did anything wrong, please just tell me and let me deal with him."

Liu Yangfan spat out his cigar in contempt. "Let you deal with him? Do you even know how much that watch costs? You think you can really handle this?"

Zhao Yue raised his hand, showing off his sports watch. "This was a birthday gift from my grandpa. Limited edition. Does he even know what brand it is? How dare he steal such a precious item? What a wonderful employee you've got!"

The shop owner was obviously astonished, but she managed to pull herself together. "Xiao-Cheng is not that kind of person. There must be a mistake."

Now the CCTV footage was displaying on the computer screen. Only one of the security cameras was facing the side of the counter. According to the time shown at the lower left corner, the four teens did enter the store shortly after 11 o'clock, and after disappearing from the frame for less than ten minutes, three of them showed up again and walked towards the counter.

What came next matched Cheng Feichi's description as well. However, this clip was not very useful; because the filming angle was a bit off, the policemen couldn't pin down the details of their movements even after carefully replaying it twice. The whole video just showed a very normal check-out process.

"He must be a repeat offender. He knew this was a blind spot and he could do whatever he wanted."

Zhao Yue struck first in order to control the whole situation by convicting Cheng Feichi without sufficient evidence. Zhou Feng and Liu Yangfan followed by saying that Cheng Feichi had been very calm throughout the whole confrontation and investigation, which proved that he had been plotting this theft for quite a while, right from the moment they came in.

Three liars make a truth. They all looked so confident and honest, making the police unable to decide.

"I didn't steal his watch, and I really don't know how it ended up in my pocket." Cheng Feichi kept denying their accusations and looked at Zhao Yue. "I wasn't paying much attention when he approached me. Now I think about it, that's probably how I fell into their trap."

"Bullshit!" Zhou Feng scolded. "Who the hell are you? Why would we waste time scheming against you?"

Zhao Yue jeered in a more composed manner. "Watch your mouth. We don't even know each other. Why would we set you up? How do we benefit from this farce?"

The police also thought Zhao Yue had a point. They watched the footage of the other two cameras inside the store and asked Cheng Feichi, "You said that you were framed by Mr. Liu. Can you get another witness to back your statement?"

Ye Qin was leaning against the door and throwing a gummy into his mouth when he heard the police's question. And Cheng Feichi was looking straight at him.

The three teens involved had already agreed to collude the moment they paid for the cigarettes and left the store. Zhou Feng was determined to teach Cheng Feichi a lesson. Since he couldn't beat him up, it didn't matter what strategy he employed. As the very target of their perfectly ready scheme, Cheng Feichi could hardly get himself off the hook. Ye Qin had already predicted this difficult situation for him before they returned to the store.

It was obvious that Ye Qin would not testify against his friends. But his role had been different, in that he was the only person not involved in the frame-up whatsoever. He was the only bystander in this farce.

He thought that he wouldn't feel nervous, but when Cheng Feichi looked into his eyes, he still felt butterflies in his stomach.

It was a weird feeling, but he soon discovered where it came from.

He didn't like bullying others. Probably he was thinking of his mother, or his sympathy with the weak was just visceral. If Cheng Feichi looked weak, poor, and hopeless, and had eagerly solicited his help, he might've helped him out even though it would put his friendship at risk.

Yet not even the slightest sign of weakness was revealed in Cheng Feichi's eyes. Instead, he looked candid; so much so that his eyes were as sharp as a dagger piercing into the pit of Ye Qin's stomach, exposing his ugly and freakish thoughts in broad daylight.

"He saw it," Cheng Feichi said. "He was standing right in front of me, behind the two guys."

The gummy stuck to Ye Qin's teeth because he chewed it too hard. He looked away so that he could pretend that he didn't see Cheng Feichi—who was still standing tall.

"I was daydreaming at the time. I didn't see anything," Ye Qin said while savoring the fruit jam in the gummy. It didn't

taste sweet. The unpleasantly sour flavor in his mouth almost kept him from uttering a clear sentence. "Sorry. Can't help."

The teens went on a late-night gaming spree.

Zhou Feng was particularly thrilled, as he had finally taken his revenge on his love rival. After a few rounds, he dropped the joystick and continued to drink, then he passed the beer to Ye Qin.

Ye Qin took a sip and frowned, pushing his arm aside before slouching back into the sofa and continuing to chew the gummy candies.

Zhou Feng gulped down the rest of the beer and threw the empty can away. "We should've followed him to the police station, so that we could see how he was questioned. Then take a picture of him and send it to Yiran."

Zhao Yue laughed, saying that they would have taken things too far if they did. The lad seemed to be quite arrogant; he must be furious right now after falling for such a shameful setup.

"Why would he even try to ask A-Qin to defend him?" Liu Yangfan also sneered. "Even a five-year-old can see that he belongs to our squad. How could that guy be so stupid? He actually thought A-Qin would help him out?"

Zhou Feng couldn't help laughing even harder. "Probably because A-Qin looks like a sweet and easygoing boy."

"Right. Look at that soft skin, those big eyes, that tiny little cherry mouth and that pinkish face; no one would ever doubt his innocence. If we didn't point it out, who would ever know that he's the real boss?"

Liu Yangfan then tried to pinch Ye Qin's face, but the latter dodged his hand and tossed another gummy into his mouth.

They joked about his lack of humor and turned to other topics, while carrying on with their drinking. When they paused

and picked up the joysticks again, Ye Qin patted Zhao Yue and asked, "He...I mean, that guy. What are the police going to do to him?"

"They'll probably hold him in custody and report it to the school. And the school will punish him and put it in his record," Zhao Yue answered in a relaxed manner. "He could also be fined. But who knows? He's left to the whims of destiny now."

At the same time, the glass front door of Yulin Police Station was pushed open from inside, and Cheng Feichi stepped out of the building. He looked up at the Bell Tower in the distance and found it was already half past three o'clock.

It was a damp, misty, and cool autumn night in Northern China. Wearing only a T-shirt emblazoned with a store logo and normal black track pants, Cheng Feichi ducked his head while walking along the empty street.

The station was not far from the store. When Cheng Feichi entered, the owner was holding a broom in her hand—she was preparing the store for the next shift that would begin in two hours.

"Let me do it." Cheng Feichi stepped forward and took the broom from the store owner. He went to the other end of the store without asking her opinion and started systematically sweeping from there.

Watching him doing the cleaning, the woman sighed all of a sudden. "The police didn't embarrass you, did they?"

"No," the young lad answered. "Seeing that I'm still a student, they just asked me some questions and let me go."

The owner turned back to sort the goods on the shelves, but couldn't help nagging him after a slight hesitation. "I told you a million times. The outside world is complicated, especially during the night shift. When night falls, all the hooligans are

out on the street making trouble. We don't mess with them, but at least we can stay away from them. Never confront them when it's possible to compromise. Because if you fight against them, you'll only get yourself hurt."

Cheng Feichi's movement froze for a second. "I didn't mess with them."

The woman turned again to face him. "I know. How would I not know what kind of person you are? But there are people that just love to make a fuss about nothing. They won't let go of you even when you did nothing wrong. You really need to learn how to protect yourself. It's for your own sake, not anyone else's. If that nonsense did become a big deal, do you want to have to drop out of school? It's already unfair that you were transferred from the university's affiliated high school to High School No. 6. If the police notified your school, how disappointed your mom would be."

The young man didn't reply anymore; his mouth set in a grim line.

After tidying everything up, the woman packed several steamed Chinese buns and two bags of soy milk and handed them to Cheng Feichi. But the latter refused the offer, ready to leave the store after placing the broom where it should be.

The woman ran after him and stuffed the plastic bag into his hands. "Take it. Nobody's gonna buy them after a whole day; they'd be disposed of as expired food anyway. I trust you'll have class later? You can't do without some breakfast."

He tucked the books under his arm and took the bag with both hands. "Thank you."

The woman then gave him 200 yuan and said, "Here's your salary for these few days."

He looked down at the two red ¥100 notes, and knew that

this meant that he didn't need to come back anymore.

Looking a bit awkward, the store owner explained in a subtle and mild manner, "It was my fault, letting a kid like you work the night shift. I didn't consider the potential dangers and risks. You'd better listen to your mom and focus on your studies. Money isn't something that you should worry about now."

He remained silent, neither taking the money nor saying anything. It seemed that he was pondering how to save this hard-earned job.

It was a windy morning. Unable to stand the cold anymore, the woman patted him on his back and urged him to go home. "So obstinate... Well, if there are any job opportunities that suit you, I'll let you know as soon as possible, okay?"

He replied with a "sure" after this promise. He put the two notes in his pocket, and thanked her again.

He reached home in the gray dawn. The house was only lit by a sheer streak of light peeping through the heavy curtains.

He walked into the kitchen quietly and put the buns on a plate when he heard the sound of a bedroom door opening from behind him.

Cheng Xin, his mother, left the main bedroom for the kitchen, holding on to the dining table to steady herself. Covered with a coat, she asked him in a weak voice, "Why did you get back so late? You said you'd get off work at two or three o'clock."

He put down everything to help her into the chair. "We had a new load come in. I helped Ms. Feng unload the goods."

Cheng Xin sat down, nodding. "Good. She's helped us a lot."

The cramped house they lived in measured less than 60 square meters, and the dining area was only three or four meters away from the kitchen. Cheng Feichi returned to the kitchen to heat the buns up when Cheng Xin noticed a book beside the stove.

"What's that book about?"

"Math Olympiad exercises," Cheng Feichi replied. "The teacher said that the CEE is going to be reformed this year. My teachers say that the bonus questions might be picked from these exercises, so I'm checking them out, just in case."

Cheng Xin could only see her son's back, but given that she had been a teacher for a decade, she still caught his true intentions.

The top three contestants in the Mathematical Olympiad would receive a huge monetary reward. Of course she knew that.

Breakfast began. Cheng Xin picked up a bun stuffed with meat and put it into her son's bowl. "Life in Grade 11 will be busier than before. Don't do part-time jobs anymore. I still can afford your tuition."

Probably because she had worked as a respectable teacher for too long, Cheng Xin talked in a rather stern and emotionless tone even now, while her feebleness somehow intensified the pressure subtly imposed on her son—though she was, in fact, trying to comfort him.

Cheng Feichi remained silent, finished the meal, and stood up to clear the table. When he spotted the blatantly branded shoebox on the end-table at the entrance, he let out a question, "He visited again?"

Cheng Xin was stacking the bowls and plates. "Hmm. The shoes are for you; they're at your disposal."

An hour later, he exited the building with garbage bags and the shoebox in his hands. He approached the garbage bins and got rid of everything.

At this moment, the early morning sun appeared from behind the buildings amidst floating mist. An elderly man was practicing tai chi in the open area. When he saw Cheng Feichi, he stopped and greeted him. "Xiao-Chi, you got up so early! You're not wearing much. Aren't you cold?"

The sun didn't beam down on Cheng Feichi's heart at all. He could only manage a smile. "Morning, Mr. Lee. I'm not cold."

A glance at Cheng Feichi reminded the elderly man of his own grandchild, who must still be lying in bed right now.

"Are you going to help with the restaurant today? Stay home. It's the weekend after all. Have a good sleep or hang out with your friends. I'll ask my son to let you cut loose today."

"Ah, thank you, Mr. Lee."

Cheng Feichi easily agreed, if only to keep the conversation as short as possible. He went back to his bedroom, took off the convenience store's uniform, and put on a coat before leaving the house again.

He had always lived at a pace so rapid that when his brain was finally allowed to rest, it rested on the run. Normally, he used the downtime to calculate the income that he'd receive by the end of the month at the curbside, or scan through the want ads of nearby stores for suitable openings. Unfortunately, High School No. 6 strictly forbade its students from working part-time outside the school—he would have to leave the corner shop in no time.

However, today, everything felt different. He had a sudden burst of speed and started dashing along the empty sidewalk. Even after two kilometers of running, he could not pull himself out of the overwhelming noise inside his head. Countless taunting faces kept flashing in front of his eyes, while shrill laughter pierced his ears with no sign of abating.

He halted, gasping, his hands pressing on his knees. But his mouth suddenly formed a sardonic curve, as if laughing at himself.

Huh. Why on earth would anyone help him?

The world was filled with irrational malice. His only true savior was himself; always and only himself.

CHAPTER 02

A whole week passed. The solar term of Frost Descent slipped away, along with the warmth in the air. Coldness had completely taken over the capital city, yet the memory of that one night's farce still lingered in Ye Qin's mind.

Nothing big happened at school—to his relief, he didn't hear about anybody getting disciplined or receiving a new bad mark on their record. But on reflection, he found these thoughts stupid. Why was he worrying about Cheng Feichi getting punished and being held in custody? Wasn't that what he wanted?

Ye Jinxiang returned from his business trip with a Patek Philippe sports watch for his son. The watch constantly reminded Ye Qin of the farce that day, so he took it off after a short while, pouting quite unhappily. Ye Jinxiang assumed that he wasn't pleased with its design and told him to choose another one himself on the official website.

Ye Qin rolled his eyes. "Why would I need this? I can't wear it at school."

It seemed that his father was in a good mood—he didn't get angry as he usually did, but instead patiently explained, "A watch reflects the wearer's status and taste, especially for men.

You'll understand when you get older."

Ye Qin wasn't interested. His had only one thought on the matter: his father was deeply entrenched in vanity, and had been for a decade now. Before Ye Qin's grandfather died, Ye Jinxiang had already started imitating the way he dressed and behaved, trying so eagerly to squeeze himself into the upper class. His ugly desperation was blatantly obvious even to the eyes of his own child. His front of gentleness and humility was nothing but a disguise of decency. If it wasn't for his handsome face, how could Luo Qiuling have remained by his side all along without complaint?

Speaking of handsomeness... Ye Qin took another look at his father. Ye Jinxiang had a manly face with clear-cut features, just like that young man's.

Ye Qin became more and more convinced that the boy really was Ye Jinxiang's bastard son. Two days ago, he pedaled to the Yulin Compound again and went upstairs. When standing at the doorway of Room 304, he heard some noise from behind the door and immediately decided to go to the next floor so that he could hide himself while secretly observing the mistress.

She was a skinny, feeble woman who coughed hard every two steps. Though her home was a mere ten meters away from the rubbish bin downstairs, it still took her over thirty minutes to get there. Ye Qin had imagined the woman might be an ailing beauty, but he was disappointed after she turned around—she didn't seem pretty, even as Ye Qin tried his best to shake off all possible bias. She was merely a middle-aged woman without the slightest bit of allure.

Cheng Feichi had to be Ye Jinxiang's bastard son. Otherwise, why would his father continue to frequent this place, ignorant of the fact that he'd already been exposed?

After Ye Jinxiang left, Ye Qin thrust the watch forcefully

into a drawer.

He was the only son. He had never concealed his self-important and hypercritical nature, nor had he ever needed to. He always went for the best quality and the highest price. Even the fatherly love he didn't cherish, he was loath to share with anyone else.

During the break before P.E. class on Friday, Sun Yiran wasn't putting on her makeup as usual—instead she was bent over her desk, crying terribly hard.

Zhou Feng was trying his best to console her by making silly faces and telling jokes, but all his efforts were in vain. Her girlfriend told Ye Qin that she had asked Cheng Feichi to attend her birthday party at the beginning of next month, and not only was she rejected, but she also witnessed him flirting with a girl from a different school.

"That girl...was in the uniform of the university's affiliated high school. She was on his arm, and asking him to show her around. None of them were taking me seriously." Sun Yiran was still crying through broken sentences. "He just left with her, without saying anything to me!"

Zhou Feng was always the one most excited by such stories. He whipped the coat off his desk, shouting, "Fuck! How dare he treat our Yiran like this?! Looks like he didn't learn anything last time!"

The hubbub gave Ye Qin a headache, and he dragged Zhou Feng off to P.E. class. Sun Yiran held back her tears and ran after them with her workout clothes in her hands. "Did you guys go after him? What did you do to him? Why did you do that? If anything bad happens to him, I'll never forgive you guys!"

Though he felt very wronged, Zhou Feng had to contain his anger in front of Sun Yiran. When they were asked to warm up, he could only vent his feelings by running two more laps around

the track than everyone else. He nearly rolled up his sleeves to pick a fight with Cheng Feichi while passing the meeting point of Class No. 1. But Liao Yifang, who had been keeping his eyes open for any signs of discontent, immediately held him back.

"Zhou-tongxue, don't waste your energy! We're going to take the fitness test!"

For these high school students with more energy than needed, P.E. classes were the most direct way to consume said energy, and were the only classes that they would never want to skip.

However, this was not the case for Ye Qin. He hated P.E. classes because he had always hated sweating. And this hatred was amplified now by a certain person.

The teacher seemed to be intentionally making life difficult for him—he asked them to assemble at the east side of the recreational yard to take the test with students from Class No. 1.

Sit-ups were for female students, while pull-ups were for males. Already knowing how much they were going to suffer, the students roared sadly and tried to avoid the test by pretending that they weren't feeling well.

In the blink of an eye, more than one third of the male students in Class No. 2 left, for which the P.E. teacher called them good-for-nothings: they were not as good as the model students from Class No. 1, neither academically nor physically.

Class No. 2 was always depreciated like this, so no one looked offended, not in the slightest—except for Zhou Feng. With outrage still written all over his face, his nostrils flaring, he gave Cheng Feichi a very fierce glare. Ye Qin was standing at the end of the queue. He glanced at the other queue, and found that Cheng Feichi was also at the end—half a head taller than the boy in front of him, he was too tall to be overlooked.

Two horizontal bars were set next to each other. Students in each queue headed for the one in front of them, from the shortest

to the tallest. This was when a sense of collective honor was unconsciously evoked. The students were all rooting for their classmates; even if someone couldn't manage to finish one pull-up, his classmates would be shouting, "Keep it up!"

When it was Zhou Feng's turn, he turned to face the other queue, thumbed his nose once, and then jumped up to grab the bar.

He let himself drop to the ground after barely finishing a third pull-up.

The P.E. teacher laughed, arms akimbo. "Some students aren't so strong, but they're willing and bold enough to give it a good try! This is way better than pretending to be sick."

Feeling like he was being praised, Zhou Feng confidently went to Sun Yiran to ask her if she had seen his brilliant performance. But Sun Yiran didn't pay any attention to him; her reddened eyes were fixed on someone from Class No. 1. Zhou Feng turned his head, only to find that she was still looking at that stupid straight-A student! What the fuck!

When Ye Qin was up, Cheng Feichi happened to have his turn at the same time. Seeing that his greatest enemy was right under the nose of his best buddy, Zhou Feng was so utterly thrilled that he spared no effort in encouraging the latter to perform better, so that Class No. 2 could recover from this Waterloo.

However, Ye Qin had barely ever had any chance to build muscle. How could he pass this fitness test? He did two pull-ups before his shoulder and back began to hurt badly. His arm felt like it was going to be dislocated, and his sight began to blur.

While Zhou Feng was still shouting "hang on, Qin-ge" and "one more try," Ye Qin was halfway through a third pull-up. An overwhelmingly sharp pain in the side of his chest suddenly made him lose his grip on the bar, and he fell.

Zhou Feng was still furious about what happened during that P.E. class in the following Monday's morning self-study session. He proclaimed that he would gather people to go after Cheng Feichi again.

"What a jerk! He was just trying to show off in front of all those girls. So stupid!" Zhou Feng banged on the table. "Plus, why did he have to catch our A-Qin beneath the bar? It wasn't even a long fall, anyway. He was just pretending to be nice and helpful. Such an asshole!"

Too disturbed by Zhou Feng's loud curse to get any more sleep, Ye Qin stuffed a piece of bread into Zhou's mouth. "Piss off."

Zhou Feng was extremely upset. After the self-study session, he followed Ye Qin into the men's room and kept harping on the necessity of fighting back against Cheng Feichi by the urinals. "A-Qin, aren't you upset about this? He definitely recognized us! That was him retaliating against us for what we did to him. He'll only go even further if we don't fight back!"

Ye Qin had no desire to recall what happened during last week's P.E. class, but Zhou Feng kept bringing it up again and again. He kept having flashbacks of Cheng Feichi catching him as he fell from the bar, which somehow made him feel wildly ashamed.

What was that guy trying to do? I wasn't even half a meter off the ground. I wouldn't have gotten hurt even if I'd completely wiped out. Why would I have needed him to catch me?

Ye Qin was afraid of getting hurt, so when he fell, he fell with his eyes closed. He was ready to be left lying on the ground with his arms and legs in the air, and to completely lose face. But when he actually hit the ground, he didn't feel any pain. Turning his head, he saw Cheng Feichi sitting very close to him and looking at him. His face was emotionless, and the accident hadn't

stirred up any emotion in his eyes. He looked as calm as he was when he was framed in the convenience store that night.

With Zhou Feng standing right there next to him, Ye Qin couldn't believe that Cheng Feichi had failed to recognize him. He was even preparing himself in case Cheng Feichi picked a fight, but Cheng Feichi only gave him a frosty look and a shove, signaling him to get up quickly, and then he himself got up from the ground before dusting his pants off and returning to his queue.

Ye Qin suddenly began to fret over what had happened. He didn't want Cheng Feichi to treat him like a total stranger, but at the same time he grew flustered that he had such feelings to begin with. What was wrong with acting like strangers? Surely they weren't supposed to hug each other and tell everyone that they were...brothers, were they?

Thinking of this, Ye Qin's agitation finally hit, and so he changed his mind and accepted Zhou Feng's proposal.

They didn't have night sessions on Fridays, but their teachers never ended class when it should be over. Therefore, when Zhao Yue and Liu Yangfan had crossed half of the city to meet them, Ye Qin's class had only just ended.

Zhou Feng leaned on the window frame to make sure that Cheng Feichi's class had not yet been dismissed, and whistled as he headed for the back gate with his buddies.

Dragged by Zhou Feng, Ye Qin frowned. "Why are we going to the back gate? It's more crowded than the front now."

Most of the students in their school were day students, and it was the time when students headed to the back gate in droves in order to get their bikes. At this time of the day, the back gate was indeed even more packed than the front. Ye Qin was certain that Zhou Feng's plan involved something lawless. Why would

Zhou Feng want such a large audience? Was he planning on getting reported?

Zhou Feng patted his chest with a smug grin. "Relax. I've planned the whole thing out with Zhao Yue this afternoon. Nothing could possibly go wrong."

Still doubting that, Ye Qin regretted having accepted such a stupid proposal and followed him all the way here. He started to look around. "What the hell is your plan? Don't go too far. You could get reprimanded."

Zhao Yue tapped him on the shoulder and laughed. "Our A-Qin has always been such a brave boy. Why are you afraid now?"

Ye Qin assumed he must look quite afraid, but he refused to admit it. Pulling a long face, he retorted, "Nonsense. If anyone should be afraid, it's you."

To prove that he was not nervous at all, Ye Qin offered to watch over them.

"Hey, take this for me." Before they got started, Zhou Feng gave Ye Qin a paring knife.

Ye Qin's eyes widened. "Don't tell me you're gonna kill him!"

"No way." Zhao Yue showed Ye Qin the large iron nail—seven to eight centimeters in length—and said, "Just gonna puncture the tire of his bike, to make him cry and walk all the way back home. If the nail doesn't work, we'll use that knife."

Ye Qin was relieved, and then immediately found this plan stupid as well. He complained, "Finish it ASAP. It's freezing!"

The boys had a clear division of tasks, and thought they were being *so* smart. But they forgot that the teaching building that housed Class No. 1 was right behind them.

Cheng Feichi had finished the exam fifteen minutes ago, but the teacher wouldn't let him leave early. His seat was near

the window, so now he was killing time by looking outside—from up here, he could clearly see those boys conducting their sneaky plan.

When the exam was over, he didn't hurry to leave as usual. He took his time locking the door and going downstairs, even taking a detour to give the boys enough time to finish their plot.

When he finally reached the parking area for Class No. 1, the three boys seemed to be long gone. Yet the one who was supposed to watch over them was still struggling in the cold wind. He was probably in a daze, or dozing.

Cheng Feichi first went to check his bike. The tires were already flat, and the saddle was scratched and covered with paint stains—maybe the saddle was attached too well for them to steal. However, it wasn't easy to determine what they'd done to the bike, as it hadn't been washed in years and was covered in heavy dust.

Night was falling. Cheng Feichi wheeled his bicycle to the entry of the parking area. The lookout boy was still there in the cold wind—he not only didn't notice that his accomplices had left, but also didn't realize that the victim was already so close to him. A sudden gust of wind made him shudder, making him jump up and down to warm up a little bit. His hands stuffed in his sleeves, he wrapped his arms around himself and kept rubbing them.

Cheng Feichi parked the bike and patted him on the shoulder.

"What took you so long? I'm frozen to the bone..." Ye Qin turned back, shivering. But when he saw who was standing in front of him, he was suddenly and nervously silenced with a burst of hiccups.

Pointing at his bike, Cheng Feichi questioned, "You did this?"

Ye Qin covered his mouth with his hand, feeling awkward

as hell. He wanted to say no and run away, but he thought by doing so, he was being a coward and would be a laughingstock among his friends.

But this was the first time that Ye Qin had come face-to-face with Cheng Feichi. And it was the first time that he realized that Cheng Feichi was more than half a head taller than him. He held his head high and glared at Cheng Feichi to maintain his dignity.

"That's right. So what?"

Cheng Feichi glanced at the knife in his hand. "With that?"

Well, there was no going back anymore. Ye Qin couldn't cower at this point, so he simply looked Cheng Feichi in the eye. "Of course. Your poor bike wasn't damaged enough? Are you asking for more?"

Quite surprisingly, Ye Qin saw a small, almost unnoticeable smile on Cheng Feichi's face.

It all happened too fast. Before Ye Qin even realized it, his wrist was already being squeezed hard by Cheng Feichi, and the tip of the knife was pointed at Cheng Feichi's stomach—only a few centimeters away from stabbing right into him.

Ye Qin's eyes widened at this horrible sight. He stuttered, "What...what are you doing?"

Cheng Feichi was way stronger than him. Ye Qin froze, extremely afraid that he would actually stab him.

Perhaps most men were obsessed with absolute power over other creatures, and Cheng Feichi was no different. He gripped Ye Qin's much thinner wrist and felt how it was shaking like a leaf. A few moments later, he suddenly tightened his grip and the knife fell to the ground with a clang.

Ye Qin was already white with fear. When Cheng Feichi dragged him forward, he didn't resist.

It was only when they were walking along the sidewalk just

outside the school and had stomped on a few ginkgo leaves that Ye Qin finally managed to speak. "Where are you taking me?"

Cheng Feichi was holding the stupid boy with one hand and pushing the bike with the other. He answered with a voice no warmer than the wind blowing across them. "The police station."

Right now, Ye Qin felt numb, but not so numb that he'd ask stupid questions like "Why are we going there?"

Obviously, Cheng Feichi wanted him to pay the price.

It would be a total falsehood to say that he was not unnerved. The damaged bike was right there. He'd been caught red-handed. It was no longer possible to escape, but Ye Qin didn't want to be questioned by the police. He tried to find a way out.

"How much does that bike cost? I can make up for all the damage."

Cheng Feichi remained silent.

Ye Qin thought Cheng Feichi was not satisfied, so he made a more generous offer. "I'll double its original price. No, triple. You can afford three bikes with the money I'll give you."

Cheng Feichi still didn't answer.

Ye Qin's mood grew irascible. The bike didn't seem special at all to him, so he became impatient again. "What's the brand? I might as well give my bike to you; it's an imported and famous brand. Much better than that one."

Cheng Feichi didn't respond. He just kept walking.

His cellphone buzzed in his pocket, and Ye Qin took it out and answered the call. Zhou Feng was shouting to him through the phone.

"A-Qin, where are you? We can't find you anywhere. That shitty bike is gone too. Fuck..."

Ye Qin was too embarrassed to tell them the truth, so he could only whisper into the phone. "Where did you go?"

Zhou Feng complained, "The saddle was screwed on there good; we couldn't get it off. So we were looking for a wrench, and while we did, we studied the surveillance camera around here. You know what? It's not even working! Ha ha ha ha..."

Ye Qin was speechless with indignation: he'd been captured, and Zhou Feng was laughing so happily!

But he could neither tell Zhou Feng that he was caught, nor solicit his friends' help. He kept his composure and replied, "I waited forever and you still didn't come. So I just went home. You guys can leave now."

He didn't say anything about the dilemma he was in right now. How considerate and loyal he was!

When he hung up, Cheng Feichi turned his head and glanced at him. Now the sky was completely dark, and the light from street lamps was so dim that he couldn't see for sure whether Cheng Feichi was silently laughing at him.

Well, he might not be laughing in my face, but he's absolutely laughing behind his sleeve.

The nearest police station was only one block away. Ye Qin became even more nervous when he saw the word "POLICE" on the lightbox, though from a distance. Millions of ways of escaping the law popped up in his head. He even thought of lying on the ground and shouting for help.

But he couldn't allow himself to be so awkward. It would be humiliating if he had claimed responsibility, but still ran away. They were schoolmates who would definitely meet each other again in the near future. If people started gossiping, what would others think of him?

Ye Qin walked slowly with his head bowed in shame and agony, while Cheng Feichi stopped and parked his bike by the wall. *Finally, we're here,* Ye Qin thought. He managed to muster

the courage to lift his head, only to find he wasn't standing in front of the police station—instead, it was a shabby and small garage.

Cheng Feichi was talking to someone inside. "Sir, I need to fix the tires."

The gate of the repair station was wide open. A grey-haired man was dealing with a bike on the ground, and he replied, "I'm busy right now. All the tools are there. Fix it yourself."

Cheng Feichi agreed. He put his bike down and rolled up his sleeves to remove the tires.

Ye Qin could only stand there, not knowing what to do or where to go.

He crept toward Cheng Feichi, flexed his wrist that had gone red because of Cheng Feichi's tight grip, and wiped his sweaty hands on his trousers. His nervous feeling was fading away. Seeing how hard Cheng Feichi was trying to repair the bike, he asked condescendingly, holding up his chin, "Why do you have to fix it? Just buy a new bike."

Instead of answering him, Cheng Feichi focused on his bike. He started by releasing the air in the two tires, then removed the damaged inner tubes and put them in a basket filled with water.

Ye Qin had never witnessed the process of repairing a bike. He was curious about why Cheng Feichi was pressing the inner tube in water. "What are you doing? Washing it?"

This time Cheng Feichi answered, his hands pressing on the tire. "I'm looking for the puncture."

Bubbles started to come from a specific point in the tire. Cheng Feichi made a mark on the puncture and then started grinding the tube.

Ye Qin kept watching his movements. He thought bikes were too complicated to repair, and the process also stained those nicely shaped hands. He then came up with another mean-

ingless comment. "So you can also repair bikes!"

The word "also" implied that he assumed Cheng Feichi was a jack-of-all-trades, and sounded too much like Ye Qin was trying to start a conversation. Yet Ye Qin didn't think about it that hard, and patiently waited for a reply.

Cheng Feichi glanced at him and tossed him a rag. "Wipe it."

Touching the dirty rag was the last thing Ye Qin wanted to do, but he still managed to hold it between his fingers as he came up with a good idea. He said to Cheng Feichi, very gently, "I'll wipe it, but you...you don't report me to the police. Deal?"

Ye Qin always seemed like a naughty trouble-maker, but he was a teenager after all. He didn't know what it was like to be thrown in jail, and was terrified at the mere thought of being handcuffed.

But being stared by Cheng Feichi in silence was probably no better than that.

Cheng Feichi had a beautiful pair of amber eyes, but they were cold enough to freeze others when he wasn't showing emotion. Feeling nervous and scared again, Ye Qin was about to say, "Fine. I'll do it now," when Cheng Feichi looked down at the tire and said, "Finish wiping and we'll talk about it."

Ye Qin was as lazy as a rich young master, coddled by his family. If he saw the oil bottle fall right beside him, he wouldn't bother to pick it up. He had never even wiped his own bike—he only dusted it off a little bit before he needed to use it. Now facing the various colors mixed with heavy dust on Cheng Feichi's bike, he could barely stand how dirty it was. Squatting, he tried to wipe the bike several times before feeling so nauseous that he wanted to puke right here, right now.

He was quite tidy, so he was constantly cleaning the rag. After he had already wasted a lot of water, the elderly man couldn't stand it and said, "Hey, go easy on the water. Prices just

rose last month."

Normally, at this time of year, Ye Qin would use warm water to clean his face or wash his hands; he could hardly stand the cold. His fingers were already stiff after washing the rag only a few times. The man's words instantly irritated him, so he replied crossly, "How much does it cost? I'll pay it off." He then motioned at Cheng Feichi and added, "And the money for repairing his bike. I'll cover that, too."

The man finished what he was doing and laughed with a cigarette clenched between his teeth. Yet he didn't answer.

Ye Qin became even more annoyed by his laughter, so he took a few 100-yuan bills and slammed the money on the table. "Is this enough?"

The man laughed a lot louder, then asked Cheng Feichi, "Kid, how did you meet this friend of yours? What a rich boy."

Cheng Feichi, who had been concentrated on fixing the tire, now answered, "He's not a friend."

The man wondered, "Then how do you...?"

Cheng Feichi, seemingly in a good mood, replied with a slightly rising intonation, "I found him on the street."

Ye Qin was incredibly embarrassed. He kept scrubbing the rag and trying to endure this painful moment. He unexpectedly realized how vulnerable he was without the help of his friends and family, and it made him both ashamed and somehow sad.

His sad feelings reached their climax when he got a call from his mother. Hearing Luo Qiuling worrying about why he hadn't come home yet, he couldn't help but sneeze as his eyes filled with tears. He quickly turned his back on Cheng Feichi and answered in a hoarse voice, "I'm hanging out with my friends. I'll be back soon."

"Did you catch cold? Go somewhere nice and warm, and I'll get the chauffeur to pick you up," Luo Qiuling said, sound-

ing concerned.

"I'm okay. I'll get a cab." Ye Qin sniffed, pretending that he didn't want to cry at all. "Where's dad? Is he home now?"

"Not yet. He said he's having a dinner party tonight. He'll be home late."

Ye Qin unconsciously glanced at Cheng Feichi, who was now fully concentrated on applying patch glue on the tube.

Ye Qin thought his dad could be using a dinner party as an excuse to visit his housebound mistress and her son, so he replied angrily, "He can go partying forever, and shouldn't bother coming home tomorrow. Or ever."

After the work was done, Ye Qin's hands were already so numb that he felt they no longer belonged to him. He followed Cheng Feichi timidly, and couldn't help but sneeze twice when they were back on the street.

The police station was right in front of them. Ye Qin was attentively planning on how to answer the police officer's questions smartly, to fight for a reduction of the possible charges. He was so immersed in his thoughts that he suddenly bumped into Cheng Feichi.

Cheng Feichi was standing quite steadily. He took out a pack of facial tissues and handed it to Ye Qin. Seeing that Ye Qin was staring at him blankly without taking the tissues, he could only point at his own face and say, "You've got something here."

Ye Qin used his phone as a mirror to check his face. The corners of his mouth, his lower eyelid, and his nose were all covered with paint stains. It must have gotten all over his face when he was wiping his tears with his dirty hands.

It took a long while to get his face clean, and then he had to struggle with the dirt on his hands. The paint that Zhou Feng

used drove him completely crazy, as it was not only hard to rub off, but also smelly as all hell.

The pack of tissues was quickly used up. Ye Qin used the last one to wipe his nose, which immediately turned red. He protested against the roughness of the tissue with a frown.

When he was done, he took out a 100-yuan bill and said, "Here. For the tissues."

After getting himself clean, Ye Qin was once again an arrogant and condescending young master.

Cheng Feichi didn't even take a look at the money. He turned around and straddled his bike.

Ye Qin was confused. "Aren't we going to the police?"

And Cheng Feichi said, "The bike is all good now."

Ye Qin remained silent for a few seconds before he suddenly realized something. "You fooled me!"

Cheng Feichi turned his head to watch two students by the curbside. They picked up a snack bag that they'd accidentally failed to throw into the bin and threw it back in. Ye Qin didn't understand why, but he also looked in the same direction.

When the two kids left, Cheng Feichi said slowly, "See? Even those students know they need to take responsibility for what they did."

After what happened when they left the bike station, Ye Qin was so angry that he didn't sleep well for days. But he also cared about his dignity, so he couldn't tell anyone about the embarrassing story.

Later, he recalled that the surveillance camera wasn't working, and that Cheng Feichi didn't take the knife with him. Then why was he afraid of facing the police? What charges could Cheng Feichi bring against him?

Cheng Feichi was definitely making a fool of him as payback!

He was completely outraged this time, and was fully prepared to take revenge on Cheng Feichi with Zhou Feng—yet Zhou Feng announced that he would stop picking fights with Cheng Feichi after several immature plans.

"He's already in a relationship with someone, and Yiran was about to give up on him. Why would I keep messing with him?" Zhou Feng was not the type of person that held a grudge for long. He said quite casually, "As long as he doesn't cause me trouble, I won't go after him anymore."

This time, it was Ye Qin who felt indignation. He felt irritated at the thought of having wept like a fool in front of Cheng Feichi. He was afraid that one day Cheng Feichi might tell everyone about it and completely embarrass him in school.

Sun Yiran's birthday arrived very quickly. A bunch of students went to the club that belonged to Liu Yangfan's family, and sat down in the largest room. Fruit and drinks were served in large quantities.

Sun Yiran had a lot of girlfriends; there were over a dozen from the neighboring classes alone. The girls were all complimenting and obeying her, letting her pick the karaoke songs first. She was the princess of the evening.

But she was still immersed in sad feelings of rejection. She picked a dozen heart-breaking love songs and kept wiping her tears as she sang along. When it came time to cut the cake, she was still sniffing. Someone asked what wishes she had made, and she threw the knife onto the table and started crying out loud.

"What's wrong with me? Why isn't he into me?"

A few girls took her to the bar table and tried their best to comfort her. Zhou Feng was also acting the fool to make her laugh. After a while, someone finally made her smile. She took the microphone and sang a sad but powerful song named *Innocent of Love*.

Ye Qin sat alone on the sofa at the corner of the room. He looked at everyone through listless eyes, feeling that he could no longer blend in with these naive and reckless teens.

Zhou Feng returned to Ye Qin with several bottles of beer in his arms. He opened one of them and gave it to Ye Qin. "Here. Let's drink together."

Ye Qin pushed his arm away and moved farther from him.

"What's wrong with A-Qin?" Zhao Yue approached them.

Ye Qin was annoyed the instant he saw Zhao Yue. Zhao Yue was the one coming up with all the awfully stupid ideas, while he was the one bearing all the consequences. He wanted to beat the shit out of him.

"Hey, it's Yiran's birthday! Why can't we just be all nice and happy?" Zhou Feng tried to ease the tension. "I just got a very interesting piece of news. Wanna hear about it?"

Ye Qin wanted him to leave as soon as possible. "Say it or fuck off."

Zhou Feng was never the type of person that could keep a secret. Seeing that most people were busy having fun, he asked everyone to lean forward as to form a circle. And then he put on a mysterious and exciting voice to spill the beans.

"Remember that straight-A student in Class No. 1? He's gay."

It was fifteen minutes to five in the morning when Cheng Feichi woke up.

His circadian rhythm wasn't working to his advantage. He hadn't been working at the convenience store for three weeks in a row, so he could have actually slept in this Saturday morning.

After washing his face and brushing his teeth, he put a pot of porridge on the stove. As he waited, he reopened the book on classic Math Olympiad exercises. Having never specifically

signed up for any classes, he merely listened to the math teacher's two-hour course on the competition, but found that he had approaches to math problems that were quite different from those of the teacher's. In order to pin down the most accurate and safe shortcut to the answers, he took out some used scribe paper to reexamine the exercises.

When Cheng Xin got up, it was not yet 6 a.m., but Cheng Feichi had already packed his bag and was ready to leave home. Breakfast was on the table, kept warm with a porcelain bowl on top.

"Mom, I'm gonna be home late today. I need to look for some books," Cheng Feichi said while putting on his sneakers.

Cheng Xin approached the bedroom door. "I recall that tutoring doesn't begin until 9 a.m. Why are you leaving so early?"

"I've left a book at school," Cheng Feichi stood up and was about to turn the doorknob. "I have to go get it. And I'll just stay there to review for a while."

Cheng Xin asked him to wait and got him a pair of gloves. "You need to ride your bike, don't you? Wear this. It's very cold outside."

Cheng Feichi's bike was right at the staircase between the second and the third floor. There was no such thing as a security guard in this outdated compound, so the bike would very likely get stolen if parked outside the building.

He held up the crossbar and the seat to take the bike downstairs when Cheng Xin, who was by the doorstep, suddenly said, "Some kids are coming here for classes today."

It took Cheng Feichi a few seconds to come up with a response. "Mom, just rest at home. You don't need to work. I've made enough money from tutoring."

"Staying home alone is boring. I want to do something useful." Cheng Xin covered her mouth and coughed, before she

continued with no emotion, "I'm just telling you my plan. Not asking you for advice."

Cheng Feichi went downstairs and left the compound on his bike. He wasn't going in the direction of his school, and turned left instead.

Recently, he'd started working in a breakfast diner from 6 a.m. to 8 a.m. each day. Normally his classes didn't start before eight, so it perfectly fit into his daily schedule. The owner would even let him leave early if they weren't busy.

There were fewer people in the diner on Saturday mornings, so Cheng Feichi even had the time to consider taking another part-time job in the evenings from Monday to Thursday, as long as he could be home before midnight. He could just tell his mom that he was doing homework at school.

He didn't want to deceive his mother, but there was no other choice aside from lying. Cheng Xin had never approved of his part-time jobs; she wanted him to focus on his schoolwork. Yet she had recently been hospitalized for half a year, which almost completely drained the family's bank account and nearly lost them the apartment they now lived in. When they could no longer afford the hospital services, Cheng Xin chose to stay at home. Cheng Feichi took a year off school to care for his mother, and during that year, they didn't have any income.

One night, Cheng Xin was sent to the hospital with a soaring temperature. Because Cheng Feichi didn't have enough money to pay the medical bills, the two of them could only sit in the corridor of the hospital. Cheng Xin had an IV drip, and Cheng Feichi held the bag as high as possible. He kept the same posture for such a long time that his blood circulation was blocked and his whole arm swelled after that excruciating night.

Ever since then, he understood the importance of wealth. He didn't mind how people looked down on him, as long as he

could prevent his mother from suffering. More importantly, he didn't want to grovel in face of temptations in the future, so he had to work hard.

The work at the diner was not demanding for him. Two hours later, he headed for a garden compound that was more than ten kilometers away on his bike. The tutoring fee was calculated by minutes, so the sooner he got there, the sooner he could leave and buy books before noon. After the afternoon classes were over, he planned to try his luck to see if he could find a job in the shopping center near his school—the school stood in an area that became quite bustling at night. Someone there might need a part-timer after 9.30 p.m.

The student that Cheng Feichi tutored in the morning had signed up for classes in three subjects: Math, Physics and Chemistry. Her parents came into the study room every twenty minutes to make sure that their daughter was safe alone with a male teacher, bringing along drinks and snacks as an excuse.

After her parents had entered and left several times, the girl became so annoyed that she was about to jump to her feet and lock the door. Cheng Feichi tried to comfort her. "Your parents really care about you."

"No one needs this kind of 'care'!" The girl seemed a bit angry.

After she closed the door, she became bolder and looked at Cheng Feichi with undisguised affection.

"Mr. Cheng, do you have a girlfriend?" she asked, flushing.

Cheng Feichi answered, "No."

"Then...then..." She had been waiting for this exact moment! She continued with more courage. "What's your type?"

Cheng Feichi's face was emotionless. He didn't even look up from the exercise book. He drew two more circles on the exercise book and shoved it back to the girl. "Finish these exercises and

I'll tell you."

The tutoring classes in the afternoon were for a ninth-grade boy named Wei Jiaqi. He was in the middle school division of School No. 6.

His parents were old clients, and had been hiring Cheng Feichi since last semester. With Cheng Feichi's help, Wei Jiaqi's class rank had moved up by nearly twenty spaces.

Normally, parents would be content with such a good result, but when Wei Jiaqi's mother heard that Cheng Feichi had been transferred from the very famous high school affiliated with the nearby university to the no-name High School No. 6, she immediately doubted his ability. She even came in between classes several times in order to negotiate the tutoring fee with him. She claimed that a certain teacher from High School No. 6 charged only a bit more than him for extra-curricular classes, which meant that she wanted to cut the price.

This time, Cheng Feichi came with the first-place certificate he'd earned in a physics competition. It had persuaded Mrs. Wei, and she stopped nagging about the fee.

In order to show his willingness for continued employment, Cheng Feichi extended the class by thirty minutes for free. When the class was over, Wei Jiaqi, a timid boy, felt quite awkward and sorry. He gave Cheng Feichi a bag of sweets and hoped he was not offended.

When he left the Wei's home, he took a wonderful deep breath and felt quite relieved. He threw a candy into his mouth and rode his bike to school.

He might lose these two jobs soon, so it was never too early to start preparing for the future.

There were many stalls and shops near High School No. 6, and want ads were all over their windows. The recruiters either

left their phone numbers or wrote their email addresses. Seeing that there was still some time before nightfall, Cheng Feichi bought a two-hour pass at the nearby internet cafe and sat down at a computer. He planned to send his resume to suitable employers, as well as search for more possible solutions to that exercise in the Math Olympiad book that he was reading that morning.

He'd just hit the power button on the computer when his phone started to buzz because of an incoming call. The name "Zhang Peiyao" popped up on the screen.

Ye Qin woke up when someone sat down in the cubicle right next to him.

The weekends were always the most boring days for him. After lunch, Zhou Feng and some friends had talked about going to the new disco in the city center, but Ye Qin didn't want to come along. They parted near High School No. 6. Not wanting to be home with his hypocritical father either, he just paid for a cubicle for two hours at the internet cafe. He played games for a few rounds, browsed the high school forum for some time, and then lay on the sofa and slept for half of the afternoon.

The wall next to him was so thin that it barely reduced the sound from the next cubicle. His "neighbor" seemed to have put their phone on the table. The phone kept buzzing for a whole minute before the caller hung up, and then started buzzing again. Ye Qin was so irritated that he was about to kick on the wall when his neighbor finally picked up.

"What's up?"

It was a low-key, masculine voice, familiar but not recognizable.

Ye Qin couldn't help but eavesdrop on the conversation.

The person on the other side clearly didn't expect this would be an issue, since he turned on speaker mode. Ye Qin was able to catch every word the caller uttered.

"I'm not at home. You can say everything over the phone."

"Don't be like that," the girl sounded kinder and more adorable through the phone. "Hey, don't be like that. I gave my heart to you. I want to be with you no matter what school you go to."

"I told you I don't care. Don't call me anymore."

"You're mad at me."

"No."

"Then why are you so indifferent to me? You didn't talk to me when I visited your school. You weren't like this before...Are you seeing someone else?"

"No."

"I'll ask my dad to help me transfer to your school, okay?"

"No."

It seemed that the girl had burst into tears because of his cold attitude toward her. She sounded like she was crying. "You're definitely mad at me. You hate me for revealing your secret and getting you expelled from school."

On hearing this, Ye Qin was astonished.

The one sitting next to him must be Cheng Feichi, and the secret that the girl was referring to might be the gossip that Zhou Feng had just told him yesterday: Cheng Feichi was gay, and he transferred to their school not only for the amazing scholarships, but also because he was running away from the resulting scandal—everyone in the university's affiliated high school knew about his shameful sexual orientation. Though the school masked the truth and details to save face, he had actually been expelled. Since no other school would accept him, he had stayed out of school for a whole year before High School No. 6 finally took him in.

"No." Cheng Feichi's voice didn't change at all, even when the girl reminded him of such heartbreaking memories. "I've forgotten all about it. You should do that, too."

After that, Ye Qin was basically listening to the girl crying and apologizing for what she did. Cheng Feichi only responded very briefly from time to time to show that he was still there.

From what he heard, Ye Qin had the whole plot—a girl had tried in the wrong way to make Cheng Feichi interested in her, and consequently pushed him even further away. Yesterday, that gossip hadn't stirred many feelings in him, as Zhou Feng didn't have any proof. It could've been complete nonsense. But after hearing it all with his own ears, Ye Qin began to gloat at Cheng Feichi's failure and humiliation.

These days, he could only be happy when something bad happened to Cheng Feichi.

Ye Qin was softly and happily humming to himself as he moved from the wall back to his computer. He was randomly browsing web pages when he saw a post with the title, "Ran into a hot guy at the recreational yard. Anyone know him?" Wondering whether it could be about himself, Ye Qin clicked it, and a photo of Cheng Feichi immediately appeared. It was most likely a sneak shot taken during P.E. class, in which Cheng Feichi's face was barely recognizable. Scrolling down, Ye Qin saw a flock of people screaming about how handsome he was. And someone replied, "That's Cheng Feichi from Class No. 1 in the 11th Grade. He just transferred to our school this semester."

And then someone anonymously uploaded more pictures of Cheng Feichi and introduced him as a hot and smart straight-A student. The whole comment section gradually became all about praising Cheng Feichi as a genius. Ye Qin kept clicking "next page" in the replies, and much to his surprise, someone wrote, "I

now pronounce Cheng Feichi as the hottest guy in High School No. 6. Any objections?"

A lot of people supported this proposal.

Ye Qin couldn't help rolling his eyes while reading the comments. He clicked the comment section at the bottom and began typing. *Hot Straight-A student? He's not even straight.*

When he clicked the "Send" button, the dialogue box kept telling him that he needed to log in before leaving a comment. He typed in his most frequently used username, "Yourbigbro-Qin_notQing," but failed to get the password right after five attempts. He was so annoyed that he wanted to just smash the keyboard, but he was afraid that Cheng Feichi would hear it. So he could only hold his temper, turn off the computer, take his shoes, and go home.

When he pushed the door of the cubicle open, he had a nasty trip and nearly fell down. The internet access card slipped from his hand and landed after moving in a parabolic path.

He looked down to find his shoelaces untied. Luckily, the doors of nearby cubicles were all closed, and no one was in the corridor when he tripped. He squatted down to try his best to fasten his shoelaces. No one knew that he liked wearing slip-ons not for the convenience, but for the fact that he couldn't deal with shoelaces. No matter how hard he tried, the knots would come untied in three minutes. The pair of shoes he was now wearing now had been bought for him by Ye Jinxiang. He would've never even considered putting them on if his mother hadn't set them by the door when he was about to go out.

He carelessly tied the laces into a snarled knot and moved forward without standing up to reach for the card that was lying near the water dispenser. He had only moved two steps forward when he saw a hand with beautifully outlined knuckles picking up the card.

He was quick enough this time. He opened the nearest door, entered the cubicle, and hid behind the door. When he was about to kick the door so as to close it, he heard Liao Yifang shouting after him.

"Cheng-tongxue, are you here searching for study materials too?"

And not even half a second later, before Ye Qin could close the door, he continued, filled with joy and amazement, "Ye-tongxue! You're here too!"

Things started to go way beyond Ye Qin's wildest imagination.

In the internet cafe cubicle, surrounded by noise from outside, the three of them were...studying. Ye Qin sat between two model students, hearing them discussing the math problems which he could make no sense of. To him, their conversation was no different from a foreign language, which only made him feel like a moron among talents.

"Ye-tongxue." Liao Yifang worried that Ye Qin might get bored, so he took a very thick chemistry exercise book out from his pack and showed him the basic knowledge review papers from Unit 2. "You haven't mastered the knowledge in this unit. You can finish it here, and Cheng-tongxue can help you with it. He can explain things very clearly."

Ye Qin immediately waved his hands. "Thanks, but no... I haven't finished the homework yet. I'll just go home..."

Liao Yifang looked very surprised. "Is that so? The homework was picked from exercises in the textbook." He then got the Chemistry textbook out of his pack and said, "I've written it all on my exercise book. Use my book. I've circled the important parts and written down some ideas that could help you do the exercises."

Seeing how Liao Yifang trying his best to help him, Ye Qin

could no longer reject him. He took the textbook and started doing the homework, as muddle-headed as he was.

The three teens focused on studying until Cheng Feichi's two-hour pass expired. They packed their things up and prepared to leave the internet cafe.

As the sky was getting darker, the internet cafe was getting more crowded. Liao Yifang protected his two fellow students with his arms as if he were a helicopter father. When they reached the cafe gate, he said very seriously, "A lot of ruffians gather here at night. Don't hang around after getting what you need."

Ye Qin pretended to agree with him, while thinking Liao Yifang was the only one that would ever think of studying in an internet cafe. When he entered Cheng Feichi's cubicle, he clearly saw that he was looking at an email box, but he didn't see the exactly what he was reading or typing.

Cheng Feichi could've been sending an email to Ye Jinxiang. The man always liked to put on airs and required his employees to report everything via email, no matter how small it was. He even had very detailed specifications for the font and layout of the email. He'd once asked Ye Qin, on a whim, to write a semester report and send it to him.

When they finally got out, Liao Yifang invited both of them to dinner. "We've been chatting so happily, but I forgot to properly introduce the two of you. Let's eat together and get to know each other."

Ye Qin didn't want to be with Cheng Feichi, so he quickly said, "Of course I know who he is. Cheng Feichi. The straight-A student from Class No. 1."

"You two already know each other? I didn't know that..." Liao Yifang said.

Cheng Feichi looked at Ye Qin, seeming curious about how

he would explain the matter.

Ye Qin stuttered, "Ah...did...didn't you give me his notes last time? The...chemistry notes? I was the one who returned them to him. And I saw him from the window that day."

"Ah...right." Liao Yifang totally believed it. "Cheng-tongxue is not only intelligent, but also handsome. It's not strange that you'd remember him for such a long time after just a glance... He was the one who caught you when you fell from the bar in P.E. class, wasn't he?"

Ye Qin nodded, feeling incredibly anxious. He and Cheng Feichi were not just acquaintances.

"Cheng-tongxue, do you know Ye Qin? We're in the same class. In our class, his nickname is Little—"

"Little buddy. They all call me their buddy," Ye Qin cut in on Liao Yifang's enthusiastic introduction. Now he understood why Zhou Feng was always trying to cover Liao Yifang's mouth—he would keep talking forever if no one interrupted him.

"Uh-huh?" Cheng Feichi seemed quite interested. "I don't know much about him. Why don't we choose a restaurant and talk details over dinner?"

Sitting in a small restaurant near the school, Ye Qin was so fretful that he wanted to pull his hair.

Cheng Feichi is absolutely doing this on purpose! He already knows that I overheard his secret, so now he's pretending that he doesn't know me to make sure that I keep his secret from Liao Yifang, all to save face.

Ye Qin was fiddling with a piece of tissue when he figured it out. He thought of Cheng Feichi as this tissue and tore it into many strips.

The small restaurants just outside the school were very eco-

nomical. Liao Yifang ordered two stir-fried dishes and a soup. When he was about to sit down, he saw the other two sitting at different sides of the table and facing each other in complete silence, so he tried to start a conversation.

"Hey, are you guys hungry? Sorry, they serve dishes a bit slower than other places. But their food tastes better than anyone else's. Whenever it's too late for me to go home, I come here and order a dish and a bowl of rice. With your stomach full, there's enough strength to make it through the entire afternoon's classes and assignments."

Ye Qin looked around and saw several wooden tables on which the paint was already starting to crack and peel, as well as a wall-mounted television on which the screen was covered with small black spots. The whole place seemed so shabby that Ye Qin doubted whether the food here was really edible.

He quietly raised his arms to prevent himself from touching the dirty table covered with oil; careful enough to not be noticed by the other two people. When he turned his head, he found several sweets lying in the dish in front of him.

"Eat these if you're hungry," Cheng Feichi said.

Ye Qin had tried sweets from this brand before, and the milk-flavored ones were his favorite. Now, he was indeed hungry. Seeing that Liao Yifang had just put one into his mouth, Ye Qin also picked one up and popped it into his mouth to suck.

Because they were all hungry, they concentrated on eating during the meal. The restaurant used fresh ingredients and never skimped on the amount of food, which surprisingly shattered Ye Qin's bias against economical food. Since he hadn't eaten eat much at noon, he ate two bowls of rice with a plate of stir-fried eggs and tomatoes.

Ye Qin habitually took his wallet out when the bill arrived, but Liao Yifang forbade him to pay. "Ye-tongxue, this isn't right.

We still have so many meals to enjoy together in the future, you know. Surely we can't let you pay the bills forever."

Cheng Feichi didn't say anything, but showed he agreed with Liao Yifang's comment. Ye Qin was speechless, and thought, *God, please help me! I don't want to eat with them anymore!* Still, Ye Qin reluctantly agreed to split the bill.

Liao Yifang's bike was parked very close to the restaurant. He took the bike, sitting on it and waving goodbye. "It was so much fun today. Let's keep in touch. We can study together and make more progress!"

Liao Yifang was so positive that Ye Qin somehow felt ashamed of himself.

After Liao Yifang left, Ye Qin walked towards his own bike, kicking the gravel on the road. He saw that Cheng Feichi was walking slightly ahead in the same direction.

"Hey."

Cheng Feichi stopped and looked back at him.

Ye Qin didn't even start thinking about what to say next until now. He said with hesitation, "Umm...that...I mean, a bit earlier..."

Cheng Feichi took several sweets out of his pocket and handed them to Ye Qin. "These are all that's left."

Ye Qin, who'd eaten as many as five of Cheng Feichi's sweets at this point, now blushed. He felt like he was being treated as a kid. "...I wasn't asking for these. I mean, I was in the cubicle next to yours."

He was expecting that Cheng Feichi would promise that he'd never tell anyone about what happened that night. But what he didn't expect was for Cheng Feichi to be extremely calm. He was standing there, waiting for him to continue, not showing any inclination to break the silence.

Ye Qin was feeling both self-conscious and awkward. He

didn't know what to do other than get straight to the point, so he did. "I overheard what you said to that girl over the phone. And I already knew your secret. If you promise that you won't tell anyone about what happened that night, about how I fell for your trick, I won't tell anyone your secret as well."

Cheng Feichi seemed slightly surprised, and then put on a quite obvious smile.

This was the first time that Ye Qin ever saw him really smiling. He used to smile in a rather unnoticeable way, but now he was actually smiling at him, with the corners of his lips clearly moving upwards and his eyes squinting. He was acting like he'd just heard a hilarious joke.

Ye Qin was about to ask why he was laughing when Cheng Feichi slightly lifted his chin, taking in a breath, still smiling. "What secret?"

Ye Qin's eyes widened. He couldn't believe how calm Cheng Feichi was. He wasn't even afraid of him telling everyone that he was gay!

The absolute nerve.

Ye Qin couldn't be as bold and calm as Cheng Feichi was. His face turned all red. He thought he was about to go crazy. He couldn't say another word, so he kicked a piece of gravel, which hit Cheng Feichi's feet. Tossing his head, Ye Qin ran away furiously. His shoelaces came untied again and fluttered in the air with his movements.

Another week passed. Everything was normal at school. Ye Qin didn't get any unusual gossip about Cheng Feichi from Liao Yifang.

He felt quite relieved. Just as he thought that Cheng Feichi must have accepted the deal and he would never need to worry about him anymore, things went wrong at home.

He skipped two self-study sessions in the evening and ran all the way back home. When he pushed the door open, he saw his mother sitting on the sofa and crying.

"Why did you tell him to come back now?" Ye Jinxiang felt quite ashamed upon seeing Ye Qin. He quickly closed the door behind Ye Qin and said, "Go upstairs now. I'm talking about something serious with your mom."

Ye Qin had come home because the housemaid had called him. He'd told her to call him when anything unusual happened at home, lest his father try to bring any strangers into the house. He didn't expect that her call would come so soon.

Luo Qiuling didn't want her son to see her crying so help-lessly, so she wiped her tears, managed to smile, and nudged him towards the stairs. "Why did you come back so early? Don't you have self-study sessions tonight? Go, go upstairs and finish your homework. I'll ask the maid to warm some soup for you..."

Taking in the sad smile on the face of his mom, Ye Qin felt intense heartbreak. Overwhelmed by outrage at his father, he suddenly threw a porcelain vase onto the floor. With a loud bang, it smashed into pieces.

Staggered by his violent behavior, Ye Jinxiang pointed at him, shouting, "What the hell are you doing? You wanna beat me up? Are you crazy?" And then his fingertip turned to Luo Qiuling. "See what a good son you've raised? How on earth can he take over my company?"

Ye Jinxiang was never the gentleman he pretended to be when he was angry. Once the hypocritical disguise was taken off, his roughness was clearly revealed. Though Ye Qin wasn't willing to admit it, he had already realized that he probably got his perversity and quick temper from his father.

Luo Qiuling was so frightened that she forgot to wipe the tears on her face. She pushed Ye Qin even harder to make him

go upstairs. "Sweetheart, just go. Stay in your room and I'll come to you right away."

Ye Qin tightened his grip on the handrail and glared with force at Ye Jinxiang. Like a young leopard daring to challenge his sire, he was silently compelling his father to tell the truth.

Ye Jinxiang walked back and forth in the living room. Perhaps it was because of his own awareness of his crimes, when he started talking again, he became gentler.

"What you think is true is not the truth. I have no idea why that woman's stuff ended up in my pocket," he said to Luo Qiuling in a seemingly very honest way. "You know, a lot of people are trying to get at me. But I can promise that I've never been interested in a single one of them. Not in the slightest. Never."

The last thing Ye Qin would do was to believe his father, but he couldn't tell his mother the truth.

The next day, everything went back to normal. Luo Qiuling was watering the flowers while talking about what happened yesterday. She sounded a bit helpless. The whole thing wasn't complicated at all. Just as Luo Qiuling had said, she had a gut feeling that something was wrong with her husband.

"But you heard what you dad said. Perhaps I was just too sensitive. I was making a fuss about nothing. Your dad is always busy at work, and he has to socialize with many people. Misunderstandings are hard to avoid, but we have to let it all go. Listen, you're still young. You have to let it go."

While Luo Qiuling was saying that, she put on a smile on her face, but Ye Qin didn't see any sign of joy in her eyes.

In the evening, Ye Qin was tossing and turning in bed. The image of Ye Jinxiang's black MPV sliding into the Yulin Compound and coming to a stop in front of building #3 was so clear

in his head. And then his ugly and angry face popped up, still shouting, "See what a good son you've raised? How on earth can he take over my company?"

Ye Qin stared blankly at the ceiling. He refused to close his eyes, even when they grew sore.

Of course he'd say that. He's got another son out there. Of course he doesn't care about mom and this family.

Cheng Feichi's cold eyes suddenly appeared in his head. According to the private detective, Ye Jinxiang hadn't reconnected with his mistress and her son until the end of last year. And every time he went to the Yulin Compound, he chose a time when Cheng Feichi was not home. On his student information sheet, Cheng Feichi stated that his father was deceased. It seemed that he knew nothing about Ye Jinxiang and Cheng Xin's secret, or that his birth father was still alive.

But...

Ye Qin tried his best to shake it off, but he just couldn't stop himself from linking Cheng Feichi with Ye Jinxiang.

That boy would eventually return to his father's family, even taking control of the Ye company. Ye Qin didn't care about being the next CEO, but the company should have belonged to the Luo Family and to his mother. Who the hell was Ye Jinxiang? And where was Cheng Feichi coming from?

At this moment, Ye Qin thought of Cheng Feichi's face, wearing a smile that could be called a blatant sneer, and his amber eyes slightly enlarged.

He must have been laughing into his sleeve the whole time. In his eyes, I must be stupid for fighting him. My efforts were of no avail; I was as hilarious as a clown.

Ye Qin closed his eyes forcefully, his eyelashes trembling in the darkness.

At the time Ye Qin had just fallen asleep with his fists clenched, Cheng Feichi, who had been unknowingly haunting Ye Qin for the whole night, had already gotten up. When he finished his morning routine and left the building with his bike, a dim crescent moon was still hanging in the sky.

Yesterday, the owner of the breakfast diner asked him to come earlier today. A regular customer had ordered a large batch of steamed buns for the temple on the Hongye Mountain, and in the meantime the diner had to serve its customers as usual, so they needed to start earlier in case they got too busy and things got out of control.

Cheng Feichi had been helping his mother with housework since childhood; for him, kneading dough and making buns were but small pieces of cake. He finished preparing 100 buns before dawn, which absolutely satisfied the owner. The owner then allowed him to leave early, and filled his bike basket with baozi and soy milk sealed in plastic cups for him to share with his classmates.

Seeing Cheng Feichi entering the classroom with a huge bag of breakfast, a student who'd also come very early said to him, "Wow, you've really got a lot of food today. Can I have some?"

"Sure."

Cheng Feichi went to his seat and put down his backpack. When he tried to stuff the backpack into the drawer of his desk, he felt something inside the drawer. He reached for it and pulled out a beautiful pink paper bag.

The student who'd followed him to his seat for breakfast looked at what Cheng Feichi unwrapped from the pink paper bag with amazement. There was a box of milk, a sandwich, and a package of nice milk-flavored toffees.

The amazed student exclaimed, "Smart guy, you're so popular! Not only are you getting more and more love letters,

you're now starting to get tasty breakfasts too!"

As Cheng Feichi had only been at the school for a little over two months, his classmates didn't really know much about him other than his amazing grades. They only knew him as a smart guy, and called him that as well.

He opened the card at the bottom of the paper bag and saw some scribbles: *A nice day starts from nice breakfast. — YQ.*

Cheng Feichi thought of all the people who could have done it, but none of their initials were the English letters Y and Q. He waited for a whole day, but there was no follow-up. He assumed there must be some kind of mistake.

But the next morning, another pink paper bag showed up in his drawer. He asked the students who'd arrived earlier than him, but no one had seen the person who came with the bag. And this time, the note on the card changed: *Did you like the sandwich yesterday? I got a new flavor for you today. — YQ.*

Cheng Feichi had been receiving anonymous breakfast all the way through Thursday, but he still hadn't figured out who was behind all this. Yet the culprit took a small step forward by changing their signature into a very intimate, perhaps too intimate, phrase in English: "Yours lovely, Qin." But the letters were still just scribbles.

Cheng Feichi stared at the signature for quite a while and extended the scope of "suspects" to the whole school. He thought of every single person that he'd ever met, and now he finally came up with a match.

In the next morning, Ye Qin entered the classroom at the last minute, yawning. He immediately noticed the pink paper bag on his desk. It seemed just like the one he'd asked Zhou Feng to pick for him.

A card was beneath the bag. Ye Qin opened it up and saw

Cheng Feichi's beautiful handwriting beneath his own scribbles.
Ye Qin, I'm the person who sits close to the window in the second to last row of the 4th group of Class No. 1.

Even the signature was in neat and perfectly formal English:
Yours sincerely,
Chi.

CHAPTER 03

DURING the morning reading session, Ye Qin scolded his deskmate Zhou Feng for his bad advice. "I told you it wouldn't work."

Zhou Feng scratched his head and wondered, "How come? Yiran was so happy when she got the breakfasts I sent her."

Ye Qin opened a search engine and turned his cellphone to Zhou Feng. "That English saying, *yours s...s...*whatever; that sign-off is usually used in formal business emails. And you told me to write 'yours lovely'?! How 'lovely' it is! Now I'm screwed."

Zhou Feng took the card from his hand. "Shit! He must have done it on purpose! It was so obvious that the breakfast was for him, and now he thought that you made a mistake?"

Ye Qin rolled his eyes. "Of course. Otherwise he wouldn't taunt me with that signature."

Zhou Feng replied, "So...what next?"

Ye Qin had no idea. The pink paper bag was driving him crazy. He patted Liao Yifang, who was sitting diagonally in front of him and memorizing new vocabulary, handing him the bag. "Mr. Class Monitor, this is for you."

Liao Yifang turned around and adjusted his glasses. "I've

had breakfast. Give it to someone who needs it." Seeming deeply touched by what Ye Qin did for him, he continued, "I just knew Ye-tongxue hasn't changed! You're still our lovely little sunshine."

"Lovely" was the last word Ye Qin wanted to hear right now. Feeling insulted, he gritted his teeth while putting on a reluctant smile, "I'm not sunshine anymore. I'm a thunderstorm."

It indeed rained in the afternoon, and P.E. class became a self-study session.

Mr. Sun, the class's main teacher, was sitting at the podium, while Zhou Feng hid behind a large pile of books to use his cellphone. He created a QQ chat group named "Qin-ge's Dream Team."

Zhou Feng: First thing to do after joining: change your alias in the group! You idiots change your usernames a million times a day; no one can ever figure out who the hell you are.

Fan: *Done.*

Ye Qin: ...

Zhou Feng: Use your full name! Come on! A-Qin wouldn't like this!

Zhao Yue: What happened? The breakfasts didn't work?

Zhou Feng: That guy returned it with a note joking about A-Qin's previous notes, which pissed A-Qin off.

Liu Yangfan: I told you so. You should've listened to me.

On the day when Ye Qin decided to punish Cheng Feichi, the four of them sat down for a brief discussion on how to make real impact this time.

In the beginning, they all wondered where Ye Qin's sudden hatred of Cheng Feichi came from. Ye Qin couldn't possibly tell them the real cause, so he switched up a few facts about that night, portraying himself as a hero of brotherhood and emphasizing how treacherous Cheng Feichi was, which evoked outrage

in Zhou Feng.

Zhou Feng shouted, "What an arrogant jerk! I told you that we couldn't let him get away. If we don't teach him a lesson and make sure he remembers it, he'll keep pulling this shit forever!"

Their long discussion did not guarantee a perfect, workable plan. They even thought of putting up huge posters on the school's notice board to tell everyone that Cheng Feichi was gay, but Zhao Yue immediately vetoed it. Now that the school had taken him in, it either meant that the school didn't care about the gossip regarding his sexual orientation or that it cared more about the benefits he could bring. Society was becoming more and more tolerant of gay people; there was even news that same-sex marriage would soon be put on Congress' agenda. Cheng Feichi wouldn't be hurt just because his sexual orientation was exposed.

"How about this?" Liu Yangfan had remained silent for quite a while, and suddenly said, "He likes guys, so we get a guy to hit on him, toy with him, and then dump him for good. That'll cause way more psychological damage than the public's useless opinion ever could."

Zhou Feng applauded his genius and praised him for becoming such a genius badass; thanks to the influence of his rich, cunning, and resourceful family.

Now they had a new direction, but they were again trapped—who was the right person for this?

"First of all, he has to be completely on our side," Zhou Feng said, stroking his chin.

Liu Yangfan followed, grinning wickedly: "And he must be very good-looking."

And then, everybody was looking at Ye Qin.

Despite everything else, everyone could at least agree on that Ye Qin was indeed very good-looking. He looked just like his mother, with his big eyes, fair skin, and slender limbs. When

he was a kid, he was a crybaby and was constantly mistaken for the opposite gender. His dark history included pictures of him dressed as Snow White in a kindergarten drama activity. After he realized the problem, he had always tried to imitate older boys who swaggered and talked in gruff voices. Describing him as "pretty" or "cute" would immediately irritate him. Gradually, he became the arrogant and condescending young master of today.

Baffled, he stared back at everyone and grumbled, "Why are you staring at me?"

Zhao Yue tapped the tip of his cigarette and said: "It's always risky to let an outsider carry out a plan. We've already got someone good enough here, why bother looking for anyone else?"

Ye Qin cursed. "Fuck!"

Zhou Feng thought Zhao Yue had a point. "I think it's a good idea. A-Qin's very good-looking. Last time at that convenience store, wasn't Cheng Feichi deceived by his appearance? He even asked A-Qin to vouch for him!"

Ye Qin's mind was full of Cheng Feichi now. He thought for a while and said, "That makes it even more impossible! He must have a grudge against me. How could he ever be...be seduced by me?"

Liu Yangfan seemed confidently at ease. "What do you know? It is in his own adversary where a man finds the strongest interest and desire for conquest."

Ye Qin was getting goose bumps. "Conquest? Shit!"

Zhao Yue tried to comfort him. "Hey, put yourself in his shoes. If you can win his heart, which was impossible for any girl in this whole school, think of how proud you'll feel!"

Anyway, this was the plan. Immediately after this, Zhou Feng came up with the terrible idea of sending breakfast to Cheng Feichi. Now that the breakfast plan hadn't worked, they created this chat group to discuss new alternatives.

Zhou Feng: A-Fan, what would you do? You're really experienced at pursuing girls.

Liu Yangfan: It's raining outside.

Zhou Feng: Oh, are you suggesting A-Qin bring him an umbrella?

Ye Qin: No way. Never gonna do it.

The best he could do was to pay one of Cheng Feichi's classmates to bring breakfast to his desk, and that was what he did every day. If they made him send an umbrella to him in person, he might as well just kill himself right now.

Zhao Yue: Can you stop being so stupid? A-Qin drove to school today, right? He could just give him a ride.

Ye Qin agreed. Now that Cheng Feichi already knew that he was the one behind all the food and cards, it was time to show up and meet him face-to-face.

He saw it as the very first direct battle with Cheng Feichi, which made Zhou Feng nervous as well. The latter took out a bottle of hair spray and sprayed it all over Ye Qin's head while mumbling, "A-Qin, do your best. We might not be as good as that guy, but we have to be confident no matter what..."

Ye Qin replied, a little crossly, "Not as good? I'll nail this shit on my first try!"

During the last class of the afternoon, Ye Qin borrowed Sun Yiran's mirror and comb and slicked his hair back. Then he pulled down the zipper of his uniform coat to look cool, and walked out of the school gate, shivering with cold.

Class No. 1 was always the last to be dismissed. When they flocked out of the back gate, it was still raining. Cheng Feichi was so tall that Ye Qin immediately spotted him even when he was walking among so many people. He was steering his bike, then mounted it and rode away slowly.

Parking just outside the crowded back gate, Ye Qin's silver

sports car was not only incompatible with all the bikes around it, but also disproportionate to the narrow road. Some girls looked at him curiously through the window, but were startled by a sudden honk. Ye Qin rolled the window down and stared at the girls with reproachful eyes—they had blocked his view.

When Cheng Feichi finally passed by his car, Ye Qin started the engine and kept driving slowly alongside him. Maybe Cheng Feichi was rushing back home because of the rain, because he didn't turn his head to look at Ye Qin even after he'd peddled for a long while and was about to turn onto the main road.

"Hey," Ye Qin shouted at him. "Get in the car! I'll drive you home."

Cheng Feichi rubbed the rain off his face and rejected the offer. "No need, but thanks."

Then he rose himself up on the saddle to pedal even faster and departed like a bolt of lightning.

Ye Qin doubted that Cheng Feichi had even seen his handsome face, or how cool he looked in his car. He followed him and shouted again, "It's raining too hard! Let me take you home. We can put your hunk of j...your bike in the trunk!"

Cheng Feichi didn't even answer this time. He rode his hunk of junk straight into main street traffic.

Normally, if someone else dared to be so rude to him, Ye Qin would already be long gone by now. But Liu Yangfan had told him that the most important trick in flirting was to show sincerity, and the devil was always in the details. No one, regardless of gender, could reject such steadfast affection.

Ye Qin contained his anger and kept following Cheng Feichi.

There was heavy traffic on the road. Though there were broad, flat streets from the school to Yulin Compound, Cheng Feichi seemed to purposely choose the narrow and poorly-main-

tained ones. Ye Qin struggled to keep up with him in his huge sports car. When he drove onto an unfamiliar road, he was surprised to see a police cordon ahead. There was only one lane open, and it could only accommodate the width of two people.

The traffic officer waved his hands at Ye Qin, asking him to pull over. Seeing that he was still a boy, the officer also checked his driver's license. Ye Qin didn't look like his picture on the license; he seemed quite irritated, and had a different hairstyle—unlike the delicate and well-behaved boy with neatly-trimmed bangs in the photo.

After spending a while comparing the two, the officer lectured, "There are signs saying 'Road Closed for Construction' and 'Detour.' Didn't you see them? Be careful. It's for your own safety. You're still young."

Ye Qin was so focused on Cheng Feichi that of course he hadn't noticed any signs. Wait...Where was Cheng Feichi?!

Cheng Feichi had outwitted him again! Ye Qin was furious.

Ye Qin was getting more and more excited by the day, but he was already at his wit's end. Cheng Feichi seemed immune to whatever he did—he changed the breakfast bags to blue ones, but Cheng Feichi still returned all of them. Once Ye Qin noticed that the card was slightly different, only to find that Cheng Feichi had corrected a grammatical error for him.

Ye Qin tore the card to shreds, and even went as far as to reduce the shreds to ashes. He grabbed the lighter out of Zhao Yue's hand and started burning them, piece by piece. He accidentally burned his fingertip but was too ashamed to let anyone else know about it. Despite his reddening eyes, he could only bury the pain and hurt in his heart as he threw the lighter out the window.

There had never been anyone who would go against his will. There had never been anything that he wanted but could not obtain. How could he stand being treated like this?

While Ye Qin remained so indignant that his eyes filled with tears, Zhou Feng returned with some juicy gossip. After finishing a can of cola, he comfortably sprawled himself on the sofa.

"I finally know Cheng Feichi's type," he announced, quite pleased with himself.

It was an autumn afternoon. The shadow of trees on the concrete changed along with the sun's movement. The bright sunshine lit up the tiny dust particles floating in the warm air.

At around one, Cheng Feichi put down his book and headed for the cafeteria. He was used to avoiding the busiest hours. If he came later, he could not only save time that would have been wasted queuing, but also save some money as the food price would sometimes go down in off hours. He could then use the money to buy dietary supplements for his mother. Autumn was the best time for nourishing the body, and his mother had lost some weight due to her worrying about her students.

On the first floor of the cafeteria, Cheng Feichi glanced at his usual seat and saw that Wei Jiaqi was reading while he was eating. The middle school section, where Wei Jiaqi attended, was a little bit far from the cafeteria. Wei Jiaqi was anxiously preparing for his monthly exam, and he was quite timid by nature. Whenever he had problems with his studies, the first one he would turn to was always his tutor, Cheng Feichi.

Wei Jiaqi was not a smart boy. Cheng Feichi always had to explain the same question multiple times before he could finally understand it. But he was hardworking, and was of the opinion that attending a great university was the only path to a better life. Cheng Feichi was very patient, and wasn't bothered by Wei Jiaqi at all. For him, it was just a couple of questions to be solved during lunch break. It wouldn't take much time.

After they finished the "mini-lecture," Cheng Feichi went to grab some lunch. The cafeteria would close in twenty minutes, so he ate faster than usual.

The rice was a bit dry. As he gulped down a bowl of soup, he saw someone sitting down in front of him.

Ye Qin was drowning in shame right now.

Zhou Feng had told him that Cheng Feichi was "dating" a boy every day at noon. The kid was short and skinny in an effeminate way; a light wind should suffice to blow him away. Yet Cheng Feichi was so nice to him that he not only always ordered food for him and helped him with his schoolwork, but also wore a warm and charming smile throughout the date, which made lots of girls look at the kid with envy. How they wished they could be this lucky boy!

"Yiran even saw him unscrewing a bottle cap for the kid," Zhou Feng sneered. "He doesn't even care if people know that he's gay. Only those girls could possibly be blind enough to be that obsessed with him."

Zhou Feng was neither cautious nor reliable, but Ye Qin only had him to count on now.

Ye Qin glanced down at himself. He was wearing a dusty pink sweater, light blue jeans, and a pair of white platform shoes. He couldn't possibly dress any more effeminate than this. As his straightened bangs slightly blocked his view, he pushed them back, revealing the fair forehead covered with a slight sweat, like pearls.

What Liu Yangfan had said was still ringing in Ye Qin ears: "You know what, we're doing it all wrong. Men all like to be seen as heroes, to be relied on, so you just need to pretend to be weak. If you could act like you've got a bag leg, that'd be even better."

Ye Qin had his doubts about this, but he hadn't ever really been in a romantic relationship. The internal logic of his argu-

ment seemed okay, or at least it sounded right to him. Gay men were men, too. They should be treated just like any other men.

So he'd come to the cafeteria dressed like this. He put a bottle of drink on the table and pushed it forward. "Drink something. I don't want to see you choke yourself."

He didn't even dare to speak up.

Ye Qin only managed to keep up an imposing act by always speaking at an unnaturally loud volume. Now that he kept his voice down, he was startled by how soft and sweet his tone actually was.

Cheng Feichi responded as expected. He stopped neglecting him and glanced at the bottle. "I'm not thirsty. Keep it for yourself."

Ye Qin took the drink back coyly and tried to open it, but failed. So he put it back on the table and pushed it again towards Cheng Feichi.

Seeing that Cheng Feichi was looking at him, Ye Qin's face turned red.

He softened his voice. "It's too hard. Can you...help me out?"

Cheng Feichi opened the bottle for him, and then took his plate to the sink.

While he was rinsing the plate, Ye Qin showed up again behind him. "Thank you. This is for you."

It was a 500ml bottle of cola. What Ye Qin had bought for himself was a bottle of sweet pear juice.

"It's nothing." Cheng Feichi shook off the water on the plate, put it in the collecting area, then turned around and left. He didn't take the drink Ye Qin offered.

Ye Qin kept following him. "You don't like coke? Then... you can have my juice."

He said so, but he didn't hand the juice to Cheng Feichi. He didn't seem willing to give it away, looking like a little cute animal protecting its food.

Cheng Feichi was amused. "It's okay. I'm really not thirsty."

It was only a three-minute walk from the cafeteria to the teaching building, but Ye Qin managed to extend it to ten minutes by talking about random things.

"Are you hungry? You didn't eat much."

"Have you tried the milk-flavored lollipops from the corner shop?"

"Do you wanna go to the bathroom together?"

"Your first class in the afternoon is Physics? Mine is Chemistry."

"This drink is so heavy. Can you hold it for me?"

…

Liao Yifang had once remarked that Ye Qin was the sunshine of his class. Cheng Feichi didn't buy it at the time, but now he realized it was somewhat true.

When they reached the staircase, Ye Qin hadn't yet made Cheng Feichi take the drink and his every gesture of goodwill was met with a cold shoulder. Extremely unsatisfied with how things turned out, Ye Qin reached an arm out to stop Cheng Feichi when he was about to go upstairs. He held his head high and announced: "The breakfast was for you. It wasn't a mistake."

Cheng Feichi stopped. "Uh-huh?"

It was the first time that Ye Qin ever confessed his love to anyone. Even though it was merely a prank, a show, he was still so shy that his face completely turned red; it looked as if it was going to start bleeding.

It seemed impossible that Cheng Feichi would make the first move, so he mustered the courage to make the offer. "I rode my bike to school today. Can you wait for me after school?"

"For what, specifically?" Cheng Feichi asked, seeming cool and distant.

Ye Qin couldn't believe that Cheng Feichi didn't take the hint at all. But he was the one who wanted to pursue Cheng Feichi, so he closed his eyes for a second and finally managed to say: "I... I wanna do my homework with you."

Normally, they had over an hour before the evening self-study session began, so Ye Qin was used to returning home for dinner. He might even play a round of computer games, if time allowed. But today, he called Luo Qiuling and told her that he wouldn't be coming home. When Luo Qiuling asked him whom he would be eating dinner with, he answered in a careless way, "Just a classmate."

The cold wind was blowing hard, but Ye Qin still only draped the uniform coat loosely around his shoulders. He ran into Sun Yiran in the corridor and she couldn't stop laughing at how he was dressed.

"A-Qin, you really make me worry. Are you dressed like that to compete with me? To be the fairest of us all? You're so cute."

Having been laughing at for the whole day, Ye Qin couldn't have cared less about what others said now. While he sat on his bike waiting for Cheng Feichi, some students from Class No. 1 joked: "You look so cool today! Which girl is going out with you?"

Somewhat proud of himself, Ye Qin managed to keep his cool. He said to himself with excitement: *None other than your classmate by the name of Cheng!*

He waited for twenty minutes, but still didn't see Cheng Feichi. He was a bit nervous now, so he went upstairs to look for him.

Cheng Feichi was still in the classroom. It was customary for him to bring some food to school. He had lunch and dinner

at school each day, and the food he brought was enough for another meal. Recently he'd needed to help Wei Jiaqi at noon every day, so he ate lunch in the cafeteria. When evening came, he would put some boiled water in his lunch box, and he had a hot meal to enjoy.

When Ye Qin rushed into the classroom, he saw Cheng Feichi pouring boiled water into his lunch box. He stared at Cheng Feichi for a while, forgetting everything that he planned to say. He looked at Cheng Feichi in astonishment and a bit of disgust.

"This is your dinner?"

"Hmm." Cheng Feichi stirred to fully mix the water and rice and sat down for the meal.

There was no one else in the classroom, as everyone else had left for the cafeteria. After making a call, Ye Qin returned to the seat in front of Cheng Feichi. He rested his chin on his hand and watched Cheng Feichi eat.

The food in Cheng Feichi's lunch box looked so sad. The stir-fried cabbage was made of the outer leaves only, and the stir-fried carrots with potatoes had only some traces of meat. It was even more horrible than what the cafeteria served.

Ye Qin couldn't stand it anymore. "Stop eating. I've ordered take-away. It'll be here in ten minutes."

While saying so, he picked up the lid of the box and was about to cover the food with it.

Cheng Feichi raised his hand to stop it. "I'm fine with my own meal."

Ye Qin argued, "But I've ordered a meal for two!"

Seeing that Cheng Feichi didn't answer him, Ye Qin began to feel bored. He put down the lid, and started judging Cheng Feichi's food. "What sort of meat is that? Is it chicken? Chicken breast or chicken thigh...You've got three more evening sessions. How can you get through tonight? ...The oil smells weird. And the

dishes are just mixed together. The different flavors are gonna get all mixed up. Aren't you uncomfortable with that? How could a human being eat this?"

Cheng Feichi swallowed the food in his mouth and lifted his head, looking at Ye Qin. "If it makes you feel uncomfortable, just go back to your classroom. I'm still eating this."

Now he's angry. According to Liu Yangfan, being angry is better than not responding; it means he actually cares about me, Ye Qin thought.

Ye Qin was still sitting there, chin resting on his hands, watching Cheng Feichi eat his meal and occasionally making comments. "Is it really that good? Did your mom make it?"

Cheng Feichi wasn't a petty guy, so he still answered him with a low "hmm." But Ye Qin couldn't be happy with his response. Cheng Feichi's mother was the mistress of his own father, and her existence made his own mother cry. He could never forget about it. He had to make that woman pay for what she did.

Five minutes later, the food arrived, but Ye Qin was still feeling annoyed. As he was eating the ribs, he intentionally made a lot of noise to show how delicious they were. When Cheng Feichi finished his dinner and stood up to clean his lunch box, Ye Qin grabbed his hand.

"This is too much for me...can you eat some of it?"

Cheng Feichi couldn't figure out his intentions. "What on earth are you trying to do?"

Ye Qin finally heard him ask the question. He was so happy that the rib in his mouth fell to the ground as he answered, "Pursue you!"

When the self-study sessions ended, Ye Qin rode his bike, pursuing Cheng Feichi all the way home.

As they passed the street with the small bike garage, Ye Qin was on cloud nine. He peddled while saying, "I was stopped by the traffic officer last time, but now he can't do a thing to me."

Saying this, he made a face at the police on watch. He didn't look like a weakling who couldn't even open a plastic bottle right now.

Cheng Feichi was incredibly thankful that Ye Qin didn't follow him to his doorstep. When the sign "Yulin Compound" was visible, Ye Qin stopped and waved goodbye to him.

Cheng Feichi carried his bike and entered the dark staircase. Mr. Lee, who lived on the second floor, opened the door and turned on the flashlight in his hand.

"Xiao-Chi, you're back."

"Yep. Grandpa, you'd better go inside. It's too cold outside. I can see the staircase without the light."

Mr. Lee smiled. "It's okay. I have something to tell you anyway."

When Cheng Feichi was back inside his home, he was still thinking about what Mr. Lee had told him. He said that a young man had been wandering around the building recently, and he'd specifically asked Mr. Lee whether a woman whose surname was Cheng was living on the third floor.

Mr. Lee was a cautious man, so he replied that he didn't know. But he supposed that the young man would come back again, so he told Cheng Feichi and his mother to stay cautious.

The first "man" Cheng Feichi thought of was *that* man. Maybe it was someone working for him.

Last summer, that man came to his home for the first time, and was subsequently kicked out by Cheng Feichi. After that, that man made sure to only come around when he wasn't home. If he hadn't been certain that man wouldn't hurt his mother, Cheng Feichi would've rather stayed home at all times to forbid

him from entering the house at all.

But lately, Cheng Xin's attitude towards that man had softened very obviously.

It had always been only his mother and him, supporting each other. The hardest times were already over. Cheng Feichi still remembered when his mother was so aloof that she told that man to stop patronizing her, even though she was ill. Even if that man had managed to worm his way into her house, Cheng Xin wouldn't take anything he gave.

Cheng Feichi looked at the fine watch on his desk, feeling extremely agitated. When he tossed the watch into the rubbish bin in its original package, Cheng Xin tried to persuade him otherwise.

"You don't need to wear it every day. Just take it."

Cheng Feichi obeyed her by picking the watch out of the bin and placing it on the table. When he was about to enter the study, he returned to where his mother was sitting.

"Next time when he comes, am I supposed to call him Dad?"

The very straightforward question made Cheng Xin panic for a second. But she regained her composure very fast; so fast that Cheng Feichi thought he misread her expression.

She said to Cheng Feichi, as calmly as when she taught Cheng Feichi to be an independent and responsible boy, "I'm your mom. I won't let anything bad happen to you. You'll understand it when you get older."

Cheng Feichi thought he had already understood plenty. He was probably being too naive and confident. But while most of his peers were still under the sure protection of their parents, he had already started to learn how to survive in society and clearly planned out his future. He made sure to stick to his plan.

Not a single, tiny mistake was allowed.

However, there was always something unexpected in his way—such as the overwhelming talk of him being gay at the university's affiliated high school, and the boy always by his side these days.

Ye Qin was determined to keep his word by putting real effort into pursuing Cheng Feichi. As long as Cheng Feichi was at their school, Ye Qin would follow him everywhere. It was like he'd planted a tracking device on him.

At first, Cheng Feichi thought that he'd give up quickly if he kept giving him the cold shoulder. But it'd been more than half a month, and Ye Qin was still pursuing him relentlessly.

By the end of November, Cheng Feichi got a job at a small restaurant in the shopping center near High School No. 6. He was supposed to serve food from 9:30 p.m. to 12:00 p.m. He told his teacher that he needed to take care of his mother, and was permitted to leave fifteen minutes early every evening. Therefore, he could start working right away when he arrived at the restaurant.

This was why Ye Qin failed to catch Cheng Feichi after evening sessions for several days.

He started to grow impatient. He had tried to dress like a girl and tried to act like a weakling, but Cheng Feichi was still so cool and far away. The biggest response that he'd ever given Ye Qin was a faint smile. Cheng Feichi looked like a reluctant but sympathetic spectator watching a bad circus show.

Ye Qin was absolutely humiliated by his reaction. He wrote Cheng Feichi's name on a dartboard and hit each character squarely with only three throws.

"Aside from being gay, does this guy have any other weakness that we could work on?" Zhou Feng wanted to help Ye Qin, so he started to think of other ways. "He's also poor. Is that it?"

Ye Qin said to himself, "Of course there's more! He's also a bastard."

"That's all?" Zhao Yue sneered. "Being poor is his biggest weakness."

Ye Qin, who was born with a silver spoon in his mouth, couldn't agree more. How could a poor guy have any sort of life? By eating rice in boiled water? By hustling here and there doing part-time jobs?

Right. His part-time jobs.

Ye Qin was suddenly inspired and heartened. He spent two days finding where Cheng Feichi went each night, and rode his bike to the small restaurant, sitting in the booth closest to where Cheng Feichi usually stood and playing PSV games. Sometimes he'd give 200 yuan to the owner of the restaurant so that Cheng Feichi was allowed to sit down with him for half an hour and Ye Qin could copy his homework.

Cheng Feichi was no longer interested in what Ye Qin wanted from him. Ye Qin even tried to give him money—twice as much as his current salary—to become his boyfriend. Cheng Feichi instantly frowned at the offer and stopped responding.

Upon reflecting on his own proposal for a while, Ye Qin found it disgraceful indeed. At the end of the day, Cheng Feichi was no kept man. So he didn't mention it again

Habit was a frightening juggernaut. It crept into your body and mind so silently that you couldn't notice it.

Not many days had passed before Cheng Feichi was used to seeing Ye Qin huddling at the table closest to the kitchen when he took dishes out for customers.

The heating was not yet switched on at this time of the year, yet Ye Qin was so fashion-conscious that he wouldn't allow himself to wear too much, which showed that he couldn't bear the

cold. The loose trousers he wore were cropped and barely covered his calves. His slim ankles were exposed in the cold air, shaking and circling very casually. Sometimes he sat with one leg crossed on the seat. One of his hands was busy copying homework, and the other hand rubbed his ankle red because of the cold. Meanwhile, he blew on his fingers to keep warm.

Cheng Feichi himself felt cold just looking at him, and he wished that he'd just go home.

Talking would be of no use, so he thought of a trick. He intentionally wrote all the wrong answers for multiple choice questions on his homework, and Ye Qin, unsurprisingly, copied them all.

On the following day, Ye Qin was scolded by several teachers in front of everyone, and was even given a time-out outside the classroom. All his fellow students soon knew about this, and Cheng Feichi was no exception.

If Ye Qin wasn't dumb, he should get the hint and stop coming to the restaurant. Or so Cheng Feichi thought.

However, before ten the same evening, Cheng Feichi left the kitchen holding two plates stacked with dishes and spotted Ye Qin sitting at his usual place. Ye Qin was wearing a goose-yellow hoodie and writing something, looking quite indignant and sad.

Tonight, Master Ye paid the restaurant owner the usual 200 yuan so that the servant boy could sit down for half an hour.

"I have to write a 3,000-word self-criticism letter... It's too hard. I've only done 800 words so far." Ye Qin blew on his fingers and then pushed the paper towards Cheng Feichi. He hung his head and begged Cheng Feichi pitifully, "Could you please help me with this? Even 300 words will do. I'll deal with the rest of it."

Cheng Feichi remained silent. Ye Qin was afraid that he wasn't willing to help him, so he chose to back down, pouting

his lips.

"200 words. Can you at least write 200 words for me?"

Meanwhile, he held up two fingers, poorly suggesting "two hundred."

Cheng Feichi looked at him for a short while and asked, "Why do you have to write this?"

Ye Qin thought he was about to say yes, so he grinned. "Because I didn't study hard enough and I wasn't paying enough attention when I copied the homework... But of course you can't write that. The central thesis is that I know that I did wrong and that I'll work harder in the future."

"Wasn't paying enough attention?"

"Yep; I was talking about yesterday's homework," Ye Qin explained as if he didn't really care. "I mistook your answers and copied them all wrong. Probably because of the dim light here... It's okay, I'll bring a lamp tomorrow."

It seemed that he didn't realize that he was being tricked at all.

Cheng Feichi didn't know whether he was only pretending to be this naive. But if he wasn't, he must be very well-protected by his parents.

Ye Qin pulled out all the stops and finally finished the letter before midnight.

When they left the restaurant, Cheng Feichi was riding his bike ahead of Ye Qin, and he frequently looked back at him. Ye Qin had been in the restaurant with him for several consecutive nights, and he didn't make it to bed until very late at night. Now he was so exhausted that he kept nodding his hooded head, struggling with the bike in the meantime. Fortunately, it was already very late and there were few people on the street. Otherwise, he would have caused an accident.

When they stopped at the intersection because of the red

light, Cheng Feichi supported his bike with one leg and looked at Ye Qin. "Go home. That's enough for tonight."

Ye Qin slowly rubbed his hands together. It seemed that the cold made him numb. He replied, "...What?"

Cheng Feichi took off his gloves and handed them to Ye Qin. "Take these and go home."

The gloves were still warm, and Ye Qin couldn't take his hands off them. Only God knew that his fingers were completely numb with cold after spending the whole night working on his letter.

Staring at the gloves, he didn't put them on until Cheng Feichi added, "At least they can protect your hands from the wind." He thought Ye Qin was judging his gloves.

Ye Qin raised his head and looked at him with a blank expression. "If I want to put them on, do I have to go home after that? But...I want to see you to the door."

Seeing that Ye Qin was too drowsy to speak coherently, Cheng Feichi knew that it was impossible to reason with him. He had to let Ye Qin continue following him.

The gloves gave Ye Qin a lot of energy. He peddled his bike vigorously in the strong wind, crying out "one, two, three" to fortify himself. When they reached the gate of the compound, Ye Qin waved his hands very enthusiastically and shouted "see you tomorrow" to Cheng Feichi.

However, tomorrow was Saturday, so Cheng Feichi didn't go to the small restaurant. He wanted to tell Ye Qin, but he instantly found it unnecessary. If Ye Qin didn't find him tomorrow, he'd just go home. It was important to make Ye Qin actually understand his attitude.

The next morning, when Cheng Feichi was on the way to the female tutoring student's home, the girl's father called to say that the whole family planned to go out, so he didn't need to

come today.

Cheng Feichi asked him whether the student had time for class tomorrow. He had already planned out the whole class schedule for this girl, based on the weak points in her studies. If she couldn't finish the schedule for this week, she'd make less progress than planned. Although the father only mumbled his response, the girl's piercing shriek was very audible. She was shouting, "I don't wanna go! I just want Mr. Cheng to be here!" as her mother tried to comfort her.

Cheng Feichi knew that he could no longer teach this girl. He stopped the bike at the curbside and sent the father a text containing his bank account number, suggesting civilly that he pay the bill for the past month.

After that, he looked up at the hustle and bustle around him, suddenly feeling at a loss. He didn't know where to go from here.

Ever since he started to know things, he was working as efficiently and endlessly as a motor. He was going faster and faster every day nonstop, to the extent that a sudden stop would make him perplexed. He didn't know how to deal with any unexpected spare time, which also flew by so quickly.

He decided to go to the library to borrow two books for Math Olympiad first, and then shop for some groceries. He could only set his mind at rest when he found something to do. While he was climbing the stairs towards his home, he was trying to decide how to cook the fish. Braise it in soy sauce? Steam it? Or make some soup? Children all loved fish soup.

Cheng Xin taught her students Chinese, and she was an expert in handling kids. Back when she had been healthier, she'd almost turned the whole house into a kindergarten. Sometimes kids would stay for lunch or dinner, so if Cheng Feichi was home on weekends, he would pay special attention to meal prep.

It was just after ten in the morning, and the kid had already arrived. Cheng Feichi knocked on the door to tell Cheng Xin that he would make lunch, and then entered the kitchen with the groceries.

Cheng Xin was sitting on the balcony, reading stories to the child. Her gentle voice escaped the closed door and went all the way into Cheng Feichi's ears. She was probably talking about *Little Red Riding Hood*.

Most kids were familiar with this story, but for Cheng Feichi, it was something that he'd read on the sly. Cheng Xin was a fantastic narrator who could enchant children with even the most ordinary stories, but she never told any of these tales to her own son. She told him that fiction was just what adults used to deceive children, and that he only needed to study hard so that she wouldn't lose face.

Seemingly indifferent to fame and fortune, Cheng Xin never made a lot of demands of her son. But Cheng Feichi knew that she was controlling him in an invisible way—a cold look and a very simple sentence from her would easily stress him out. Therefore, he instinctively refrained from doing anything wrong and only worked harder.

He knew that parents in other families weren't the same as his mother, but he would rather believe that this was his mother's unique way of loving him.

At least his mother treated him differently, not like the other kids. The doctor said that staying in good moods was good for her health, and he was also willing to make her happy.

He pared two apples and reached for a glass bowl in the cupboard. They seldom used this kind of bowl, so he rinsed it carefully. When he turned back to the chopping board, he found one apple was missing.

The person who had taken it was not ashamed at all. He

leaned on the refrigerator and took a bite, and there came a clear sound of biting into the fruit's flesh.

Ye Qin had been standing by the kitchen door, watching Cheng Feichi working on the apples very attentively without noticing him.

"Why are you here?" Cheng Feichi went blank when he saw Ye Qin.

Ye Qin had never seen him so startled. What a surprise! He pointed at the ceiling and answered: "I don't know. Guess I just fell from the sky and arrived in your house."

Still amazed, Cheng Feichi actually did look upwards at the ceiling. When he realized how embarrassing that was, he lowered his head and said: "Who's that little girl? You took her here, right?"

Seeing that Cheng Feichi knew he was lying, Ye Qin was a little frustrated. He took another bite of the apple and mumbled: "Yep, she's my sister."

Actually, she was Zhou Feng's sister. Ye Qin heard that someone living in the Yulin Compound was tutoring her. He casually inquired about the teacher's name, and found out that the teacher was Cheng Xin. He had been looking for a way of getting closer to Cheng Feichi, and this was a real godsend!

So, he volunteered to adopt Zhou Jiang as his own sister and to escort the eight-year-old girl to and from the compound. Yet when he'd entered Cheng Feichi's house, he was not home. Now he finally knew that Cheng Feichi was working as an at-home tutor.

What a poor family, Ye Qin thought and lay down on the couch. The heating made him so drowsy that he fell asleep. When he woke up, Cheng Feichi had just gotten home.

"She is really your sister?" Cheng Feichi asked in hesitation.

"Who else could she be?" Ye Qin was also busy brainwashing himself while lying to Cheng Feichi. "It's a hundred percent true. Didn't you notice how much we resemble each other?"

While they were having lunch together, Cheng Feichi kept comparing the faces of Ye Qin and his so-called "sister," but failed to spot any resemblance. Instead, the little girl looked like she was related to a friend of Ye Qin's; the one who swaggered in front of him in P.E. class whose surname was Zhou.

Cheng Xin smiled. "Xiao-Chi prepared the meal. Perhaps it doesn't suit your taste."

"It tastes really good," Ye Qin answered politely, as it was his first time meeting Cheng Feichi's mother. He didn't complain, and instead filled Zhou Jiang's bowl with fish soup while saying, "Drink it. And I'll get you more later."

Forced by her "brother," Zhou Jiang had drunk three bowls of soup, so she kept going to the bathroom the rest of the afternoon. Ye Qin was quite at ease. When Cheng Feichi was washing the dishes, he took the opportunity to look around the compact house. After a short while, he ran to the kitchen and knocked on the door.

"May I enter your bedroom?"

Cheng Feichi thought he wanted to look for his homework again. After the washing was done, he returned to his room, only to see that Ye Qin was sprawled on his bed. He'd covered his head with his hood, and part of his belly was revealed under his clothes. It was slightly moving up and down with the gentle rhythm of his breath.

When he sat by the desk, Ye Qin woke up and started wiggling on the bed. He said quite bashfully: "Sorry...May I sleep on your bed?"

Aren't you already lying on it without my consent? Cheng Feichi thought. But when he thought of how exhausted Ye Qin

looked yesterday and how he waved goodbye to him so happily in the cold wind, he didn't complain or refuse.

After waking up, Ye Qin managed to look more energetic. He sat on the bed, looking at the compact room and asking Cheng Feichi random questions. "Your room is so small...Do you have a game player? What about a basketball? Lego? At least you have a RC car? ...You've only got these award certificates and trophies? No way...you're so boring..."

Ye Qin stood by the glass display cabinet and touched one of the spotless metal trophies. The trophy made him feel cold, and even more sure that this was not a world he could understand. He looked at Cheng Feichi, who was putting away books at his desk.

"You've got so many awards. Haven't you got any pictures of you receiving them?"

Cheng Feichi was brought up short by this question and then shook his head. "Never."

"You couldn't afford it?" Ye Qin blurted out.

Unwilling to answer, Cheng Feichi turned his eyes to the desk, continuing to organize his books.

Ye Qin couldn't help frowning after checking the whole house. Today he came here to see how shrewd his father's mistress was, but he didn't expect this. The woman's behavior was as unremarkable as her appearance. She was benign. Sometimes she even looked weak. Ye Qin was never into bullying; if the mistress hadn't made his mother cry, he never could've hated her.

Theoretically, if she was Ye Jinxiang's mistress, she and her son wouldn't be so financially destitute. But now he'd seen it for himself. Every item in the house was telling him that they were poor. When Cheng Feichi opened the wardrobe to hang up his coat, Ye Qin saw that all his clothes were old and monochromatic, mostly black or gray. He only had five or six coats in

there, including the school uniform, while Ye Qin's wardrobe was filled with multiple kinds of denim clothes, outdoor jackets, baseball jackets, trench coats, and new down coats in various colors and styles.

Was Ye Jinxiang such a stingy person? Or were the mistress and her son so proud that they refused his financial aid?

Ye Qin was gradually becoming more upset. He sat back on Cheng Feichi's bed and took his new cellphone out of his pocket: "Sit still. I'm going to take a photo of you."

Cheng Feichi didn't see this coming. He lifted his head, trying to stop him, when Ye Qin pressed the button. The handsome eighteen-year-old lad basking in the warm afternoon sun was forever caught in a perfect photo.

When the winter solstice came, the capital city welcomed the first snow of the year.

The small restaurant was particularly popular tonight. A lot of people—young people just off work, exhausted middle-aged men looking for a special treat—came here for delicious dumplings as a Chinese tradition. They would also drink with friends to cheer things up during this traditional holiday.

Everyone in the kitchen was all wound up. Ye Qin couldn't get Cheng Feichi to sit down with him, even with money. Sitting all alone outside the kitchen, he felt quite bored, so he approached the kitchen door.

"Is there anything I can do? I could really use something to warm me up." Ye Qin stretched his neck so as to see better.

Cheng Feichi couldn't tend to him. He supposed the pampered boy couldn't bear the toil and would back off very soon.

What he didn't expect was for Ye Qin to be still washing the dishes when he finished his shift. Tidy dishes were stacked by his side. He was even more devoted to the task near the end;

when sweat trickled down on his forehead, he only managed to wipe it with his arm, without noticing the foam he accidentally got on his face.

"I'm almost done. Wait a second!" Ye Qin said to Cheng Feichi, his hands still working on the dishes.

In the end, the restaurant owner gave Ye Qin 200 yuan for cleaning the dishes, sending Ye Qin to cloud nine. Ye Qin seemed to forget how much money he had spent here for nothing. Holding the two notes in his hands—which had turned white because of how long they'd been soaked in the water—Ye Qin planned on buying a new pair of woolen gloves.

Once they got out of the restaurant, Ye Qin was overwhelmed by the cold. It seemed that the warm air he breathed out could freeze instantly. The snow kept on falling for a whole day as if there had been a hole in the dark sky. Ye Qin suddenly sneezed in the blowing wind, which triggered a headache. When he summoned up the courage to reach for his bike despite the cold, Cheng Feichi walked to him.

"Forgot gloves again?"

Ye Qin shrank from Cheng Feichi, preventing the latter from seeing the guilty look on his face, and uttered a low sound of admission.

Cheng Feichi took his gloves out of his pocket. Yet, when Qin raised his hands so that Cheng Feichi could put the gloves on them, the latter slightly bent down and used the soft inner surface of a glove to wipe off the oil stains Ye Qin had accidentally gotten on his own face.

Ye Qin naturally closed his eyes. When he opened them again, he saw that Cheng Feichi had already turned back and walked towards his bike. He dusted the snow off his saddle and exerted himself to wheel the bike towards the main road.

While putting the gloves on, Ye Qin sensed a subtly strange

vibe between him and Cheng Feichi. Neither of them were talking now, but he felt that it was a perfect time for saying something—if not asking for something.

"Hey," he said, walking behind Cheng Feichi. "Do you know what's special about today?"

Cheng Feichi didn't look back. "It's the winter solstice."

"And?"

"No idea."

Ye Qin noticed that Cheng Feichi was somehow not willing to look back, so he had to make him do that for him.

"It's the forty-fifth day since I started pursuing you," Ye Qin raised his voice, "and it's also my birthday."

Cheng Feichi stopped.

Not knowing exactly why, Ye Qin felt that his heartbeat was accelerating. He swallowed hard. The blowing wind covered the slight tremor in his voice. "Don't you have anything to say... to me?"

He probably had never known how soft his voice was when he dragged out the sound. As if he was acting spoilt, Ye Qin sounded as if all the sunshine was shining down on him, making the frozen air around them less unbearable.

Cheng Feichi finally turned back. His feet stepped on the thick snow on the ground, making creaks in the almost palpable silence.

The street lamp cast its dim light all over Ye Qin. It was enough to ignite his eyes, revealing the sparkles of expectation in them.

Cheng Feichi fixed his eyes on Ye Qin and slowly let out a breath. He compromised. "Happy birthday."

Almost at the same time, the clock tower inside High School No. 6 chimed.

Ye Qin counted to twelve along with the chimes and said

pitifully: "Aww...My birthday's over. I haven't made a wish."

Cheng Feichi continued to push the bike forward. The snow on the pavement was thick enough to reach their ankles. Each step of theirs left winding trails of footprints and ruts. Ye Qin carefully trod on Cheng Feichi's footprints, feeling particularly safe and relaxed.

Because of the traffic, the snow didn't accumulate on the main road. Cheng Feichi mounted his bike and pedaled for merely several meters when he heard Ye Qin grumbling. "Why isn't it moving?"

Cheng Feichi went back to check his bike. The tire of Ye Qin's bike seemed to be leaking air, which meant it could be punctured.

Ye Qin immediately looked frustrated. "No way. Bad luck right after my birthday!"

After checking the tire, Cheng Feichi stood up. He pedaled each bike with one hand, while Ye Qin was looking for somewhere to stay through the night.

"At this time of night, we can still get an hourly rate hotel room and have a bath there...or stay at the internet café for the night. Right, I need to call my mom first." When he took out his cellphone, Ye Qin said to Cheng Feichi, "You should probably call your mom, too."

With both of his hands occupied, Cheng Feichi didn't say anything in response. Ye Qin got through to his mother and was talking naturally in a sad voice: "Mom, I probably can't go home tonight...My bike broke down in the middle of my way back home...had a flat tire...It's too hard to get a taxi now. I'll just make do with a hotel room...It's okay. I've got a schoolmate with me...Not Zhou Feng. He's from Class No. 1 and you don't know him...Of course it's true! He's really from Class No. 1 in our school..."

Ye Qin's voice was gradually lowered. He didn't sound happy. After a short while, he approached Cheng Feichi and handed the cellphone to him. "My mom wants to talk to you."

Seeing Ye Qin's ears go red, Cheng Feichi understood what might have happened. He let Ye Qin hold one of the bikes, and put the phone to his ear. "Good evening, ma'am."

Ye Qin's mother sounded like a gentle and caring woman. She asked what exactly happened and whether they needed any help. Cheng Feichi volunteered that he was from Class No. 1 and they were heading for the bike station. Hearing that Cheng Feichi was likely to be a responsible guy, Ye Qin's mother felt more assured and simply reminded them to keep safe before hanging up.

Ye Qin put the phone back in his pocket and asked in hesitation: "We're going to get it fixed right now?"

Cheng Feichi merely nodded.

Ye Qin pouted his lips, looking as upset as a naughty boy who was forced to go home.

They went to the same bike station. From afar, it seemed that no one was in it, for there was no light, but the locked door was still easily pushed open by Cheng Feichi.

Before Ye Qin could make a sound, Cheng Feichi hushed him up with one finger pressed to his lips and talked in a low voice. "The owner is sleeping in the backroom. We'll leave as soon as it's finished."

Ye Qin had never sneaked in anywhere before. Anxiously, he tugged at Cheng Feichi's clothes and asked: "Is this breaking and entering?"

Weren't you bold and reckless when your knife broke and entered my tire? Cheng Feichi thought. He tried to spook him a bit: "Obviously. Be quiet. Don't let him hear you."

Hearing this, Ye Qin covered his mouth with his own hand, and turned on the flashlight on his phone to illuminate the room. He didn't realize that Cheng Feichi was joking until he saw Cheng Feichi's smile.

Cheng Feichi was busy polishing the bike's tire. "The owner is very nice. Every time my bike's broken down, I come here to fix it. He saw that I frequented here, so he told me the iron door couldn't be locked firmly, and that if I need to fix my bike at night, I could just push it open and come right in."

No wonder the owner seemed so familiar with Cheng Feichi last time, Ye Qin thought as he looked around the station. None of these things look valuable at all. Surely no one would come here to steal them.

It was very quiet. Ye Qin only heard the grinding sounds and the breaths of Cheng Feichi and himself. Ye Qin slowed the rhythm of his breath to match with that of Cheng Feichi, feeling that he was breathing as slowly as a sleeping tortoise.

He couldn't help laughing at his strange simile. Hearing his laughter, Cheng Feichi looked up at him. He quickly regained his composure and said, "You just transferred to this school. How could you become so familiar with the owner in such a short time?"

"I always passed by this place when I walked home from the university's affiliated school." Cheng Feichi stopped working for a short while and asked, "Didn't you know that?"

Ye Qin suddenly felt nervous, worrying that Cheng Feichi might have found out about his investigation. Then he pushed this idea aside; surely he was careful enough. So he answered very calmly, "Of course I knew which school you were in. Everybody knows."

Still worrying, he added, "Have you...met me before?"

Cheng Feichi answered without looking at Ye Qin. "No.

The time when we met in the convenience store was the first time."

Ye Qin was digging a pit for himself and fell into it unknowingly. He recalled the previous unhappy encounters with Cheng Feichi and was very embarrassed. "At the convenience store...my friend didn't like you, and I was just helping him... He's my friend, after all. I didn't do it on purpose..."

Surely Cheng Feichi knew that Ye Qin didn't cause trouble for him on purpose—he was just a naughty and naive accomplice of his wicked friends. Though he didn't know why Ye Qin was trying to get close to him, he didn't think the reason would be anything surprising. Maybe Ye Qin just heard the rumors about him and thought being with him would be fun.

"What about now?" Cheng Feichi asked in a semi-serious manner. "Are you doing it on purpose this time?"

In the darkness, Ye Qin became a hundred times more sensitive than usual. Cheng Feichi was talking in such a low voice, as if he was whispering to him. The magnetic charm in Cheng Feichi's voice dazzled him and suddenly made him blush. Thankfully, the room was so dark that no one could see him in this state. Meanwhile, his heart started pounding like crazy, banging on his eardrums in disorder. He could hardly hear his own voice.

"Yep, I am." Ye Qin tried his best to sound as confident as Cheng Feichi. "Didn't you know that?"

The light was concentrated on Cheng Feichi's hands, casting a shadow on his well-structured features. Ye Qin raised his phone stealthily to see the expression on Cheng Feichi's face.

When he managed to see Cheng Feichi's thick eyelashes quivering as he blinked, Cheng Feichi turned his head to avoid his stare. He took out a small notebook and tossed it to Ye Qin. "Write a memo to tell the owner that I've been here tonight."

Ye Qin put the paper on a small stool and crouched by it so that he could start to write. After he finished it, he handed the note to Cheng Feichi. "Mr. Cheng, could you please check this? Did I write anything wrong?"

Ye Qin lifted his head while saying this. Obviously, he still remembered how Cheng Feichi had corrected all the wrong characters in his "love letters."

Cheng Feichi gave an indiscernible smile and glanced through the memo. Then he put a tick by Ye Qin's handwriting and gave him 100 points for his good job.

After leaving the bike station, Ye Qin suddenly realized something: "No, it's not right. Full marks should be 150 points. You just gave me 100...so I only managed to pass the exam?"

Cheng Feichi nodded. "Well, if you did it yesterday, I would've given you 150."

Ye Qin turned his head to look at the clock tower. It was almost one o'clock. Feeling the impulse to yawn, Ye Qin did so and then murmured: "Birthdays are always the best."

Seeing that Ye Qin could barely keep his eyes open and keep himself from shaking in the blowing wind, Cheng Feichi became more serious than usual to force him to go home. "I promised your mother I'd keep you safe. You should really go home now. I'll have to go, too."

Ye Qin's home was near High School No. 6. Ye Qin kept dawdling, but they still reached the gate of the compound where he lived. He took off the gloves and handed them back to Cheng Feichi, saying feebly, "My home is close. You put these on. Tomorrow I'll buy a pair...a pair of woolen gloves."

After making sure that Ye Qin entered the gate, Cheng Feichi turned back and was about to leave. Ye Qin suddenly recalled something and shouted to Cheng Feichi from behind. "Mr. Cheng! I've left something in your notebook. Don't forget

to check it out!"

Cheng Feichi pay much mind to what Ye Qin had said.

The General Graduation Examination was around the corner. Though he was confident enough, he still needed to save as much energy as possible to prepare for the test.

Ye Qin was probably preparing for it as well, as he didn't show up for a couple of days. Cheng Feichi didn't meet him even during the examination. It seemed that Ye Qin had suddenly disappeared.

Breakfast was still on his desk every day. Cheng Feichi came to the school earlier than usual to catch who delivered it, only to find it was a schoolmate who was junior to him. The boy told him that he'd been paid to do it. The cards were prepared in advance, and he only needed to put one in the bag each time.

This was what Ye Qin normally did. He was just such a lazy and clever teen; he acted as fancy took him.

As for why he would wash the dishes that night, it was probably because the young master suddenly wanted to experience the challenges and toil of real life. It was probably that the sun had risen in the west that day.

The exam ended on the last day of December.

Cheng Feichi left the examination venue very early and went home. While organizing his books, he found the note Ye Qin had left among a pile of drafting paper stacked on the desk: "158XXXXXXXX, call me call me!"

After the scrawl, Ye Qin had drawn a plump heart.

The three-day New Year holiday started tomorrow. Cheng Feichi would be fully occupied except for tomorrow morning.

So tonight, he was allowed to stay up late. Cheng Feichi took out the detective story he hadn't yet finished and leaned against the bedpost.

The hand of the clock on the bedside cabinet was approaching the number zero. He looked back at the book. He turned a page and read the first two paragraphs, and then he read the last page again.

He started over another time after that, yet failed to concentrate on the story again. He closed the book, turned off the light, and lay down to relax his nerves, which had been strained since the start of exams.

He had good graphic memory. The numbers he just glanced over lingered in his mind.

When it was only two minutes to midnight, he took out the obsolete cell phone that he usually used only for making and receiving phone calls from below his pillow. And he started to write a text message.

CHAPTER 04

YE Qin had not gone to the club that belonged to Liu Yangfan's family for a long time, but tonight he showed up again and spent the whole night with his friends.

"You haven't been here for what? A thousand days? We thought you stopped hanging out with us for good." Zhao Yue exhaled a puff of smoke.

Ye Qin hadn't smelled that smoke for a long time, thus he was not accustomed to it at first. He frowned and tried to move away from Zhao Yue. "Last week I had a cold, so I've been staying at home."

Zhou Feng added, "Well, that I can tell you that's no lie. Each winter, A-Qin catches a bunch of colds and runs a couple of fevers. Calling in sick is part of his usual bag of tricks."

Liu Yangfan gently shook the wine and smiled. "I thought you took a leave to chase that guy. Zhao Yue bet that you wouldn't stick to it after this month, but I think you will. Don't let me down."

On hearing this, Ye Qin was upset. He pointed to the glass of wine on the table. "Pour some wine for me."

Zhao Yue put the cigar back into his mouth and poured the

wine for him. "Hey, what about this time? Now we're all here; tell us. We'll help you out."

"Help? What for?" Sun Yiran left the group of people who were playing board games and walked towards them. She sat down near Ye Qin and asked, "Is A-Qin chasing a girl?"

Zhao Yue laughed. "Yep, he totally is. Yiran, help him out with your own experiences."

Ye Qin looked even more upset. Sun Yiran thought Zhao Yue was telling the truth, so she continued while grabbing Ye Qin's shoulders. "Who is this girl? Who took my cute Qin-Qin away without my approval? Isn't there a law against this?"

Ye Qin felt dizzy as she shook him too hard. He raised both of his hands to vow that there was no such girl. Zhou Feng and Liu Yangfan helped him out, and they finally made Sun Yiran believe this and let it go.

As the boys left for the billiards, Ye Qin stayed on the couch with the excuse of feeling sick. He asked Sun Yiran, "Right... When you were wooing Cheng...that straight-A student, did you leave him your number?"

Sun Yiran was cracking melon seeds. "Sure."

Ye Qin continued hurriedly, "Did he call you?"

Sun Yiran had already recovered from her failed pursuit, so she answered quite easily. "Nope."

Ye Qin felt somehow relaxed. He hadn't lost face.

"Why are you asking this?" Sun Yiran had an idea. "Oh, it must be that the girl you like likes him."

Ye Qin rolled his eyes. That's Zhou Feng's story, okay?

Looking back at his own story, Ye Qin was no luckier. He had been chasing after Cheng Feichi for such a long time and even gave him his number, but Cheng Feichi hadn't called him yet. The guy hadn't given him any response, let alone done anything proactive. Ye Qin had been waiting for so many days for a

single phone call from him.

He even had the whole procedure of answering his call planned out. He had to let the phone ring five times, because he couldn't let Cheng Feichi know that he had been waiting for it. When he picked it up, he would yawn to pretend that he'd been sleeping and was upset about being woken up. Therefore, Cheng Feichi would feel sorry and say yes to anything; even if he went a little bit too far.

For example, after he washed a couple of dishes, Cheng Feichi was so touched that he'd said "happy birthday" to him, not realizing that it wasn't his birthday at all.

Thinking that being pitiful was indeed the best policy, Ye Qin was so proud of himself. He'd made very thorough plans about how to answer Cheng Feichi's call, yet when he got himself all prepared, Cheng Feichi didn't call him at all.

It's so shameful! Ye Qin was completely upset. *I have your number, but I won't call you! Let's wait and see who'll make the first call!*

He made a good plan, but the reality was nothing like that. With three cups in his belly, he couldn't control himself and quickly dialed Cheng Feichi's number; which was already too familiar. As soon as it connected, he shouted, "Who is it?"

The caller was asking the one receiving the call who he was. Only Ye Qin could ever do this after getting drunk.

The person on the other side of the phone remained silent for a short while before replying cooly, "Cheng Feichi."

The three syllables immediately enchanted Ye Qin, making him even more dizzy. He lay on his stomach on the sofa and rested his jaw on the soft cushion, squinting as he asked, "Where are you?"

His voice could instantly turn to "soft" mode, making it

difficult for Cheng Feichi to be angry with him. Cheng Feichi could only answer, "At home."

"Why...why don...don't you...why...why don't you ask me out...why?" Ye Qin stammered and finally managed to make a complete inquiry.

Cheng Feichi couldn't help but chuckle upon hearing such a naive question. The boy had called him so late at night just to ask him why he didn't ask him out.

The irritation of being suddenly woken up soon disappeared. Cheng Feichi asked him patiently, "What about you? What are you doing now?"

Ye Qin turned around and shifted to a more comfortable position. He answered without opening his eyes, "I'm...I'm enjoying New Year's Eve. We're playing cards, eating snacks, drinking wine, playing billiards...and...and what...Anyways, this is just so boring."

Cheng Feichi's recreations only included playing sports on the campus yard and reading at home. All the things that Ye Qin just mentioned were totally unfamiliar to him, so he thought for a while and asked, "Then, what *is* interesting?"

Ye Qin was still giddy as he answered. "Being with you."

Cheng Feichi didn't answer, but he didn't hang up, either. Ye Qin really thought he was dreaming, so he continued, "I still have so many plans for us. I want to send you flowers, take you to fine restaurants, the cinema, and amusement parks. I want to eat ice cream with you, play in the snow with you, spend birthdays with you and wash dishes after we eat together. Oh, cross that one off; we've done it. And I want to enter the new year with you... New Year's Eve is just tonight! You just couldn't have called me earlier, could you?"

While complaining, Ye Qin counted each item with his fingers and felt sorry for himself; for the boy who wasn't accepted

by the person he was pursuing. He even forgot that he had been the one to make the phone call. How unreasonable it all was!

Listening to Ye Qin's endless and illogical accusations, Cheng Feichi didn't retort. He merely took a deep breath and answered after quite some time, "I just texted you."

When Ye Qin woke up in the lounge in the club, he dug out the text from Cheng Feichi from piles of well-wishes, feeling totally overwhelmed. Cheng Feichi had sent a "Happy New Year."

He couldn't separate the reality from his wild dreams, so he could only ask Zhou Feng, "Did I say anything crazy on the phone?"

Zhou Feng had been playing cards for the whole night. He knew even less about what had happened. "You probably did? You cried and begged him to marry you."

Liu Yangfan brought them some beverages. "Only you could do that; you just would not let Yiran go. Don't freak A-Qin out."

Ye Qin was so nervous that he tried hard to swallow his saliva, hoping for a different answer from Liu Yangfan. "Then what did I say?"

Liu Yangfan put on a wicked grin. "Why don't you ask him?"

Ye Qin kept feeling uneasy about this accident for three whole days. He thought that he'd exposed the whole conspiracy against Cheng Feichi behind his efforts in chasing him. Cheng Feichi was so smart; he would know as soon as Ye Qin started talking.

Ye Qin replied to Cheng Feichi's text with a heavy heart. He wrote "Happy New Year" with a doddering heart emoji at the end.

More than ten minutes later, he still didn't get any response from Cheng Feichi. Ye Qin threw himself on the bed again.

—Now it was completely over.

The school's winter sports meet started on the first day after they returned to school. The students were lined up at the recreational yard, and the queues of the No. 1 and No. 2 classes were close to each other. Ye Qin stood in the line with his head hung low, trying his best to hide himself.

Liao Yifang was at the head of the queue of Class No. 2. Holding a small notebook, he raised his voice. "This afternoon, we're having a long jump contest. But Chen Haoyu, the representative of our class, is sick. Is there anyone who can take his place? This is for the honor of the whole class!"

The original entry list had been submitted before the General Graduation Examination back in December. Ye Qin had decided to have a good rest during the three-day sports meet, so he didn't sign up for any of these contests. Zhou Feng, however, would participate in the 5,000-meter long-distance running race in order to impress Sun Yiran. Ye Qin predicted that Zhou Feng wouldn't even get through the first 500 meters.

Liao Yifang tried to motivate his classmates, but no one answered his call. Zhou Feng the long-distance runner gestured for Ye Qin to volunteer. "Hey, why don't you sign up? It's just for fun."

Ye Qin was very afraid that he would be seen by Cheng Feichi, who must be standing in Class No. 1's line now. He answered timidly, "No way."

"It's nothing! You'll finish in a few minutes. I remember that you got first prize in the long jump contest back in the middle school."

Ye Qin was speechless. "One of the three people most likely to win was late for the contest. One was sick, and the other was not his usual self. If you were me, even you would have won first place."

"Well, you must've been good enough for it regardless,"

Zhou Feng kept persuading him. He approached Ye Qin's ear and talked in a low voice. "I saw the name of that straight-A student in the entry list of the long-distance running race. The long jump and the 5,000-meter run take place at the same time. With us each participating in one event, we can grab all the girls' attention. Who's gonna look at him anyway?"

Ye Qin was shocked. "He signed up for the 5,000-meter race?"

According to the rules, the students who didn't participate in the contests were not allowed to leave the recreational yard without legitimate reason. The students in Class No. 2 were supposed to stand by the tracks. Cheng Feichi was going to run twelve and a half laps. There was no way that he wouldn't see Ye Qin.

Once the box of imagination was open, there was no way to close it.

Liu Yangfan's pet phrase came into Ye Qin's mind, "It is deceit that a man hates most." Perhaps Cheng Feichi, upon seeing him, would run off the track in outrage and give him a hard beating. After all, the guy was able to do thirty pull-ups in one go; in the whole high school, he had no rivals. Even the judges wouldn't be able to stop him.

Ye Qin still remembered how Cheng Feichi stared daggers at him the night at the convenience store. If Cheng Feichi was to take revenge on him for all the things he did, he would have to cut him to pieces to give vent to all his anger.

Still giving his heartening speech to the whole class, Liao Yifang suddenly heard something in the crowd. After searching for a while, he looked at Zhou Feng with excitement. "Zhou Feng, you seem to be willing to have a try. Just do it. There's no need to be afraid. No matter what result you get, we will all be proud of you."

Zhou Feng answered at once. "I'm in the long-distance running contest. I can't compete in long jump at the same time."

Liao Yifang checked his little notebook, disappointment on his face.

This was when Ye Qin raised his hand. "I'm in. I want to sign up for the long jump contest."

Cheng Feichi was warming up by the track.

Usually occupied, he especially needed to save energy as much as possible, so he avoided contests that would burn him out and only planned to participate in the 100-meter short-distance run.

However, now he had to run 5,000 meters. And nobody knew why. Probably the monitor got it wrong when submitting the name list, or someone had intentionally changed it. No matter what the reason, it was no longer possible to find out—even if it was, it wouldn't matter now, as the race was about to begin.

Someone passed a bottle of water to him. "Drink some water so that you won't pass out after the first lap."

Cheng Feichi recognized this person as one of Ye Qin's friends who framed him at the convenience store that night. He'd also tried to provoke him into a fight in P.E. class before.

He didn't take the bottle of water, but this person still reminded him of Ye Qin. Before the race started, he glanced at the place where Class No. 2 was supposed to be, but didn't see Ye Qin. Probably Ye Qin was somewhere else for other contests.

But that was just impossible. Delicate as Ye Qin was, riding a bike would wear him out. How would he participate in any sports events?

At the same moment, the delicate Ye Qin, who was standing in the southwest corner of the recreational yard, sneezed for no particular reason.

He took off his coat so he could move more easily, so now he was merely wearing a pink sweater. Liao Yifang, who sent him to the site of the contest, praised him. "Bright colors really do look good on you. You're really the most good-looking guy in our class!"

Recently Ye Qin had grown accustomed to wearing bright soft colors to look young and delicate, so today when he left home, he didn't even think twice before he put on this pink sweater. He glanced down at his clothes, feeling so ashamed of its color that he tried to take it off.

Liao Yifang tried to persuade him. "It's so cold. You should keep it on. If you catch a cold, we'd be devastated."

If someone overheard him, they'd probably think that Ye Qin was about to sacrifice himself on a battlefield.

At this moment, Ye Qin was called upon to enter the site. He shook his arms and legs to relax a little bit and joined the line of contestants near the sand pit.

Ye Qin had a lot of friends, but few of them knew that he had been a weak kid. He once suffered from pneumonia, and after that he frequented hospitals. At that time, some expert suggested Ye Jinxiang to let him train with the sports team at school. After training for over half a year, he still didn't like sports, but he indeed became stronger. He even unexpectedly became skilled in long jump.

With such a background, he made full use of all his strengths and skills and finally got second place in the long jump contest, while the first prize went to an official member of the school sports team.

Liao Yifang was calculating how many high scores Class No. 2 had obtained, and now he was more than thrilled: "Ye-tongxue, you're not only our sunshine—you're also our secret weapon!"

Ye Qin was also a little bit high on his own fumes right now.

Yet unlike Zhou Feng, after quickly running his fingers through his hair with pride, he still managed to reply in a humble manner. "It doesn't really count. The only reason why I could get such a good result is that other people are so busy studying instead of exercising."

"Speaking of doing exercise, do you still remember Cheng-tongxue in Class No. 1? Studying never prevents him from being good at sports." Liao Yifang gazed afar towards the running tracks. "Right now, he must be in the middle of the 5,000-meter race. Let's..."

Upon hearing Cheng Feichi's surname, Ye Qin immediately winced. He didn't even let Liao Yifang finish the sentence before he fled with the excuse of refueling his energy.

After lingering at the corner shop for dozen minutes, Ye Qin returned to the recreational yard with a lollipop in his mouth, thinking that the long-distance race must be over.

Candidates for the 100-meter race were getting ready as requested. Numerous boys and girls spread across the recreational yard were cheering for this sports event. Their roars pierced through the heated air, making the track under their feet quiver.

Races that emphasize the athlete's explosive power, such as short-distance races, always attract most of an audience's attention. Seeing that the game was so intense, Ye Qin also joined the crowd—after all, he didn't want to go back to his own class yet. He saw a bunch of boys dashing for the finish line. A few seconds was all it took for an athlete to outpace another one. Getting excited in such an atmosphere, Ye Qin also leaned forward to see who would excel in this race.

And...he saw a familiar face.

Ye Qin didn't know any excellent runners in this school, while members of the school sports team were not as tall as this boy...No way! He just finished a long-distance race, and now here he was? What was he? A perpetual motion machine?

The girls next to Ye Qin began to shout "Fighting Class No. 1" to show their support. This was when Ye Qin suddenly realized that he was going to expose himself. He quickly fled. But unluckily, this time, he tripped over his own two feet and fell to the ground. Even the lollipop nearly left his mouth.

Lying on his own stomach, Ye Qin felt so dizzy. He recalled that he'd put on someone else's sneakers before doing the long jump, and he didn't pay any attention when tying the shoelaces—it was already a miracle that the laces had stayed fixed for so long.

Hearing the cheering behind him, Ye Qin managed to stand up, thinking that Cheng Feichi should have won the race by now. With his head hanging down, he took two steps forward when he suddenly saw a pair of long and slim legs wrapped in normal sweatpants.

Looking up, he saw a young man breathing heavily, but still seeming to be quite at ease.

Cheng Feichi was sweating after two consecutive running races. He wiped the beads of sweat on his forehead, evened his breath, and asked Ye Qin, "Why did you run away?"

All of a sudden, Ye Qin felt that his legs could no longer support himself. He almost collapsed to the lawn in front of Cheng Feichi.

He already began racking his brain for a clever way of protecting himself if Cheng Feichi was going to beat him up for revenge. Seeing a hand held out in front of him, Ye Qin thought he was going to punch him, so he automatically drew back with fear.

"Why are you dodging?" Cheng Feichi asked, looking very honest. He took the drink bottle from Ye Qin's hand, opened it, and then handed it back to him. "Drink."

Ye Qin froze right there. He didn't dare to take it. At Ye Qin not taking the bottle back, a smile appeared on Cheng Feichi's lips. He gave the bottle a gentle shake. "So...this is for me?"

Class No. 2 ranked first with highest scores for the first day of the sports event. In the evening, Liao Yifang applied for event expenses from the head teacher so that they could dine out to celebrate this success. They booked a large private room with three big round dining tables at the family restaurant near the school gate.

The whole class gathered here, with everyone sitting very close to each other. Before the dishes were served, Liao Yifang invited each athlete who won points that day to the small pulpit in the front of the room so that they could be praised and applauded. He gave special mention to Ye Qin for being sent on an unexpected mission and successfully completing it.

Thanks to the heated atmosphere and Liao Yifang's heartening speech, everyone stood up and gave Ye Qin a big round of applause. Even Zhou Feng, the most mischievous boy who never agreed with Liao Yifang, chimed in eagerly: "Hear, hear! Hear what the monitor says! Qin-ge's the best!"

Ye Qin was extremely abashed. He didn't think that he deserved such attention—after all, the collective honor never was his priority.

But this was not the only thing that kept him hesitating. After the dinner began, Ye Qin elbowed Zhou Feng. "Hey, did you do well in the race?"

Zhou Feng's mouth was stuffed with a huge chicken leg. He made an awkward laughing sound. "Heh heh...didn't even finish it."

Ye Qin rolled his eyes. "And you're still so comfortable with everyone's applause?"

Zhou Feng didn't feel embarrassed at all. "The class monitor insisted. How could I not accept it?"

Ye Qin had been so busy working on Cheng Feichi that he didn't notice until now—Zhou Feng and Liao Yifang somehow seemed closer. Zhou Feng then told him that he had accepted Liao Yifang's offer of help and had been to his home to prepare for the General Graduation Examination.

"At least he really helped me out this time. I passed the exam. Otherwise, my dad would beat me again," Zhou Feng commented while chewing the chicken. "Well, he's not bad. Just a bit dumb."

Ye Qin thought Zhou Feng was dumber than Liao Yifang, but didn't say it. He kept pumping Zhou Feng for more information. "So who won first place? I mean, in the long-run race."

"Dunno. It was probably that straight-A student, you know. I lagged way behind him in the first lap. Shit."

"You talked to him?"

Zhou Feng wiped the oil off his mouth. "Speaking of which, I'm so mad at him! I gave him a bottle of water before the race and he refused!"

Ye Qin didn't quite understand what he meant. He blinked with confusion. "Why?"

"You got me. Why would he do that?" Zhou Feng suddenly had an idea. He slapped on the table and said with confidence, "He must've been waiting to accept water from some girl instead!"

The meal was halfway done when a bowl of fish was served. Ye Qin never liked fish, so he put down the chopsticks and left the room. He went to the men's room and called his mother on the way.

"Hey, mom...yeah, the meal's started now...we're just having the normal sorts of meat, chicken, duck, fish and so on. Nothing

spicy. I'm totally okay with the dishes...I went for the long jump and got second place. I didn't care much about it...it's okay. I'm not a porcelain doll..."

Luo Qiuling kept nagging about tiny things. Maybe people just became more worrisome and cautious as they aged. Ye Qin held the cellphone between his cheek and shoulder so that he could wash his hands. When he turned around, he gasped as he nearly hit a very tall person.

When Ye Qin saw who the person was, he mumbled to the phone, "Nothing. I just ran into a schoolmate. It's the guy who helped me fix my bike last time...I know, I know. Got to go."

He stuffed the cellphone back into his pocket and suddenly recalled that Zhou Feng thought Cheng Feichi had been waiting for a girl. Feeling a little uncomfortable and awkward, he cleared his throat and managed to find a decent conversation starter. "Your classmates are also dining here tonight?"

Meanwhile, he kept glancing slyly at Cheng Feichi. From how Cheng Feichi had behaved earlier at the recreational yard, he didn't seem to have any doubts at all.

Cheng Feichi nodded and then looked at Ye Qin from head to toe. "Model Student of Class No. 2?"

Ye Qin quickly looked at himself. Oops—he'd forgotten to take off the ribbon that Liao Yifang had put on him earlier tonight.

Feeling overwhelmingly embarrassed, he turned around and tried to take it off. When he raised his elbow, his sweater somehow got in the way. Cheng Feichi stepped forward to help him. When approaching Ye Qin's nape, he said, "It looks good on you, Sunshine."

Ye Qin was absolutely caught off guard when he heard his cute nickname from Cheng Feichi's mouth. His eyes widened and his face reddened in just a blink of an eye. He clutched the

ribbon in his hands and had already cursed Liao Yifang a million times before he explained with difficulty, "It was Liao Yifang...many other people have one of these too."

He was referring to the other athletes in his class.

They hadn't met with each other over the past two weeks, but such a conversation erased the time and distance between them. They were as close as before.

Ye Qin was finally sure that Cheng Feichi didn't know a thing about his scheme. After that threat was cleared, Ye Qin's arrogance returned. He questioned Cheng Feichi about why he didn't reply to his text message on New Year's Eve.

"You texted me?"

Cheng Feichi took out his phone and pressed on the buttons to check his message box. He didn't see the text that Ye Qin was asking about.

Ye Qin leaned forward to look at the screen of his phone and complained, "Such an outdated model! It can't even get texts! Now we all use smart phones. Who's still using these..." He suddenly had an idea. "How about this? I'm gonna buy you a new cellphone. Same as mine, but a black one; you like it?"

Cheng Feichi couldn't be any more familiar with Ye Qin's habit of paying his way out of everything. For Ye Qin, money could solve all problems. Therefore, upon hearing this, Cheng Feichi just gave Ye Qin a cold look.

There was something in Cheng Feichi's expressionless face that made Ye Qin quail. He could only say, "Okay, okay. Forget it. I'll just buy it for someone else."

Cheng Feichi was dining here with just the athletes from his class instead of the whole class, so they were seated around a single table at the end of the corridor. They reached the private room first, and Ye Qin walked towards it. Cheng Feichi stood behind him, watching and waiting for him to go inside.

Ye Qin still wanted to talk Cheng Feichi into accepting his gift. He gave Cheng Feichi a soft kick on one side of his right shoe: "Then...how about a pair of sneakers? That'll be fine? I just wanna thank you for helping me with the bike last time. Look at your shoes. They're totally worn out. How could a champion wear shoes like these?"

Cheng Feichi looked at his shoes. He hadn't noticed earlier, but his clean white shoes were covered with dust after the running races, and there was even a hole in the upper mesh of the right shoe.

"No need for that. I have other shoes at home." Cheng Feichi continued after a few seconds, "Champion? How did you know I won?"

Of course Ye Qin wouldn't tell him how he tried to get detailed information from Liao Yifang. He turned his eyes away and answered, "Of course you're the champion. If not you, who else could be?"

After the sports event, the semester was halfway over.

Ye Qin was possessed by an invisible pressure. He didn't want to be laughed at as someone who couldn't win the heart of a mere classmate after a whole semester, so he started to spend more time consulting his three buddies.

Ye Qin: He's not replying to my texts again. What now?

Liu Yangfan: ...

Zhao Yue: ...

Ye Qin: Stop it! HELP ME OUT!!!

Liu Yangfan: I thought he already fell for you. Zhou Feng told us so.

Ye Qin: WHAT???

Zhou Feng: Yep. He opened a plastic bottle for you. Isn't that sweet?

Ye Qin: Are you fucking kidding me?? It didn't mean any-thing!

Zhao Yue: LOL.

Ye Qin: What are you laughing at?

Zhao Yue: I laugh because it must be difficult for you. You could never swear in front of him.

Ye Qin: ...

Liu Yangfan: I think the build-up part is enough. Now we just need an opportunity.

Ye Qin: What kind of opportunity?

Liu Yangfan: You can only figure that out by yourself.

Ye Qin: Zhou Feng, remove him from the chat NOW!!!

Zhao Yue: Hahahaha...well, I suggest that you stop circling around. Just tell him.

Zhou Feng: Like: stop hesitating and be my boyfriend!

Ye Qin: ...

Liu Yangfan: Speaking of which, it's A-Qin's very first love!

Ye Qin: Bullshit! A bullshit first love!

Ye Qin was always willing to learn from others, but he wouldn't blindly copy others' experiences. After all, he himself was the one who was going to deal with Cheng Feichi face to face. He must combine the best parts of his buddies' suggestions and come up with a perfect plan. He must choose the perfect time, the perfect location, and the perfect way of interaction so that he could win Cheng Feichi once and for all.

However, imagination and theories were thousands of miles away from real life. Things turned out to be a lot more difficult than Ye Qin had expected.

This Saturday, Ye Qin took Zhou Feng's sister to Cheng Feichi's house for class again. Ms. Cheng was telling stories to the little girl, while Mr. Cheng was trapped by the big boy who

brought a thick book of Chemistry exercises and asked him to explain the difficult ones.

"How much do you get for an hour as a tutor? I'll double it."

"I won't take your money for nothing," Cheng Feichi answered.

This was easy. Ye Qin took out another book of Physics exercises and said: "You can teach me Physics as well."

Schoolwork became Ye Qin's bargaining chip. Cheng Feichi found it both hilarious and absurd. "It's not about how many subjects I'm gonna teach you. There are so many excellent teachers out there. I'm not your best choice."

"No, you are," Ye Qin replied unswervingly. "You're the only one that I want, Mr. Cheng—"

Emphases were put on the final two words, and Ye Qin even said them in a sing-song tone. Cheng Feichi was so startled that he nearly let an apple slip from his grip.

Not knowing how to reply, Cheng Feichi tossed the apple to Ye Qin. "Peel it. Let me see if you have any potential."

Ye Qin surely knew that Cheng Feichi was just avoiding the answer, yet he started peeling anyway. But he was so bad at peeling apples that he ended up cutting his own finger.

Cheng Feichi reentered the room with a home first-aid kit and noticed that Ye Qin was secretly wiping tears from his face. It was something new to him, as he hadn't immediately realized that Ye Qin was so vulnerable.

It was just a small cut on the fingertip that barely bled. Cheng Feichi held Ye Qin's wounded hand, trying to get the cut disinfected and wrapped up in a band-aid.

Ye Qin kept pouting while mumbling, "Why are your knives so sharp?"

Cheng Feichi gently squeezed Ye Qin's finger. "You've got

tender skin. My rough hands can't be cut."

These words cheered Ye Qin up. He stopped whining about the pain and resumed bargaining. "You see, I'm wounded and it's thanks to you. Can you be my tutor now?"

Ye Qin was probably the only one who could make connections between things that were so unrelated. Seeing that his eyes were still red, Cheng Feichi just couldn't say no, so he pulled the book closer to himself and asked, "Which one got you?"

Now Ye Qin had gotten a good teacher, but he didn't really concentrate on studying.

The important examination was already over, and then came the exciting sports meet as well as a number of festivals. Few students could still remain highly disciplined. Many girls, in particular, started working on handicrafts together whenever classes were dismissed.

Ye Qin saw what they were so busy working on: mittens and scarves in various colors and patterns.

"How could someone wear this? Does it really work? Why couldn't you just buy a nice one?" Ye Qin frowned at the scarf that Sun Yiran had made.

"Why?" Sun Yiran snatched it back. "It's the energy and time I spent on it that really counts. How could some other random scarf compare to this one?"

Zhou Feng approached Sun Yiran with a sycophantic look. "Who is it for?"

Sun Yiran rolled her eyes. "Not you."

Zhou Feng sprawled listlessly on his desk for a whole self-study session. Ye Qin didn't look happy either, seeming immersed in his own thoughts.

Liao Yifang handed them their exercise books and asked, "Did you guys run into any learning problems? As the saying

goes, when everybody adds fuel, the flames rise high. Why don't you tell me about it and we can figure a way out?"

Zhou Feng roared in sadness, "I ran into relationship problems. Can you really help with those?"

Liao Yifang adjusted his glasses and answered very carefully: "Though puppy love isn't something that the school encourages, it's actually a process of experimenting with relationships, So it's also a sort of learning. Why don't you share your problems with me? I'll tell you how I see things."

Zhou Feng then asked him how to make his crush fall for him too. Liao Yifang thought for a while and answered: "In terms of studying, we adjust our methods according to the nature of the pupil. It's the same when it comes to making friends. You have to know what that person likes and give them it."

Zhou Feng thought he was talking nonsense, so he joked as a response, "Like me giving you Qu Yixian's exercise book as a gift?"

Liao Yifang was caught off guard by his answer and then smiled bashfully. "Well, I've bought that already. Now I'd prefer Wang Houxiong's book."

One could never really trust a nerd for relationship tips. Zhou Feng soon forgot all about Liao Yifang's answer while Ye Qin took a mental note of it. He also remembered that Sun Yiran mentioned the importance of spending time and energy on a gift. Therefore, he went to the stationery shop just beside the school gate and bought many strips of plastic paper specially designed for making lucky stars.

He also thought about knitting scarves, but eventually forgot about it because he thought it was too girlish. At any rate, Cheng Feichi had no use for that either. Last time when Cheng Feichi held his hand after his injury, he didn't even want to let go of his hands, for they were as warm as a hot water bottle. Unlike

Cheng Feichi, Ye Qin's hands were cold all year long.

Speaking of necessity, Ye Qin was suddenly reminded of how frozen the atmosphere was in Cheng Feichi's home, and how Cheng Feichi's room was stuffed with books, certificates of honor and trophies. He didn't even have a photo frame to decorate the room! Ye Qin was impressed by a glass jar full of colorful, paper-made lucky stars when he entered the stationery shop. The shop owner even told him that these stars would glow in the dark. Wouldn't that be a wonderful decoration for Cheng Feichi's room? Ye Qin decided to make paper stars without a second thought.

So, over the next few days, Ye Qin stopped skipping classes and seemed to be quite docile and obedient at his seat. Only the students sitting around him knew what he was really up to behind the large pile of books.

Ye Qin had a really difficult time when he started working on the stars, for he hadn't done any origami work ever since he graduated from elementary school. All he did that involved his hands in more recent years was building Lego. Sun Yiran couldn't stand how slow and clumsy he was, so she taught him how to make stars in a very detailed way and shared with him useful tips. For example, one would have to squeeze the rims of the star with one's nails to make the star look plump.

Ye Qin always kept his nails short, so he used a ruler instead. Gradually he was able to make decent paper stars.

After he succeeded in making a small bag of stars, Sun Yiran reminded him, "Did you write anything on the strips before folding them?"

Ye Qin didn't understand. "Write what?"

"Write your blessings or wishes on the side of the strip that's gonna be folded up. That's how you can make your dreams come true."

Ye Qin complained about her not mentioning it earlier while undoing all the finished stars.

But seriously, what should I write? Ye Qin was bewildered. He thought about "I wish my mom would be healthy and happy forever," but he was making stars for Cheng Feichi after all. He struggled with it for a whole class and finally made a decision.

Zhou Feng watched him writing for a while and then asked him, looking quite worried, "A-Qin, you don't really mean that, do you?"

Ye Qin was too occupied to notice the connotation in Zhou Feng's words. "Mean what?"

"You actually fell for that guy?"

This one sentence was enough to make Ye Qin jump to his feet. "I'm only pretending! If not, how can I make him believe me?"

He immediately wrote "Cheng Feichi, you're such a fool" on one strip of paper, made a star of it and tossed it into the jar. He announced with super confidence, "When I got him on the hook, I'll let him open this particular star. Only the most unimaginable fool would ever fall in love with him!"

On the last day of the semester, the students came to school only to grab their grade reports for the final exam.

The school organized a lecture on proper time management for the winter vacation to keep the students from wasting their time. The students that were about to start the final year of high school all gathered in the school hall, making the place overly packed.

Ye Qin carefully hid the jar in his backpack and held it with both arms, afraid that he might break it into pieces. He searched for Cheng Feichi in the queue of Class No. 1, only to find the overly tall lad talking to a girl nearby.

Somehow, Ye Qin was annoyed by this scene. He took his phone out and texted Cheng Feichi: "Huh."

Phone signal was never stable in the hall. Cheng Feichi didn't get back to Ye Qin for over ten minutes: "?"

Ye Qin always hated it when people simply texted him with punctuation. He thought that leading with a modal particle was enough to show that he was super annoyed right now. How dare he toy with him like that!

Though feeling even more annoyed now, Ye Qin still replied: "I'm sitting behind you."

And then he waited and waited, but Cheng Feichi never turned around to look at him, not even once. Then he got a reply. There were only four words in it: "Listen to the lecture."

Ye Qin could hardly be more annoyed than he was right now. He plonked the pack on the floor heavily.

But he immediately regretted it and bent down to see if the glass jar still remained intact.

After the lecture, a few students from each class were supposed to stay and clean the hall. Liao Yifang made Zhou Feng stay and Zhou Feng took Ye Qin with him.

Ye Qin kept glancing at Cheng Feichi while picking up the garbage on the floor. Cheng Feichi was the only reason why he stayed to do such a trivial thing.

Because vacation was around the corner, everyone was in high spirits even when doing the cleaning work. The whole hall was filled with joyful laughter. Ye Qin saw a bunch of girls surrounding Cheng Feichi. The laughter burst from the crowd was enough to rip the roof off, but he just couldn't do anything.

Zhou Feng's classmates were usually boys, as he was a science student, so to him, the girls' laughter had a magical charm. He wanted to join the group when Ye Qin asked him, "Don't you

want to be with Yiran?"

"Yiran went home to give her father that scarf she's been working on." Zhou Feng wasn't sad at all about not getting Sun Yiran's special scarf. Instead, he asked Ye Qin, "Did you give him your lucky stars?"

Ye Qin didn't answer.

Suddenly, he didn't want to give out the stars anymore.

Liao Yifang was the only one in the hall who was actually cleaning. He had sweated so much that his face was covered with beads of perspiration, and he took off his glasses to wipe his face.

"Hey, hey, don't put the glasses back on!" Zhou Feng shouted, as if he'd seen some sort of miracle. "A-Qin, come here! Let's see what our class monitor actually looks like!"

The features usually hidden beneath the black-rimmed glasses were pretty and refined. Liao Yifang's eyes were big, clear, and sparkling black, while the skin on his small face was tender and white; a stark contrast to his dark eyes. The gentle glow from his glassy eyes made him look innocent and soft.

Zhou Feng seized Liao Yifang's wrists and scanned every inch of his face in amazement. "I should have made you take your glasses off earlier. Your dear gege would have treated a beautiful face like that much better."

Ye Qin was speechless. Zhou Feng was just the kind of guy that wanted to make any good-looking person call him "gege," as if they wanted his protection. When they were in the middle school, Zhou Feng was constantly trying to make Ye Qin call him "gege," only to receive fierce beatings. Later, he had been working on Sun Yiran, again in vain.

It was probably the first time that Liao Yifang had been asked to do such a thing. Plus, he was always such a nice boy who never guarded against anybody. As a result, he finally succumbed to Zhou Feng's relentless efforts and let out "gege" in an unin-

tentionally soft voice.

Zhou Feng's mind went blank because of the surprise for quite some time. As soon as he felt himself again, he tried to get Liao Yifang repeat it.

The three boys were the last to leave the hall. Ye Qin didn't want to hear Zhou Feng talking to him all the way back home, so he got his bike and left earlier than him. He pedaled out of the school through the back gate and, as soon as had made a turn, he suddenly saw Cheng Feichi standing on the street next to a maidenhair tree.

He barely muted himself when he automatically called Cheng Feichi "gege" and was so mad at himself that he nearly wanted to slap himself secretly as a punishment. He internally scolded Zhou Feng for his stupid requests and halted his bike with composure.

When he sat on the bike, he was much shorter than Cheng Feichi. He put on his "super-annoyed" look and asked, "You're waiting for me?"

Cheng Feichi didn't give him a direct response. "I didn't ride a bike to school today."

The two boys walked on the sidewalk. Ye Qin made Cheng Feichi carry his backpack with the excuse of having to hold his bike. Cheng Feichi was therefore walking with two backpacks on him, but he still seemed quite at ease.

Ye Qin noticed that there was a cute animal made with small balloons on the slider of the zipper on Cheng Feichi's backpack. He asked without showing too much interest, "Did you make this cat?"

"I did," Cheng Feichi answered, "and this is a dog."

"Uh-huh." Ye Qin turned his head to look at the tall Bell Tower inside the school. "You know how to make those things?"

"Hmm. I worked in a supermarket once. I made balloon animals for kids."

Ye Qin looked down upon such fancy but useless stuff. *These are totally for little girls,* he thought. After they walked across the street at another traffic light, Ye Qin couldn't help glancing at the small animal again.

"Besides cats, what else can you make?"

After these months, Cheng Feichi was already too familiar with how different Ye Qin's words could be from his real thoughts. He wouldn't make a meaningless argument about what exactly the animal was, either. Instead, he took out a new balloon from his pack, blew it up, tied it off and then swiftly twisted it like he was performing a magic trick. In just ten seconds or so, a balloon flower with five petals appeared in his hands.

"Is it for me?"

Ye Qin was asking this question while his hands already reached out for the flower.

Cheng Feichi then made a two-colored lollipop with a yellow balloon and a red one. Ye Qin put it in the basket of the bike, looking much happier than before. He kept asking Cheng Feichi for more in excitement.

Cheng Feichi had found the balloons in the backstage of the school hall. There weren't many balloons left after the girls in his class took more than half of them. After making a peach heart, Cheng Feichi only had one balloon left with him.

Ye Qin was not satisfied with all the balloon crafts in his hands and on his bike. He was still asking for more.

Looking at the radiant happiness in Ye Qin's eyes, Cheng Feichi was feeling unexpectedly good as well. So he asked him patiently, "What else do you want?"

Ye Qin pondered the question for a long time. He didn't make any response until they passed the next traffic light and reached a quieter place. He poked Cheng Feichi's backpack. Cheng Feichi didn't know what he meant and looked back at his pack.

"You want a cat like this?"

Ye Qin shook his head and whispered something.

Cheng Feichi didn't hear him and instead made a small cat for him. It was in the same color as Ye Qin's clothes.

Ye Qin threw the balloon cat on Cheng Feichi and shouted, "What I want is you! Nothing else but you! Just give me a quick answer *now*!"

CHAPTER 05

ON the first day of the winter vacation, it snowed again in the capital city.

Ye Qin wrapped himself up from head to toe with a duvet. When Luo Qiuling came upstairs for the third time and told him to have breakfast, he managed to poke his head out of the quilt and shouted back, "I'm not hungry. I'll have it a bit later."

After that, he retreated into the nest of covers.

The room was well-heated; Ye Qin was not feeling cold either. Yet he just didn't want to get out of bed at all. Actually, he had been hiding from his family members since last night when he came back home from school. Luo Qiuling asked him what happened, but he just kept shaking his head under the covers and requested his mother in a muffled voice to leave him alone. He didn't sound like he was sick, so Luo Qiuling had to let him be. She knocked his bedroom door every now and then and asked whether he needed anything to eat.

Ye Qin really didn't need to eat anything. On the contrary, he needed to vent his anger.

Over ten hours ago, he told Cheng Feichi about his feelings and confidently pushed Cheng Feichi to give him a positive

answer, only to be turned down.

...Well, he didn't really say "no." Nor did he give any direct response. He just replied while looking towards the road ahead, saying "This is it," as if having completely filtered out what Ye Qin just said.

...He might as well just say no! Ye Qin was still freaking out about the whole thing. He would never say such degrading words again! But what is done is done—this would definitely remain one of the biggest jokes in his entire life.

His cellphone kept ringing a million times before he could no longer stand it. He reached out for it and answered the call under the covers. "What?"

It was Zhou Feng, shouting in a crowd of noisy people. "A-Qin! I'm at Times Square. Come! Now!"

Ye Qin frowned. "Why?"

"That merit student is working here! You'd never believe it! I just went out for a walk and saw him right there. It was like I was stalking him, you know? The KFC restaurant on the first floor. He was at Counter No. 2 and taking orders!"

Ye Qin replied, "...No."

"Why not?" Zhou Feng didn't have a clue about what happened. "You already gave him the stars?"

Ye Qin hung up the phone, clenching his teeth with fury. He rid himself of the quilt when he suddenly saw the whole glass jar of handmade stars. He threw his cellphone away as hard as he could. The phone rebounded when hitting the wall and fell onto the ground with a loud noise.

For three days in a row, Ye Qin didn't contact anyone. He locked his cellphone in the drawer and didn't even touch his computer, let alone go to an internet cafe. His daily routine merely consisted of having meals, sleeping, and using the bathroom—

back to the most basic lifestyle.

The fourth day soon arrived. Zhou Feng, Liu Yangfan, and Zhao Yue all came to his home. Ye Qin welcomed them with his body still completely wrapped in the duvet and took them to his bedroom. He told them to make themselves comfortable and then returned to his bed.

Zhou Feng worried, "My Qin, how are you, really? Are you like...isolating yourself?"

Zhao Yue picked up the glass jar on the nightstand and consoled Ye Qin. "Hey...even if it's a no, you don't need to be upset. We still have so many ways to get to him."

At first, Ye Qin was just feeling abashed because he failed to honor his big talk of winning over Cheng Feichi in this very semester. After blowing off some steam, he just wanted to hide himself so well that he wouldn't show up in front of Cheng Feichi unless he stepped up his game.

And then he felt that avoiding people made him feel good. He no longer needed to be anxious and worried all the time. He might as well have more rest until he had enough of it.

He mumbled under the duvet, "Leave him alone. I'll take care of it."

Liu Yangfan laughed at Ye Qin's response. "It seems that our A-Qin hasn't given up." As he was speaking, he picked up a balloon animal from the bay window. "What it this? A dog? Where did you get this sort of thing?"

Ye Qin suddenly jumped to his feet and snatched the balloon from his hand. "Get your hands off my stuff," he said grumpily.

The four of them had been friends for almost forever; a clear sense of "personal belongings" had been nonexistent in this small group. Thus Ye Qin's possessiveness today surprised them all. Zhou Feng's best efforts to mediate between the two boys

went in vain and they left Ye Qin's house on a bad note. Ye Qin sat by his bed for quite a while, the balloon cat in his arms, in which the air was almost gone.

He didn't know what on earth was wrong with him. He had a bad temper, that was true. But he had never been so unpredictable and bewildered about himself. It was as if he was becoming mentally ill. He found nothing interesting, not even a fine meal, a delicious drink, or a good sleep.

Luo Qiuling worried that her son may have had a bad time at school, so she phoned the head teacher of Ye Qin's class. After the call, she went into Ye Qin's room. Sitting by his bed, she asked her son hesitantly, "Darling, tell me, and tell the truth. Do you have a crush on a girl?

Ye Qin immediately got out of the bed. "Who said that?"

"You're my son. Of course I can see through you." Luo Qiuling couldn't get any useful information from Mr. Sun, other than the fact that Ye Qin wasn't making much academic progress. So she was merely guessing when posing this question. She continued, "You know, I won't be a helicopter parent. I totally respect your romantic freedom. It's just that...you should at least let me know who she is, right? You're such an innocent, sweet boy. I worry that you might get hurt."

Ye Qin curled his lip. He couldn't agree with his mother regarding being an "innocent" boy. He and Cheng Feichi hadn't reached the end of their game. It was still unclear who would be the last man standing.

Speaking of romantic freedom, the marriage between Luo Qiuling and Ye Jinxiang was a love match. Luo Qiuling was a college student coming from a rich family, but Ye Jinxiang was a mere salesman who barely made ends meet, not to mention their age difference. This was why Ye Qin always secretly referred to

his dad as "the old man," expressing how he thought his father was way out his mother's league.

Judged by all these objective conditions, this marriage was an ill-matched one. Considering Ye Qin's experience over the past years, he could tell that his mother didn't experience as much romance as she had imagined before marriage. Ye Qin thought his mother was the one indeed "hurt" by a relationship, so he couldn't figure out why she was asking this question. Did she intend to break them up, or was she just asking out of concern?

On a second thought, he stopped worrying. He and Cheng Feichi weren't even in a relationship in the first place.

"There's no such girl," Ye Qin answered, without showing a slight hint of his worries. "Surely I won't introduce to you someone who doesn't exist."

Luo Qiuling asked a few more questions nicely, but failed to get any concrete answers. She did not push Ye Qin, but changed the subject by talking about the family trip this year. They were heading to the Island M to celebrate the Spring Festival, thus Ye Qin could ask the maid to pack things up for him in the next few days.

Ever since Ye Qin's maternal grandfather passed away, the family spent almost every Spring Festival abroad. Ye Jinxiang's parents both died very young, so after getting married they usually spent the Spring Festival with Luo Qiuling's father. After her father's death, Luo Qiuling didn't want to upset herself by reliving the memories in the old house, so she would always arrange a trip overseas for the whole family.

This year was no exception. Because Ye Qin could hardly bear with chilly weather and would easily catch colds during the winter, Luo Qiuling set a tropical island in the Southern Hemisphere as their destination. She was the one who decided everything about the trips in the previous years, but this time

was different. Someone had an objection.

At the dinner table, first Ye Jinxiang was dissatisfied with the plain dishes; he complained that eating such stuff was no different from living a monk's life, and it was far from enough for him after a long day at work.

Luo Qiuling explained, "Our son hasn't been feeling well over the past few days; I'm afraid his stomach can't handle greasy food."

A few minutes later, she told Ye Jinxiang that the destination for their winter vacation would be Island M, where the weather would be perfect for Ye Qin to get back to good health.

"The Southern Hemisphere is so far away! It'll cost me two days just traveling to and fro. What about my work?" Ye Jinxiang snorted. "You're the one who made him so girly. A boy even more delicate than a girl!"

Ye Qin knew how feeble he was, but he couldn't stand Ye Jinxiang judging him and his mother in such a way. He put down the bowl with a bang. "If you're really so damn busy, you can just stay home and do your work. I'll go with mom."

The father and the son were at each other's throats. Ye Jinxiang had to vent his anger, so he picked up Ye Qin's academic report card and scolded him for how bad he was doing in each and every subject. He said Ye Qin was a disgrace, not in the least resembling his own excellent younger self.

Ye Qin was only patient enough to let him finish his words for the sake of his mother. He did not offer any retorts to his father, but replied, "Then go look for a son that resembles you!" And then he went upstairs without ever looking back at his parents.

He returned to his bedroom, picked up the glass jar, and was about to smash it on the ground. Eventually, he managed to quench the fury rising in him. When he calmed down, he took out his cellphone, charged it up, switched it on, and started edit-

ing a text message.

A week after winter vacation had started, Cheng Feichi got a text message from Ye Qin again. He asked him whether he had a WeChat account.

Cheng Feichi had heard about this app. A social media app like QQ, it was hugely popular recently. He didn't know why Ye Qin was asking this question. He thought that he had made himself extremely clear on the last day of the term, and it was impossible for Ye Qin to not take the hint.

He had never thought much about making friends with Ye Qin. To him, it was merely a normal social interaction between two schoolmates. He wouldn't refuse to talk to anyone that shared common interests or got along well with him.

Ye Qin was born rich, whereas Cheng Feichi wasn't even in the same league. For Cheng Feichi, Ye Qin was trying to get closer to him mostly because he found something rare and interesting in him. Once Ye Qin had explored everything about him, they would be bombarded by disagreements and conflicts. Cheng Feichi knew better than anyone that this sort of friendship would never last, because eventually the discord would grow strong enough to kill everything good between them.

As for the kind of affection beyond friendship which Ye Qin claimed that he wanted from him, Cheng Feichi considered it to be even more unreliable and vulnerable. Previously, he didn't take Ye Qin seriously, as he asserted that the passion Ye Qin had for him wouldn't last for even a month. After all, they hadn't given each other a good first impression. Though they gradually got to know each other in recent days, it wasn't enough for them to be more than friends.

Cheng Feichi was surprised that Ye Qin was still trying now. Surely, he was willing to be a friend to him, but that would

be all. He was a sensible person. If Ye Qin wouldn't give up on him, they might as well just return to being total strangers.

When the message arrived, Cheng Feichi was occupied. He saw it, but didn't have the time to reply. Somehow, having a legitimate reason to ignore whatever Ye Qin said made him feel relieved. But he ignored that feeling, too.

When he finished, he saw three more notifications on his phone.

If not, can you read MMS on your phone?
Oh right, your phone doesn't come with color display.
But there's a photo that I wanna show you.

Ye Qin sent a lot of text messages to him. Normally, he was very emotional, and so were his messages. By reading the words he wrote, Cheng Feichi could easily imagine his facial expression when he was typing these messages. This time, it was one of the rare cases where Ye Qin sounded calm. Cheng Feichi decided to reply to only one of the messages, and he wrote, "No."

Ye Qin didn't complain as usual. He changed to another topic, telling Cheng Feichi that tomorrow he would leave the country for vacation with his family and wouldn't come back until two weeks after the Spring Festival. Cheng Feichi didn't see the message until he got home. It was already past eleven. Everything and everyone should be sound asleep now. So he put his cellphone down, not replying anymore with the excuse of not wanting to disturb Ye Qin's good sleep.

Chinese New Year's Eve came on the 9th day of February. Cheng Feichi got up very early to prepare the necessary ingredients for the big meal this evening. As a tradition, most of the vendors would close up in the middle of the day and return to their families.

On his way, he ran into Mrs. Feng, who just came back

from the market. She insisted that Cheng Feichi take a bag of pork belly that she just bought. She said that she bought more meat than she needed for making dumplings, and he could take it home and make some dishes out of it.

"Though your mother was born and raised in the north, she has a stomach for southern foods. She doesn't like dumplings, so you can make braised pork belly with bean curd sheets. This is perfect."

Cheng Feichi could only take the bag and promised Mrs. Feng that he would visit her right after New Year's Day.

When Cheng Feichi was walking back home, he ranked from high to low the importance of the families that he should visit as a gesture of goodwill. Cheng Xin hardly went out to meet these acquaintances, so Cheng Feichi had started taking care of the relationships with neighbors and relatives several years ago. He wasn't sure whether it was appropriate to visit a particular relative first thing on New Year's Day, and decided to consult his mother. After all, it was a relative a lot more senior and closer to him, whom he regarded as the only family to him other than his own mother.

He opened the door and saw Cheng Xin was making dumpling wrappers.

"I thought we weren't making dumplings today." Cheng Feichi was curious.

Probably because the New Year always brought people happiness, Cheng Xin looked happier than she ordinarily was. "Well, though I don't like dumplings, you guys need to have some anyways."

So there will be more people visiting and celebrating the festival with us. Cheng Feichi suddenly stopped worrying. He washed his hands and started making dumplings for dinner.

No one came on New Year's Eve, but Cheng Feichi didn't think too much of it. It was freezing outside and their house was small. If someone really came and dined with them, it was not convenient weather for hurrying back home at night, and they couldn't offer them a cozy place for an overnight stay either. In the early morning of New Year's Day, Cheng Feichi got up to do some cleaning. But Cheng Xin told him that it was inappropriate to tidy up the room on this particular day and pushed him out to pay New Year's visits to the neighbors' house instead.

All these years, Cheng Feichi and his mother lived here. Life was never easy for an incomplete family, but thankfully their neighbors were very helpful. Cheng Feichi knocked on their doors one by one, and all the neighbors welcomed him with happy faces and bags full of snacks. Mr. Lee even gave him a huge Want Want Lunar New Year Snack Pack. Cheng Feichi politely declined, but Mr. Lee insisted.

"Take it. You and my grandson are the same age. I know young boys like you always love these snacks."

Cheng Feichi returned home with so many snacks that he was suddenly reminded of a certain young boy who always had a lollipop in his mouth. Ye Qin was indeed that kind of boy who really liked these snacks. If he were here, half of the snacks would be gone by the time he got home.

Cheng Feichi hadn't checked his cellphone since last night. Now he was wondering whether Ye Qin had sent him a text message with his New Year's blessings.

A few kids were playing with a kind of small firecrackers that would make explosive sounds without being lit up. They were competing with each other, trying to make the loudest sound. The laughter traveled through all the stairs and windows to Cheng Feichi's ears, making him feel relaxed and cheerful. He soon reached the door of his home. Looking at the couplet

in lucky red and hearing the muffled conversation sound from inside, Cheng Feichi never felt that the Spring Festival could be this good until now.

Yet every bit of happiness went to pieces the moment he opened the door.

There was a pair of leather shoes at the entrance. Only one, not two as he expected.

Cheng Xin was the only daughter. Other than her own parents, she didn't have any living immediate family. Yet the leather shoes seemed sophisticated and stylish, far from the kind of shoes that elderly people would normally wear.

"Xiao-Chi, you're back."

Cheng Feichi heard his mother talking to him. The door of the kitchen opened from inside, letting out the blinding white vapor that came from the cookers. Everything was blurred in front of him.

A man approached him, becoming gradually clear in his sight. This was a middle-aged man who put on the smile of the nicest father, bent down to take the snack bags from his hands as naturally as a daily habit, and said something that the neighbors who actually witnessed his whole childhood always said to him, "You've grown so tall."

Cheng Feichi very swiftly tilted back to avoid being touched.

Looking beyond the man's shoulder, he asked his mother, "Mom, who is he?"

The man's face froze for a few seconds but he, as a powerful and respected adult, was mature enough to quickly adjust himself. He answered in a gentle voice, "You can just call me uncle."

Cheng Feichi didn't respond. He walked past the man and entered the living room. Cheng Xin came forward to get the bags he was holding. "What took you so long? The dumplings

are getting cold."

The man followed Cheng Feichi into the living room. Hearing his footsteps, Cheng Feichi didn't answer his mother, but turned around and stared at the man. "This is my house. What the heck are you doing here?"

Cheng Xin didn't expect her son's violent rage. She tried to smooth things over. "Calm down. This gentleman is our guest."

Cheng Feichi left everything on the table and walked back towards the door.

Cheng Xin grabbed his arm. "Where are you going?"

"To get some fresh air." Cheng Feichi replied.

Cheng Xin said, "It's so cold outside. Stay here. The meal's ready."

The man was apparently still working on a good relationship with Cheng Feichi. He scanned the young lad from head to toe and give him a compliment, "I bought that coat according to the size your mom gave me. It fits you very well."

Cheng Feichi froze for a second. He looked at the down jacket he was wearing. When Cheng Xin gave him this coat a few days ago, she said that the last time she bought him a new coat was many years ago. Now seeing that the coat was on sale, she bought it for him to make up for it. Of course Cheng Feichi would never let his mother down. He kept very good care of this jacket and saved it for New Year's Day.

How could he have known that the coat was a gift from this man?

"I don't know your favorite color, so I bought the gray one. It's a versatile color. If you don't like it, I'll take you out and buy another one after the meal."

The man was obviously not good at pleasing others. He meant to ask for Cheng Feichi's opinion, but his words sounded very distant and condescending. Cheng Feichi felt as if he was a

beggar in front of the man.

When Cheng Feichi started to undo the zippers of the coat, Cheng Xin tried again to appease him. "Don't rush to take off your coat. I just turned on the heating. It's gonna be a while before the room is warm enough…"

Cheng Feichi didn't listen. He still took off the new jacket which he had happily worn for less than two hours. Seeing the somber look growing on that man's face, Cheng Feichi flung it down on the dresser at the entrance. "One of us has to piss off. If he doesn't leave, I will."

At this time of the year, most of the stores were closed. At a fast-food restaurant, a female colleague who took the shift from Cheng Feichi the day before yesterday was cleaning the table. When he entered the restaurant, she was surprised. "Hey handsome, aren't you cold like that?"

Cheng Feichi answered her with a "Happy New Year," and then headed for the staff lounge.

The girl kept up with him, still holding the plates. "Why are you here? You wanna see the manager? He's not here."

Cheng Feichi stopped. "When will he come back to work?"

"I'm not sure. Probably not until the day after tomorrow."

Cheng Feichi thought for a few seconds and said, "Are there empty shifts today or tomorrow?"

The girl's eyes lit up. "You wanna change your shift? Didn't you say that you wouldn't be available until the day after tomorrow?"

Cheng Feichi compressed his lips slightly. "I suddenly became available."

"Wait a second! I'm calling the manager!" The girl put down the plates, ran towards the lounge and returned in less than three minutes. She looked at Cheng Feichi with a sad face.

"The manager needs you to call him. He wants to make sure that I didn't push you to do this..."

Cheng Feichi took his phone out of his pocket and realized that it was already out of juice after last night. The girl gave him a charger. After less than five minutes, the outmoded phone could be switched on again. He called the manager, telling him that he was free today and tomorrow, and that he wanted to take Wu Rui's shifts.

Wu Rui was the girl. She had been doing part-time jobs here for a long time, just like him.

"You told us that you needed to stay home with your mom, didn't you? What's the rush?" the manager asked through the phone.

"My mom isn't alone now," Cheng Feichi answered. "I had nothing to do at home, so here I am."

Cheng Feichi took the shift from Wu Rui, while the latter soon put on some makeup and left. When she walked past the glass wall of the restaurant, she turned her head and gave him an air kiss. "Thank you, handsome! If you ever want to change shifts in the future, just let me know!"

A lot of part-time workers worked here. When Cheng Feichi just got here, everybody called him "handsome". He was not very comfortable with this nickname, but it was still better than "that straight-A student".

While the phone was still charging, a text message arrived, much later than the time it was supposed to be received. It was from a strange number, whose registration location was also strange to Cheng Feichi. It simply said, "Happy New Year."

A few moments later, another one came. "Is your shit phone still working?"

Cheng Feichi smiled. A tiny sign of joy finally appeared on his face. He replied, "Happy New Year." Then he changed into

his uniform and started working.

On New Year's Day, many people flocked to the fast-food restaurant. In the middle of day, the restaurant became so crowded that no seats were available anymore. A lot of customers had to order take-out. Cheng Feichi stopped cleaning the tables and helped his colleagues packaging the food, to take the stress away from people working at the counter.

When things got less crazy, it was already four in the afternoon.

Cheng Feichi was having his meal while checking his phone. The strange number texted him again four hours ago, "Have you had lunch?"

Cheng Feichi replied, "On it now."

A new text soon arrived, "A late lunch! I've already had my lunch here."

Cheng Feichi was typing when another one got in. "Wait. Do you know who I am or not?"

Cheng Feichi typed something with one hand, but changed his mind before sending it. He deleted everything and typed merely three words, "No, I don't."

"Darn it!"

Hundreds of thousands of miles away, Ye Qin threw the cellphone onto the ground. A few moments later he dashed to the balcony to pick it up and then slumped down on the hanging chair nearby. He gently swung himself back and forth with his feet randomly tapping on the floor while editing a new text message.

"I'm Ye Qin. This is a temporary number that I use overseas."

Cheng Feichi replied, "Mm."

As cool as he always was.

Pursing his lips, Ye Qin suddenly grinned wryly. He began typing very fast. "Do you know how much it costs to send an international SMS?"

Cheng Feichi replied, "No."

Ye Qin burst out laughing. "Ten yuan!!!!!!!!!!!lol"

After this message, Ye Qin waited for more than ten minutes, but Cheng Feichi wasn't replying anymore. Ye Qin began to regret his words. Perceiving that Cheng Feichi must be worrying about the huge cost, he quickly sent more messages to Cheng Feichi, explaining that he made up the price and the real cost must be just one yuan or something.

But Cheng Feichi was still not responding. Ye Qin was incredibly upset. He turned his eyes away from the screen and saw a barbecue party down on the beach. A giant arch made of balloons was standing there, decorated with more colorful balloons forming the shape of "Happy Birthday."

It reminded him of the balloon cat he had left back home. Before he left the country, the cat was already a tangle of deflated rubber. He wanted to let Cheng Feichi see it, so he took a photo of the sad cat, but later recalled that Cheng Feichi's phone couldn't display photos.

He didn't know why he wanted Cheng Feichi to see the deflated cat. He was too emotional and capricious. Probably he was feeling annoyed then, because of his father's awful attitude. He wanted to vent his frustration.

But this gave him more reasons to continue working on Cheng Feichi. After all, he had gone this far. How could he give up now? Luo Qiuling was hardly ever tough enough to confront her husband, but Ye Qin couldn't bite the bullet anymore. As long as he couldn't get actual proof, he had to get to the bottom of this potential scandal.

The sea breeze took the strangers' laughter all the way up

to the second floor. Ye Qin had made up his mind and cheered himself up before he woke up the cellphone screen and started typing again. "When's your birthday?"

Cheng Feichi had two continuous shifts that day. When he finally had a break, it was already the early morning of the second day of the new year.

He saw a bunch of missed calls from Cheng Xin and an unread message, asking whether he was coming home last night.

Normally, Cheng Xin would just ask when he would come home. This time she posed a different question, which meant that someone might be staying at their place that night.

Fortunately, the dawn was approaching. Cheng Feichi took off the uniform and took a nap in the corner of the restaurant. After the day broke, he called Cheng Xin back, telling her that he had slept at a classmate's home and didn't hear the phone ring.

Cheng Xin's voice didn't reveal any emotion. She just said, "Come home. It's not appropriate to stay at your classmate's house when you should be with your family."

Cheng Feichi asked bluntly, "Is that man still there?"

Cheng Xin was silent for a moment and replied, "He wants to celebrate your birthday with you."

Cheng Feichi suddenly froze.

Ever since he could remember things, he'd never had birthday celebrations. Mrs. Feng, who knew him from the first day of his life, told him the struggles Cheng Xin went through to give birth to him. That was a particularly cold winter. There was snow even after the Spring Festival. It snowed for a whole night, and she had endured the pain the whole time. There was no heating in the local public health center, so she could only count on a small charcoal stove to keep warm. She gripped the bedside handrail so hard that her sweat soaked the sheets completely. If

it were not for the loud cry of the new-born baby, the doctors wouldn't have found her lying unconscious on the bed, on the brink of dying because of postpartum hemorrhage.

At last, Cheng Xin pulled through, thanks to the efforts of the medical staff, but the sequelae had been undermining her health ever since. She was too feeble to have a normal life. It made Cheng Feichi grow up tortured by a sense of guilt. He believed that his birthday was not only a day of suffering for his mother, but also the beginning of all the disasters that doomed their small family. That no one ever mentioned his birthday actually gave him a sense of relief.

He didn't want parties and gifts. He just wanted to grow up, as fast as he could.

He wanted to be a game-changer in his own life, but he didn't want to take a shortcut through anyone else. Thus the man that appeared at his home was severely repugnant to him. He couldn't understand why his mother had given up on fighting, but he wasn't the one who could judge or oppose her. To express his attitude, he could only be emotional and even a bit aggressive.

"Don't bother. I never celebrate my birthdays," Cheng Fei-chi answered. "I'll be back home once he's gone."

After hanging up, Cheng Feichi let out a deep breath. His phone suddenly started vibrating continuously. More than a dozen of text messages flocked in, lining up on the screen of his phone.

This was normal. The messages were delayed because of the unstable phone signal. One of the texts came from Zhang Pei-yao. She asked him how his Spring Festival was and whether he was available for hanging out with her tomorrow. Cheng Feichi turned her down.

The rest of the messages all came from Ye Qin. The first one was about the date of his birthday. After three unanswered mes-

sages, Ye Qin's fury began to grow.

Reading the second to last text message, Cheng Feichi could easily picture how furious Ye Qin had become. "Why are you so cold and stubborn? Were you born from a stone?"

Shortly afterwards, the last message sounded weak and apologetic. "Okay, it was me born from a stone…If you don't wanna tell me, fine. I'll go ask your head teacher once the next semester begins."

Ye Qin was like an elementary schoolboy who could only seek his teacher's help in the face of whatever problem he encountered.

Cheng Feichi could not withhold his smile anymore. He looked up at the clock on the wall, realizing that it was time for Ye Qin to wake up. And then he replied, "The day after tomorrow."

For the next two days, Cheng Feichi had been staying outside.

It didn't feel bad to not go home every evening. Cheng Feichi had many co-workers helping him out and accompanying him in the restaurant. The manager also came two days after the Spring Festival when the public holiday ended. Hearing that Cheng Feichi had nowhere to go, he allowed Cheng Feichi to use his own private lounge. The room was right next to the kitchen, so the noise could be a bit disturbing. But it was better than sleeping out there in the dining area.

On the third day after the Spring Festival, Cheng Feichi picked up his phone to check the time and then opened the message box. There was nothing new.

Ye Qin said that he would come back before the semester began, which was about a week from now. *Probably he's having such a good time in that foreign country that he has no time to spare for me.*

In the morning, Cheng Xin called and asked him again whether he was going home. Cheng Feichi said no again. Cheng Xin, very unexpectedly, started to try to persuade him. "He's leaving tomorrow. You don't need to care about me. Just come home and have a dinner together."

Cheng Feichi found it ridiculous. She was his one and only *mother*! How on earth could he not care about her? Even if he managed to stop caring about her, he wouldn't be able to resist his own feeling of sickness and strangeness when he saw that man.

There was an insurmountable wall between himself and that man. Each day of the past over ten years had piled up to form this overwhelming barrier. He wouldn't be easily bought off by a few clothes, a watch, or some useless nice words.

The restaurant was even busier than it had been on New Year's Day. During the break, Cheng Feichi quickly finished his meal and casually checked his messages. Ye Qin texted him, asking him where he was. Cheng Feichi didn't think much and replied, "Home." And then he resumed his work.

At dusk, Wu Rui just got back to work. When Cheng Feichi was packing the take-out food, she came to him and said, "Your phone keeps beeping. A bunch of messages are coming in. Mind you, I didn't mean to peek at your private messages; it's just the font size is too big. A glance was all it took to read them."

Cheng Feichi asked her what kind of messages they were. She used exaggerated gestures to indicate an unusual length of words. "It just keeps repeating 'I'm frozen' for like a thousand times. It's from a strange number. It doesn't look like a local phone number. Probably it's some kind of scam."

Cheng Feichi let out a stifled laugh. Ye Qin's foreign number did look like those on the unwanted telemarketing phone number lists.

But...wasn't he in the Southern Hemisphere? How could he

feel cold there?

When the restaurant was busy, the shift work schedule didn't mean anything anymore. Everyone was so occupied that they hardly had the time for dinner, if not a minute to chat.

When they could finally slow down a bit, it was already dark outside.

Cheng Feichi soon checked his messages. On the top of all the messages saying "I'm frozen," he saw something unexpected. "I'm waiting for you downstairs. Come and take me home!"

When he was back in the Yulin Compound, even the concierge was off duty. He rode the bike on the bumpy lanes, hearing nothing but the blowing wind. He mocked himself for being such an idiot. Ye Qin must be making fun of him. How could he really be waiting here in the cold wind?

But the thought fled from his mind just one or two seconds later.

The closer he became to the No. 3 Building, the clearer he saw the boy huddling up at the back of the stairs.

Having heard a creak of bicycle wheels, the boy give a few shivers and managed to stand up. He first tried to recognize who it was on the bicycle, and after confirming his assumption, he dashed towards Cheng Feichi and shouted, "You liar! How dare you lie to me, saying that you're at home?"

Ye Qin's voice was hoarse, and he didn't sound as intimidating as he was trying to be. The street lamp nearby let Cheng Feichi see Ye Qin's reddened face, pale lips, and the pair of flip flops he was wearing.

Ye Qin also looked at himself and said awkwardly, "I was too eager to leave...I didn't change my clothes when I get on the plane." Thinking of the reason why he quit his beautiful vacation and returned home early, he became angry again. "Why didn't

you give me a heads-up about your birthday before I left? There was no direct flight from the island I was on to Beijing! I went to their capital by boat, but when I arrived the tickets had been sold out. I had to stay an extra night there and took the earliest plane back. You know what? Even the earliest plane got delayed! I nearly couldn't make it home to see you tonight!"

Ye Qin couldn't stop complaining, but the volume of his voice gradually went down. He seemed hurt and embarrassed, dragging the hem of the coat to cover the beach shorts which did not match his coat in the slightest. He sniffed while grumbling, "And you lied to me! But I'll forgive you...it's your birthday."

He didn't mention a thing about the many hours he'd waited in the cold winter night.

The lamp was behind Cheng Feichi, so Ye Qin couldn't see his face very clearly. Seeing that Cheng Feichi was not giving any response, he felt even more unsure of himself. "Where were you? Why are you still working during the festival...How poor you must be..."

Before he could finish the sentence, a piece of clothing dropped on his head. Cheng Feichi put his uniform on Ye Qin, threw the bicycle in the corner behind the gate and took Ye Qin's arm.

The uniform was thin and smelly. Ye Qin didn't like wearing it, so he kept moving his arms to rub Cheng Feichi's forearm, now exposed in the cold air.

Cheng Feichi grabbed his hand but was surprised by how cold it was. He turned his head to face Ye Qin. "Why don't you just call me?"

Ye Qin could finally touch something warm. He kept up with Cheng Feichi and, finally satisfied with himself, he got closer to him, answering with both confidence and vulnerability, "I couldn't use my foreign number here to call you..."

Ye Qin started telling Cheng Feichi how he left in a hurry with nothing but a cellphone and his passport. He exaggerated the details to spice up the story.

Cheng Feichi wondered, "How did you get here?"

Ye Qin answered, "My mom asked a chauffeur to pick me up at the airport."

"Why don't you just go home?"

Ye Qin blinked his eyes and quickly came up with an answer. "I don't have the key, and the housemaid left for vacation. So I couldn't get into the house."

Very reasonable. Cheng Feichi stopped asking and took Ye Qin out of the building, heading towards the gate of the compound.

Ye Qin kept looking back. "Aren't we going to your home...? You don't have the key with you?"

Cheng Feichi paused shortly. "Did you knock on the door?"

"I did," Ye Qin said. "No one answered. Otherwise I wouldn't be standing outside."

Cheng Feichi turned his head and saw the windows of both the kitchen and the living room were dark.

He didn't say anything to explain that he actually had the key with him, but instead he walked away from the building, taking Ye Qin straight to the chain hotel near the compound.

At the entrance of the hotel, Ye Qin retreated and moved behind Cheng Feichi. "Are...are we going to get a room?"

Normally, "getting a room" should mean staying in a place like a hotel to have a rest. Ye Qin, however, was intentionally misinterpreting the phrase.

"Aren't you cold?" Cheng Feichi didn't let go of his arm. Instead, he asked Ye Qin with an expressionless face, "Do you have any other places to go?"

Ye Qin could only finish the check-in procedures and enter

the elevator with him. *I'm also a man. What do I have to lose?* he kept telling himself.

They entered the room and turned on the heater. The room had hardly started getting warmer when Ye Qin immediately took off Cheng Feichi's uniform. He paced slowly around the room and inspected it like he was the boss of the place. "The window can't open? The drapes are so dirty...The bed is tiny! And when's the last time they cleaned the sheets? Or have they ever done that? Can we really sleep here?" Then he ran to the door of the bathroom. Cheng Feichi was filling the teapot with water there. He asked Cheng Feichi, "Hey, why don't we stay at the Hilton Hotel in the city center? It's on you this time, but I'll pay you back later."

The pot was full of water. Holding it, Cheng Feichi passed by Ye Qin without looking at him. He bent down to see where the power sockets were. "I don't have enough money with me."

Ye Qin grimaced behind Cheng Feichi's back and swallowed up his complaints. His feet bare, Ye Qin ran to where he could feel the warm breeze from the heater.

The water boiled, Cheng Feichi disinfected the cup with hot water, then filled the cup and handed it to Ye Qin.

Ye Qin frowned at the tasteless boiled water. "I want to drink soda water. Do they have room service here? I'm gonna make a call."

Cheng Feichi insisted that he take the cup. "I'm not saying that you should drink it. Just hold it so your hands will get warmer."

When Cheng Feichi returned with a bottle of soda water, Ye Qin began to realize that he was a bit too demanding. Cheng Feichi was obviously upset and tired, while he was still constantly making things difficult for him; not a bit afraid of being

left alone out there on the street.

He took the bottle that Cheng Feichi opened and took a gulp. Then he asked, "You were still working on your birthday?"

Cheng Feichi merely said, "Hmm," indicating that he didn't want to go any deeper regarding this topic.

They sat at the bedside shoulder to shoulder. Ye Qin moved closer to Cheng Feichi. "Let's buy a cake! It's on me."

Cheng Feichi replied with a low voice, "I don't need it."

"What sort of birthday it is without a decent cake?" Ye Qin jumped from the bed to the floor. "I came all the way back here just to celebrate your birthday with you. It won't do without a cake!"

Cheng Feichi raised his head to look at Ye Qin, but soon lowered it. "You didn't have a cake on your birthday."

It took Ye Qin quite a while to realize that Cheng Feichi was referring to his last birthday on the Winter Solstice Festival. On that day, he washed a lot of dishes while waiting for Cheng Feichi at the small restaurant. Of course he couldn't tell Cheng Feichi that that day wasn't his birthday at all. He lowered his voice out of guilt.

"Well...that...that was different."

Somehow, he made Cheng Feichi laugh. Cheng Feichi chuckled and patted the bed. "Come on. Lie down and tuck yourself in. Your knees are so cold that they've turned red."

Seeing that Cheng Feichi was still able to laugh, Ye Qin finally could stop worrying. Covering his legs with the baggy coat, he demonstrated to Cheng Feichi the posture he used while waiting for him in the doorway. "I squatted there like this, so my legs weren't cold. My toes are a bit cold though."

Cheng Feichi gave in. He dragged Ye Qin to the bed and covered him with the quilt.

Ye Qin automatically curled up to form a round heap. With

only his head out of the quilt, Ye Qin looked more like a ball than when he was squatting. Cheng Feichi couldn't help grinning, so he looked away and cleared his throat.

"Are you hungry? What would you like to eat?"

They had the delicious cake Ye Qin wanted after all.

Ye Qin found the number of his favorite cake shop and called it using Cheng Feichi's phone. Within an hour, a six-inch cake was sent to the hotel.

He opened the plastic package of the birthday candles with one hand while talking to his father on his cellphone. "I'm with a schoolmate...You don't know him...He's very outstanding. He's a straight-A student from Class No. 1, okay? You can ask mom if you don't believe me... Alright, alright, I'll go home tomorrow."

After the conversation ended, Ye Qin still felt annoyed. Ye Jinxiang clearly heard "Class No. 1," yet he didn't panic at all. Ye Jinxiang was indeed a foxy man. He must have done all-round preparation to hide the bastard and the bastard's mother.

Cheng Feichi looked at the two candles in the shape of Arabic numbers "1" and "8" in Ye Qin's hands and asked him, "Didn't you say that your foreign number is out of service here?"

Ye Qin answered him impatiently, "My father has the card that can make it work."

Then he suddenly realized that he shouldn't bring up his father at the moment. Looking at Cheng Feichi, Ye Qin didn't see any interesting response. He was so curious that he put the candles on the cake and asked in a casual way, "Your family...I mean, your parents. They've never celebrated your birthday?"

Cheng Feichi stayed silent for quite a while. Finally, he answered in a cold voice, "I don't have a father."

Because he accidentally asked a stupid question, Ye Qin didn't dare to do anything rash. On the next day, he got up particularly early.

But he was still later than Cheng Feichi. When Ye Qin was brushing his teeth with the unbearably hard toothbrush provided by the hotel, Cheng Feichi had already returned with breakfast.

Among several freshly made stuffed buns was buried a sandwich, which was already warm now. Cheng Feichi picked out the sandwich for Ye Qin. "Eat it. I'll call you a cab when you're finished."

Ye Qin began to regret telling his father that he would come home today. He came up with something new. "The maid won't be back until this afternoon. If I go home now, I'll have to stand around outside the house."

Cheng Feichi checked the time on his phone. "I'll ask them to postpone the check-out time to 2 p.m. When you leave here, remember to check out."

Then he folded his uniform, carried it under his arm, and was ready to leave.

"Hey." Holding the sandwich in his mouth, Ye Qin stood up to stop him. "Where are you going?"

"I need to work."

Ye Qin became anxious. "No way. You can't leave."

Cheng Feichi stood by the door, looking at him. "What now?"

From Cheng Feichi's reaction just now, Ye Qin deduced that Cheng Feichi was not angry at him for what had happened last night. So he became more confident and pointed at his legs. "I don't have trousers or shoes. I'll be frozen once I get out of here."

Half an hour later, Ye Qin was standing in men's department of VNIQLO, with Cheng Feichi's uniform tied around his waist. He kept picking and choosing: this pair of trousers was too out of style, while others were of poor quality. He just

couldn't find something that satisfied him.

But Cheng Feichi needed to get to work on time. Jeans, casual trousers, sweatpants: he picked one pair out of each and shoved Ye Qin into a fitting room.

Ye Qin didn't come out after a long time, making nonstop ruffling sounds. When he finally opened the curtain, he only revealed his head and a sad face. "These are so ugly. Can't we go to another store?"

He had never worn such cheap trousers; so weirdly designed and poor quality. None of them were good enough for him to make do with.

"No, we can't." Cheng Feichi turned him down without a second thought and handed him a pair of white casual shoes that he randomly got from the shelves.

Several minutes later, he got out of the fitting room, rather bashfully. He even tripped himself on his way out, yet Cheng Feichi was alert enough to catch him.

Cheng Feichi looked down and saw the loose shoelaces. "Wrong size?"

Ye Qin managed to stand up straight and held Cheng Feichi's arm to keep his balance. He looked pained and sounded as if he was going to cry. "I don't know how to tie shoelaces…"

After putting on new trousers and new shoes, Ye Qin unexpectedly went back on his word.

He didn't go home as he said. Instead, he followed Cheng Feichi to the fast-food restaurant and stayed at the table closest to the heating radiator for the whole day.

In the afternoon, Wu Rui couldn't stand it anymore. She went to the kitchen and found Cheng Feichi preparing the food. "The boy that came with you is your didi? He's still there. He's drunk eight glasses of free water so far."

Cheng Feichi sighed and changed shifts with Wu Rui so that he could send Ye Qin home.

After work, he called Mrs. Feng to apologize for failing to visit her first thing after the Spring Festival. Mrs. Feng surely didn't blame him for it; it seemed that she had somehow known why he didn't come home. She even tried to defend Cheng Xin.

"Don't blame your mother. Things have been difficult for her all these years. There were many people who didn't mind taking care of you along with her, and they pursued her, wishing to marry her. Many of them were quite well-off, but she turned all of them down for your sake." In the end, she sighed. "Though I didn't know that she was still holding on to this after all these years."

Cheng Feichi didn't quite understand her last sentence. From his perspective, Cheng Xin was aloof and indifferent. She didn't look like someone obsessed with anything. What could it be?

After he packed his stuff and left the lounge, Cheng Feichi looked a bit absent-minded. Ye Qin walked towards him and waved his hands in front of his eyes to get his attention.

"What are we going to eat tonight?" Ye Qin asked him excitedly. "I heard that there's a dessert shop upstairs. Can we have a bite after dinner?"

How well he knew the nearby properties! He hadn't wasted the whole morning just waiting for him.

Cheng Feichi knew how he loved desserts. After all, almost the entire cake had gone into his belly yesterday.

Ye Qin had a very good plan, but his plan couldn't keep up with the changes. They didn't realize that today was Valentine's Day until they'd strolled in the mall for some time. All the decent restaurants were packed. There were no tables available in

the fast-food restaurants either.

Ye Qin followed Cheng Feichi with an upset face, complaining that they should have just dined at where Cheng Feichi worked. At least they could enjoy the heating there.

Cheng Feichi had been followed by Ye Qin for a whole day. With the boy who did everything on a whim, Cheng Feichi experienced all sorts of weird things and unnecessary troubles. Right now he didn't even have the energy to be mad at him. He let Ye Qin sit on a public bench nearby, and went in search of food.

They were at the pedestrian zone close to Times Square. In the evening, the whole zone was lit up by glorious lights, neon billboards, and smiley faces. The mall was swarming with happy couples...and girls selling flowers.

Cheng Feichi returned when a girl just started latching onto Ye Qin. She was very good at her business, holding a rose and begging Ye Qin to pay for it. "Sir, why don't you buy two roses? I wish the two of you will be together forever."

Ye Qin didn't have a dime with him, so he could only shake his head and both of his hands. "I'm single. Why would I need that?"

The girl was still trying to make him buy the rose. "Then one rose is enough. It will bring you good luck in love."

Ye Qin was used to spending money without any limit, so it was difficult for him to say no. Seeing that Cheng Feichi was coming this way, Ye Qin felt as if he'd finally clutched at a straw. "Come! Buy a rose for me! I'll give you the money later."

Cheng Feichi could hardly sigh now. He paid for the rose and stuffed it into his pocket.

Ye Qin had doughnuts for dinner on the way home. He didn't complain and hadn't yet stopped savoring the sweet taste when he got out of the taxi.

"Tastes good?" Cheng Feichi asked him.

Ye Qin nodded very happily. "You had one yourself. Don't you think so?"

Cheng Feichi didn't find any pleasure in eating ring-shaped bread glazed with colorful jam. Far from giving him any feeling of fullness, the doughnuts were so cloying that they made him feel sick and thirsty.

He held onto such thoughts, and didn't say it out loud. That would make Ye Qin upset. When they got to the less crowded roadside, he let Ye Qin stand still and squatted down to tie his shoelaces for him.

On this pair of new shoes, the knots easily got loose. Ye Qin was a naughty boy, so the impact of him stepping and jumping on the ground also made the laces slip. This was the third time that Cheng Feichi had tied the laces for him. The first time was at the fitting room, and the second was in the fast-food restaurant. Wu Rui was surprised by how nicely Cheng Feichi treated his "didi."

Cheng Feichi didn't think much of it, so he didn't say anything in response. But now he suddenly felt something different.

He tied stable double slipknots for Ye Qin, while the latter kept moving his toes. Cheng Feichi could see the toe cap bulge and then shrink back to normal.

Then they kept walking. Silence prevailed for a long time.

When they walked past the pedestrian bridge, the street, and finally arrived at the gate of the compound where Ye Qin lived, Ye Qin pointed at Cheng Feichi's pocket. He asked Cheng Feichi in a low voice whether he was going to give him that rose or not. At this moment, Cheng Feichi was finally able to pin a name to the different thing he had felt earlier. It turned out that the sticky, ambiguous, and unspeakable tenderness that permeated the air between them, was the so-called thing called

"romantic chemistry."

And this chemistry was just like any other chemical reaction. It was necessary to get both sides involved.

Ye Qin couldn't bear the embarrassment of waiting in silence. He picked the rose out of Cheng Feichi's pocket as if the rose had belonged to him from the beginning. After that, he asked Cheng Feichi to wait for a moment, and ran into the night.

Cheng Feichi thought it was time for him to leave, but somehow, he felt his feet were glued to the ground.

Could it be the reason was that he hadn't said goodbye to Ye Qin yet? Out of courtesy, he should wait until Ye Qin returned and bid farewell to him properly.

Ye Qin returned holding a palm-sized glass jar with both hands.

"Happy birthday!" He put the jar directly into Cheng Feichi's hands, and then warmed his own hands by breathing into them and rubbing them. "It's a bit late, but you don't mind it, do you?"

Cheng Feichi was still holding the jar, amazed. Hearing Ye Qin's question, he immediately nodded.

Ye Qin grinned, revealing two canine teeth. He yawned; his eyelashes moistened by the tears squeezed out from his eyes. He waved his hands listlessly. "Go home. My mom's gonna give me a video call, so I can't see you off. I'm going back now."

Cheng Feichi walked all the way back home.

He always went home on foot from High School No. 6, especially at night. But this time he felt different.

Probably because the stars in the jar were glowing.

Cheng Feichi looked at them; looked at how the glimmering stars lit up his skin and formed a small ocean of shining

spots like a miniature galaxy. Looking at them, Cheng Feichi was reminded of Ye Qin's bright eyes when he said "happy birthday" to him.

He also couldn't forget that yesterday was the first birthday he had ever celebrated in his life.

And this small jar of stars was the first birthday gift he had ever received.

CHAPTER 06

AFTER the Spring Festival, the weather became warmer again. Every day, when one opened the window and took a deep breath, they could sense a clear increase in the temperature.

The new semester was about to start in less than three days. The students were busy either catching up with their homework or having fun. As for Ye Qin, he was doing both things at the same time.

Zhao Yue invited his friends to seize the last chance of having fun before the term started. Though Ye Qin and Liu Yangfan were at odds with each other before the festival, it was no big deal when it came to their longstanding friendship. After all, disputes and fallings-out on a small scale were commonplace to them. From the minute they reunited, the two immediately returned to being good friends and started copying others' homework together in the noisy karaoke lounge.

Ye Qin was copying Zhou Feng's homework. Though he was not a brilliant student, he could recognize how clearly and thoroughly Zhou Feng was analyzing and answering the exercises. All of his answers were correct. It was a strange thing. Ye Qin hit Zhou Feng's head with his pen to stop his awful performance and asked him whose homework he'd copied.

"The class monitor's, of course," Zhou Feng answered with the microphone in his hand. "He was helping me with my homework two days ago. I stole his homework when he wasn't paying attention, and spent the whole night copying his answers."

Ye Qin resumed his work. He changed a few answers to pretend that he did the homework by himself, while secretly scolding Zhou Feng for being an asshole who abused Liao Yifang's trust.

Obviously, he forgot how many times he'd copied Cheng Feichi's homework with the excuse of pursuing him and learning from him.

Liu Yangfan wasn't as lucky as he was. He was in the international school. His courses were very different from those in High School No. 6, and the homework assigned for the winter vacation mainly consisted of essays and social practice reports. As he couldn't make use of Zhao Yue's homework either, he kept complaining that he should also have an excellent student around that excelled in all subjects; someone who could even write English essays for him.

Ye Qin was immediately reminded of Cheng Feichi. He was amazingly good at English. Ye Qin heard that he even took part in the school-level English debate contest.

Having just given Cheng Feichi such a thoughtful birthday present, Ye Qin naturally thought that their relationship had improved by leaps and bounds. So he texted Cheng Feichi, asking him to hang out with his friends in the club.

They would get to know each other eventually. It would be better if they met up now so that there wouldn't be any embarrassments in the future.

However, Cheng Feichi didn't reply. Ye Qin waited until the night fell. He guessed Cheng Feichi was still angry at his

friends for what they did at the convenience store last semester. *But what's the point of being so petty? You've taken revenge on me, after all.*

So he sent another text. "Why don't you reply? It's okay. I'll get another lounge for the two of us. You don't have to be with them all the time."

Still, no response.

Ye Qin wasn't happy about it, but still refrained from bombarding Cheng Feichi with text messages. He thought that Cheng Feichi must be fully occupied now and persuaded himself to be a considerate suitor.

The first day of the semester arrived. Ye Qin texted Cheng Feichi and told him he wanted to pay his debts. But Cheng Feichi still didn't give him any response. This was when Ye Qin started to feel something strange.

At the opening ceremony, they were seated wide apart, so there was no chance for them to talk. When Ye Qin went to Cheng Feichi's classroom during the break in person, the teacher was talking nonstop. Ye Qin could only looked at Cheng Feichi from outside the classroom, and asked the students sitting near the window to pass notes to Cheng Feichi.

He kept waiting for him, but all his patience and efforts were in vain. He went to Cheng Feichi's classroom again at the major break before the night session began, but Cheng Feichi wasn't there. Ye Qin didn't know where he went for dinner.

Still, Ye Qin wouldn't give up. At the first night session, he let Liao Yifang pass his graded math examination paper to Cheng Feichi on his way to the Teacher's Office. Ye Qin wrote next to his grades, "Mr. Cheng, I'll come for you after class."

To his surprise, when the bell rang, his exam paper was sent back with another piece of paper between the pages. On this

additional paper, Cheng Feichi wrote every step of deducing the correct answer. Every inch of this paper was covered by his handwriting.

In order to prevent Ye Qin from finding other excuses to meet him, Cheng Feichi wrote out every possible way of solving the problems. He even made a thorough analysis of why Ye Qin would make mistakes on this exam. Other than helping him with learning math, Cheng Feichi didn't write any unnecessary words. What a serious, efficient, and responsible tutor he was!

After the night session, Ye Qin waited for Cheng Feichi at the bike parking area. He wanted to ask Cheng Feichi what he meant. Yet Cheng Feichi didn't come at all. He left for home directly through the front gate after school, without his bike.

Ye Qin couldn't understand what happened. Last time they had such a good time together! He got a rose from Cheng Feichi, and Cheng Feichi accepted the stars he gave him. And what now? Only a few days later, Cheng Feichi just wanted to get rid of him?

If he was upset about Ye Qin asking about his father that night at the hotel room, he must be the slowest person on earth!

Ye Qin wasn't good at being cheeky. He had tried so hard. Cheng Feichi was pushing him to his limits.

During the following days, Ye Qin held himself back from coming any closer to Cheng Feichi, just like how a young master should behave. By convention, in the second week of the new semester, respectable entrepreneurs and alumni were invited to deliver speeches to students. The students were gathered in batches in the School Hall. Class No. 1 and Class No. 2 were in the same batch. When they gathered in the hall, the two groups were no more than five meters away.

Now you can't get away from me! Ye Qin thought. But what he didn't think of was that once they entered the hall, Cheng

Feichi immediately got out of his sight. He asked Cheng Feichi's classmates, and they told him that he had left early because he had some other things to do.

Since it was in public, Ye Qin refrained from smashing his cellphone on the ground. He clutched his cellphone, his knuckles turning white because of the tight grip.

If he didn't realize by now that Cheng Feichi was avoiding him, he would be a downright fool.

In the early spring, everything was no longer gray and withered. The empty recreational yard void of noise made by students was even more peaceful than exam halls.

Cheng Feichi left the School Hall, walked across the running tracks and lawns, and reached the classroom. He sat down and randomly opened a book on the desk.

He told the head teacher that he needed more time to prepare for the preliminary contest of the Physics Olympiad that would come in March. But only he himself knew the true reason for refusing to stay there for even one more second: he didn't want to listen to one particular speech.

He didn't want to see that speaker, but he couldn't help trying to figure out why he would be here.

If he had remembered correctly, the headquarters of that man's business was in S-City, so he wasn't always here in the capital. During winter vacation, Cheng Xin told him that he had already returned to S-City, so maybe this time he really was invited here to speak to the students.

As for where he would go after the speech, Cheng Feichi had no idea. He was becoming increasingly anxious. He couldn't help worrying about how that man could affect the normal life of him and his mother.

So he asked the teacher again for leave, saying that he need-

ed to check up on his mother.

Mr. Shen, the head teacher of Class No. 1, hesitated when he signed Cheng Feichi's written request for leave. "If you really need help, you can always talk to me. You came from an urban household, so it wouldn't be so easy for you to apply for a student loan. But it's not entirely impossible, right?"

Cheng Feichi knew that Mr. Shen was worrying that he might be reported again for doing part-time jobs outside the school, so he explained, "Don't worry, sir. I'm definitely going home this time."

When he arrived at the Yulin Compound, Cheng Feichi saw that, under a parking barrier that angled slightly upwards, a black business car was trying to squeeze itself out from the limited space. The car was unsurprisingly scratched by the bar.

The chauffeur got out to argue with the concierge controlling the barrier. In the back seat sat a middle-aged man. The door couldn't be pushed open, so he rolled down the window instead to back up his chauffeur, asking the concierge if he knew how many barrier systems could match the value of this car.

Having been working here for over a decade, the concierge had met all kinds of unreasonable people. He immediately retorted, "If you knew how shitty this barrier was, why would you still drive this way? The surveillance camera is on. It clearly recorded how you tried to squeeze your car out of here. Do you want the police to watch it and give you their opinion?"

The middle-aged man stopped shouting while the chauffeur was choked by this strong argument. Cheng Feichi made sure that the concierge was tough enough to deal with this farce and continued peddling via the sidewalk, heading for home.

Cheng Xin was surprised that he came home early. "Don't you have a lecture today? Why are you back so early?"

Cheng Feichi saw that there were two cups half-full of hot tea, so he asked directly, "Who was here?"

Cheng Xin didn't try to cover it up. "A friend."

Cheng Feichi couldn't ask which one it was, because his mother was still the head of the family. When it came to the private life of his mother, he didn't have a leg to stand on.

Cheng Xin had started to take her medicine again recently. At the moment, she looked tired, feeble, and sleepy. Cheng Feichi took her to her bedroom and accidentally saw an open book on her desk. There was a photo lying on it.

In this photo, Cheng Feichi saw three people in their graduation gowns standing in front of the capital's Normal University. Obviously, it was taken during the graduation season. The girl in the middle with shoulder-length hair was Cheng Xin, and next to her were two young men. Together, they made V-signs to the photographer. Everyone who saw this picture could tell that they must be close friends.

Cheng Feichi remembered this picture from his childhood. He saw it once, but after that Cheng Xin never let him see it again. Last time, he only paid attention to the slightly taller man on the left side because Cheng Xin was turning towards him and standing closer to him. However, this time he had more time to look at the other man. Much to his surprise, he found his face somewhat familiar, too.

Before he could think about the weird feeling, his phone started to ring all of a sudden.

It was Ye Qin. Cheng Feichi hesitated for a long time, but didn't answer the call in the end.

When he finished washing the two cups, Ye Qin texted him. This time, Ye Qin stopped pretending to be nice and considerate. His text was imbued with fierce anger. "If you keep avoiding me, I will never talk to you again!"

Cheng Feichi put the phone down. Staring at the jar of stars on his bedside table, he stood still for a while.

He had to admit that he was indeed avoiding Ye Qin these days.

Previously, he considered Ye Qin as a friend, so he answered his requests, calls, and texts. He had a clear definition of their relationship, and he could make sure that things wouldn't go wrong. However, after Valentine's Day, he lost control. He could no longer be calm and clear about the relationship between him and Ye Qin.

Ever since the first day of his life, he always followed rules, always weighed pros and cons before taking a leap. He was extremely alert when things were about to go off the rails. Whenever he sensed danger, he would automatically react with an invisible safety net, isolating himself from the source of it. He wouldn't let the risks become close to him and develop in his proximity.

He knew better than anyone else that indulgence nurtured greed—the more sweet and charming something was, the more risks it would bring with it. He couldn't let himself indulge in what he had with Ye Qin.

The clock was also ticking. He had no time to waste.

For normal high school students, the College Entrance Examination would officially be on the top of their agenda in the Spring Term of the second school year. Most of the students didn't quite know what kind of future they wanted, thus on most occasions, their academic decisions were made with the help of their parents.

Class No. 1 was the top-ranking class in High School No. 6. Some students had obtained offers from excellent universities, while some other students from the privileged class were preparing

for studying abroad. They were passing to each other the publicity materials of tutoring classes for tests like the IELTS, TOFEL and SAT in the classroom.

Cheng Feichi had seen these materials several times now, but he never gave any thought to them. He was gearing up for the coming National Physics Olympiad. Attending this contest was a last-minute decision. He had a rather complicated profile—taking a gap year and being transferred from one school to another made it more difficult for him to be recommended for admission to famous universities. But he checked online and found that these universities preferred students who had won prizes in National Science Olympiads. He couldn't give up something that would make his future more predictable, so this contest was important to him.

To make more thorough preparations, he quit the job in the small restaurant and even signed up for a relevant tutoring course with the money he'd saved in the first two months of this year. The Mathematical Olympiad was in the second half of year, so he didn't have to worry about it until the Physics Olympiad was over.

One day he came home after the evening session. When he was getting all the study materials ready for the tutoring course on the next day, Cheng Xin knocked on his door, entered his room, and gave him a temporary visitor pass to the International High School.

"Tomorrow at 9 a.m. at the gate of your school. Someone will pick you up and send you there."

Cheng Feichi said he had classes tomorrow. Cheng Xin glanced at his books on the desk and said, "You can skip class once. It's okay. This briefing is more important."

Cheng Xin was not only his mother; more importantly, she was an experienced teacher. Surely Cheng Feichi would like to

179

follow her advice.

However, when he reached the school gate on the next day, he realized that this briefing was more of a face-to-face meeting between the admission officers from foreign universities and the Chinese students. The students' grades and performances had already been submitted to the officers.

Cheng Feichi called his mother at once and asked her why she wanted him to be there. Cheng Xin, however, just asked him to learn about the information available there and they would discuss it after he came home.

Cheng Feichi got on the bus with many questions in his head. The bus was nearly full of students. He greeted Liao Yifang, and then saw Ye Qin sitting in the back row close to a window.

Even before Cheng Feichi got on board, Ye Qin had already seen him.

Surprise was his very first reaction. He heard that Cheng Feichi was extremely poor. How did he have the money to study abroad?

On a second thought, he probably came because the briefing was free of charge. Why wouldn't he make use of the opportunity the school provided for everyone? These poor students didn't have enough money to actually travel abroad to broaden their horizons, so he guessed the best they could do was to travel to the International High School.

Ye Qin indulged himself in looking down on Cheng Feichi and judging him in a condescending way for quite a few minutes. And then he looked away, staring at the view outside the window, but secretly paying attention to the conversation between Liao Yifang and Cheng Feichi.

"Cheng-tongxue, I'm surprised you're here! You never mentioned to me that you're planning on applying for these universities."

"Yes, it was kind of last-minute."

"Which university do you prefer? Probably we could sign up for its interview together."

"I haven't decided yet."

"Hey, why don't you just sit next to Ye Qin? You don't have to look for a seat elsewhere."

Hearing this, Ye Qin shuddered all of a sudden and turned his head to look at Cheng Feichi. The latter was also looking at him, but then turned his eyes away. He said to Liao Yifang, "It's okay. I'll sit with my classmates there."

At 9 a.m. sharp, the teacher got on the bus and they set off for the International High School.

Zhou Feng, who was sitting in the front row with Liao Yifang, was clearly having a good time. He carried a giant bag of snacks and distributed them to the students. When he came to Ye Qin, he comforted, "Don't be so upset. We're out having fun! Look how beautiful the scenery is! And you have so many snacks. Cakes, chips and milk. Ah! What a good life! Why are you still trapped in those unpleasant troubles? Hey...don't cry! What did I say wrong?"

Compared to the old Ye Qin, recently he was abnormally sensitive and fragile. Last night they came to the Haidilao restaurant to look for him, and saw him sitting alone with a Doraemon toy in front of him, pouring both chili oil and tears into the hot pot.

Ye Qin explained that the tears came because the chili oil was too spicy, and he claimed that he was a crybaby that would weep just because of a small cut or feeling cold. He insisted that it was a result of instinct, but Zhou Feng still found it somehow strange.

Later, Liu Yangfan joked in private, "If you didn't know what's going on with Ye Qin, you'd think that he's been dumped."

Right now, Zhou Feng saw out of the corner of his eye that

Cheng Feichi went to the empty seat in the last row of the bus, and he sort of knew what happened.

"Who was crying?" Ye Qin threw the napkin Zhou Feng gave him onto the floor, and shoved him away. "You enjoy your snacks! Leave me alone!"

When they arrived at their destination, Ye Qin left the bus ahead of everyone else, and the rest of the group couldn't catch up with him.

Liao Yifang was panting heavily after him. "Hey, we're supposed to head eastward like everyone else. Let's follow them…"

"Just go with them. Don't follow me!" Ye Qin didn't even look back at him.

"I'm going with you." Zhou Feng ran to Liao Yifang and gave him the large snack bag, carrying two or three snacks under his own arm. "You can go back and stay with them, class monitor. You're here for the universities, but we're just here for fun."

Zhou Feng was not a serious person, but he didn't get it wrong this time. Ye Qin came here because his father insisted. He himself didn't care about studying abroad at all. As for Zhou Feng, his parents still wanted him to stay in the country. His grandfather, who had spent the most of his life in the military, proclaimed that he would send Zhou Feng to the army if he couldn't be admitted to a decent university. He would never be expected to study abroad, so he just came here to have fun and meet his friends.

A phone call had brought Zhao Yue. Liu Yangfan couldn't come, as he was in the middle of some social practice activity. The three boys sat side by side on a lawn, each of them with a bag of chips in his hand, chatting and admiring the beautiful girls in this school.

Ye Qin had already distracted himself from crying. He

didn't cry because of sadness. He was just too angry.

Yes, he was feeling very angry. Cheng Feichi took his birthday gift and suddenly kept himself a thousand miles away from him. He even pretended to be a total stranger to Ye Qin. Did he mean to make him die from an angry and broken heart?

Ye Qin was very upset. He chewed the chips and cursed Cheng Feichi for tens of thousands of times.

"A-Qin, you really don't wanna learn something about the universities? You're not happy at home. Probably you'd feel better in a different environment," Zhao Yue said.

Ye Qin said absent-mindedly, "My dad wants me to study overseas, but my mother doesn't want me to go. I couldn't bear living without my mom either."

What he didn't say was that he was afraid that his mother would be taken advantage of by his father or someone else, if he didn't stay by her side.

"While one's parents are alive, one should not travel too far," Zhou Feng suddenly quoted Confucius, which was something completely not his style. "The ancients were never wrong."

Zhao Yue kicked him. "Considering everything going on in *your* family, I think you'd prefer going abroad as far as possible."

Zhou Feng chuckled. "No one knows me better than you guys."

The snacks were all gone very soon. Zhao Yue and Zhou Feng left to buy some more, while Ye Qin was still lying on the lawn, his mind wandering.

The sky was clear and blue, but his head was a total mess. He stared at the sky and started to think of random things. Wasn't Cheng Feichi a loving son to his mother? He'd told him that he did all the housework at home, and his mother seemed not in good health. How could his mother live without him?

Right, I forgot about Ye Jinxiang. Probably he'd give Cheng Feichi, his dear son, the precious opportunity to study abroad. This is for the future of his own beloved son. Of course he'd spare no effort.

Ye Qin felt even more annoyed.

At noon, Liu Yangfan finally returned to school and joined their squad. All of the meals served in the school cafeteria were set meals, different only in the style of cooking: some were Eastern, some Western. The food was delicious and the dining environment was clean.

Zhou Feng kept admiring how good the food and the cafeteria were. The food they had in High School No. 6 was rubbish; they had potatoes, tomatoes, and bean sprouts galore, but there was hardly any meat. To say that their food was no better than pig feed was not an exaggeration.

Ye Qin couldn't help but think of Cheng Feichi's meals. He always dined in the school cafeteria and only bought the cheapest meals. The potatoes he ate were not neatly peeled, while some potato lumps had turned weirdly black and had even sprouted. The price matched the quality, though; the cost of it couldn't compare to half a bottle of the drinks he usually had. He couldn't imagine how he could bear with it.

...Stop, why am I thinking about him again?

Ye Qin picked up the fork and stabbed the steak several times to vent his anger.

In the afternoon, Sun Yiran came too. She entered the activity room where the four boys were, complaining that since no one had called her, she got up late. A second later it began to rain.

Liu Yangfan had just finished his meal and started to feel sleepy. He joked that Sun Yiran came with a timely rain. The nonstop spring rain forbade students from idling around in the campus, so they just stayed in the room to play cards and chat.

After a while, another bunch of students came to the activity room, making the room even more crowded and noisy. Liao Yifang came too. He was a responsible class monitor indeed, handing out many brochures and presenting the admission policies of various universities to students who didn't come to the briefing this morning.

The only one who was listening was Ye Qin. He didn't like playing cards, so he just leafed through the brochures, guessing which university the person in his mind would choose.

Liao Yifang seemed to understand everything going on in Ye Qin's head. "Cheng-tongxue, the straight-A student in Class No. 1, will probably go for universities in Country F. An admission officer talked with him for a long time." A bit of envy crept into his voice. "He's developed in an all-round way, and he got good grades in the General Graduation Examination. He's just the kind of student that every school wants."

Zhou Feng sneered. "Then what? Does he have the money to pay for it?"

A girl from the No. 3 Class chipped in. "The universities can offer him scholarships, can't they?"

"Would that be enough to cover his daily expenses in a foreign country?"

"That of course depends..."

Someone threw a pair of twos on the table. Liu Yangfan responded with a "bomb" and said loudly, "Like father, like son. He was born as a poor boy, so he should stay poor forever. There's no use dreaming about becoming rich and important all day."

Most of the students surrounding him came from well-to-do families. None of them said anything in response. A few of them were from ordinary families that had used all the available resources to support their academic pursuit beyond the borders. They felt offended by what Liu Yangfan said, but they weren't

blunt enough to confront him and only dared to discuss him in private.

Somehow, Ye Qin felt pierced by Liu Yangfan's words, too. He dropped the brochure and left the room to take a breath.

The International High School was well equipped, but it was not as big as the public high schools. The space in the corridor was as limited as that in the classrooms. If he turned right and took two steps forward, he could reach the gentlemen's room on this floor.

He got in, washed his hands and woke the cellphone screen. He looked at his chatting history with "CFC" in the message box and wanted to delete it all. However, when he was about to commit to deleting it, he heard someone talking in the staircase behind the wooden door.

"Tell me which school you plan to apply for. I'll have my father keep his eye on it."

Ye Qin felt he knew which girl this voice belonged to, but he couldn't come up with a clear answer. But the male voice that came after it made him stunned.

"What for?"

The voice was cold. It must belong to the one who was no longer replying to his messages.

The female voice became softer, as if playing the woman card. "He could search for more information on that university. I'm trying to make a decision too…If I knew that you were going abroad, I wouldn't have tried so hard to defend you in front of others. When you leave the country, no one will ever care about it…"

Ye Qin had no idea of what the girl was talking about. Cheng Feichi answered very calmly, "I said that I didn't care about it. You don't have to explain to others anymore."

Feeling comforted, the girl replied happily, "I knew that you wouldn't be so cruel to me. It's been such a long time. Even

if you were mad at me, you would've forgiven me by now...When I texted you over winter vacation, you didn't reply. Do you have some time for me now? The briefing today has ended...What about tomorrow? Let's meet at the usual spot, okay?"

The conversation had gone this far. If Ye Qin didn't notice the weird relationship between this girl and Cheng Feichi, he would be a fool.

Ye Qin was extremely curious about what was going on. Was the rumor wrong? Had it turned out that Cheng Feichi wasn't gay? No way. Liu Yangfan had asked others to do fact-checking, and nearly all the senior students in the university's affiliated high school knew that Cheng Feichi had been kicked out of school because of the scandal. If it was a misunderstanding, how could the school leaders make such a careless decision?

Ye Qin was still feeling overwhelmed, while Cheng Feichi answered emotionlessly, "No. If you really want the best for me, delete my number and leave me alone from now on."

In the afternoon, the students were preparing to leave, but the bus that had brought them here broke down all of a sudden. Somehow, it couldn't start. The driver was trying everything to repair it.

The International High School was not close to the downtown area, so they could hardly get cabs. Zhou Feng complained that they should've driven here themselves instead of taking the bus. He nudged Sun Yiran back into the activity room. "It's raining out there. Let's go back inside and rest for a while."

Students from other schools had already left. The room didn't seem so packed with less than thirty students in it, all coming from High School No. 6. The teacher who went with them told them to stay put. They would leave as soon as the bus

was ready. Then she took the several students in other classrooms to this activity room.

Cheng Feichi came, too.

Upon his arrival, the atmosphere in the room grew strange, and the students all kept their voices low. After all, they had just gossiped about him. Some students kept secretly examining him, but they didn't dare to stare at him.

Ye Qin was swiping his screen in the corner. During rainy days, his cellphone always had bad reception. Even the web page of the school forum could hardly load. When he finally got in the forum, a new post was already there for discussing the gossip that the new school hunk was going abroad.

This time, the students were not admiring how excellent the guy was. Instead, they all became insiders in Cheng Feichi's life. They said that he was a poor boy who didn't even have decent food or clothes. Someone had seen him applying for student aid before. They all thought that he was just an ugly duck, not expecting the bombshells afterwards.

The netizens didn't need to be responsible for their words, so they just kept coming up with unrealistic comments. Someone even said that the boy was sponsored by a sugar mommy. And certainly there was a retort with the same argument at its core: "You're just jealous of his pretty face."

The unsupported comments soon lost their attraction. People were diverted to other aspects of Cheng Feichi. Some girls started to complain how cold and hard to impress Cheng Feichi was. Someone said that she'd sent him nearly twenty love letters but got no reply. Another girl said that he failed to remember her name even after she asked him out three times. Ye Qin kept browsing the following pages, and saw someone asking if anyone still remembered the anonymous girl who sent Cheng Feichi breakfast every day and whether she was still doing so.

Ye Qin, the "anonymous girl," immediately felt offended. He logged out of the forum and put the cellphone back into his pocket. Staring at the scene out of the window, he listened to the rain and slowly sank into his private thoughts.

The bus wouldn't be ready any time soon. The students were so bored and upset. Liao Yifang tried to organize some party games to kill time. He asked everyone to sit in a circle and pass the parcel.

They used a bag of chips as the parcel. The stupid game that only kindergarten kids would play and enjoy clearly couldn't entertain high school students. In particular, when the first one that got the parcel was asked to improvise something, the students started to complain out loud.

"Are you kidding me? I begin to wonder if it's actually the 21st Century. Are we still going to be forced to perform like kids?"

"We aren't kids. We don't like to show off anymore."

"If I'm going to suffer from these shitty performances, I might as well just go out and suffer from the annoying rain."

...

Seeing that Liao Yifang didn't know what to say, Zhou Feng proposed to replace the performance part with Truth or Dare. The person who got the parcel got to choose between answering a question truthfully or performing a dare. The students were interested again and agreed.

Zhou Feng wasn't a good student, but he was clever. In the first round, he winked at the students to suggest that they gave him the parcel so that he could do some romantic tricks to impress Sun Yiran.

No one expected that Liao Yifang would stop the first round abruptly, and the parcel was on the way to Zhou Feng. According to the rules, Ye Qin, who was sitting in the middle,

was determined to be the one who got the parcel.

When asked to choose between truth or dare, he was still a bit lost. "What truth? What dare?"

"Then you'll go with the truth," Sun Yiran helped him made the call. "Let me pose the question!"

When Zhou Feng had finished explaining the rules to Ye Qin, Sun Yiran also came up with the most interesting question with the girls. Looking at the wry smile on her face, Ye Qin knew that this wouldn't be an easy one.

"Listen to me carefully. This is a very tricky question." Sun Yiran cleared her throat. "Do you have a crush on someone? God blesses those who are honest. You can't lie to us!"

Ye Qin had never played this game before. His mind went blank when he heard the question. When Zhou Feng nudged him, he could finally react and then, by some chance, he nodded.

When the parcel was again in his hands in the second round, Ye Qin looked at the excited faces of the students and started to feel that it was all planned.

Sun Yiran had already prepared a new question that followed the previous one. "Is your crush here today?"

The students laughed even louder. Ye Qin knew that Sun Yiran was just horsing around with him. He could be serious about this question, or just take it as a game. He could say "no" and end the whole childish joke.

But he hesitated.

The students formed a big circle. He knew very well that Cheng Feichi was sitting right in front of him and probably staring at him just like everyone else.

Maybe Ye Qin was still trying to hold on to something. Maybe he was trapped in his own game. Maybe he was thinking about something that he himself couldn't clarify. After all, Cheng Feichi had never directly rejected him, right? So probably,

he could be a tiny little bit special to him...right?

Ye Qin was eager to prove something. His head was a total mess. He even heard deafening drumming in his ears. Everything became blurry. The only clear idea was that he wanted to try one more time.

So, amidst the laughter of the students, Ye Qin closed his eyes, took a deep breath and confessed, "Yes."

It was like throwing a bomb into the crowd.

The students went crazy, especially the girls. They kept looking at each other. Some of them even became so shy that they covered their ears to avoid others' questions.

Zhou Feng whispered to Ye Qin, "A-Qin, are you losing your mind? So many people are watching you. In less than half an hour, the whole school will know."

Ye Qin said nothing, keeping his head low.

There were no more than thirty people present. One could easily exclude the impossible options and deduce the most probable result. Soon they started to exchange their answers. Different names were called while the girls mentioned immediately blushed and requested them to hold their tongues.

As the initiator, Sun Yiran was surprised, too. Someone asked her if Ye Qin was talking about her. Though she started the farce, she didn't see this coming. She just asked the question as a joke! How could she predict that Ye Qin would admit it so directly?

Finally, Zhou Feng came to rescue them. "Hey, that's enough! A-Qin was just joking. Don't take it too seriously. Who here could be Ye Qin's crush, other than me? Of course it could only be me!"

The students booed Zhou Feng. They all knew that Ye Qin and Zhou Feng could be nothing more than close friends. Yet Ye Qin didn't comment on his words. The rest of the students soon

lost interest in Ye Qin, seeing that they could no longer get anything out of him.

Liao Yifang continued with the games. After several rounds, the heat of the discussion was dying out.

The bus was finally ready at 5 p.m. Sun Yiran also left with them. She asked Ye Qin, who was sitting in the row in front of her, "Hey, you said there's someone you adore...Is that true?"

Now Zhou Feng was sitting next to Ye Qin. He answered before Ye Qin could say anything. "Of course not. A-Qin isn't the kind of person that would easily fall for anyone, is he?"

Sun Yiran rolled her eyes. "I'm not asking you. I want to hear his answer."

Women were usually sensitive about such things. Sun Yiran was so curious about this gossip that she just had to get an answer from him. Ye Qin leaned on the back of the seat, pretended to be sleeping and gave a mere "umm" sound in response.

It was impossible to get a name out of Ye Qin's mouth anymore. Sun Yiran didn't want to give up so easily, so she looked around at everyone on the bus.

Just as Zhou Feng had said, she couldn't figure out which girl would attract Ye Qin so much. Ye Qin looked like a cool playboy, but actually he was the most innocent and the youngest one among in their inner ring. The rebellious stage of his adolescence just starting, he was still too immersed in the unrealistic illusions about the world to have real affections for anyone.

Having obtained no result, Sun Yiran pursed her lips and returned to her seat with disappointment.

When she turned her head back, by pure chance, she caught Cheng Feichi looking in her direction from the back row. When he found that she was looking at him, he quickly turned his eyes away from her to the view outside the window.

Somehow, her heart gave several nervous beats. Sun Yiran patted on her chest and persuaded herself that Cheng Feichi was someone she'd liked in the past. *How could he be...? With...Ye Qin?* She tried her best to quell her unreasonably strong suspicion and crazy speculations.

When it was nearly 7 p.m., the students were dismissed at the gate of High School No. 6.

The school already closed. Cheng Feichi headed to the back gate along the fence to fetch his bicycle. The rain stopped gradually. The wet and bumpy road reflected the colorful lighting from all directions, resembling a giant and vivid oil painting on canvas. Water splashed from the pits as Cheng Feichi stepped on the road.

When he pedaled across the first traffic light, Cheng Feichi saw a silver sports car by the curbside. He saw Ye Qin standing near the car talking on the phone with someone, his hooded face unable to be seen clearly.

The red light continued for an entire sixty seconds. It was enough for them to see each other. Ye Qin obviously saw him, because he immediately moved the cellphone to the other hand and turned his back on Cheng Feichi. He talked for another thirty seconds on the phone and got back in his car. The sports car suddenly jerked forward as soon as the light turned green, splattering Cheng Feichi with water from the ground. The left side of Cheng Feichi's trousers were all drenched and dirty.

Upon his arrival at home, Cheng Feichi changed his trousers first. Cheng Xin was preparing dinner this time: a simple rice porridge, with pickles and steamed buns. Cheng Xin probably believed that her obedient son wouldn't let things get ugly at the dining table, so she chose to ask Cheng Feichi about the briefing over dinner.

Cheng Feichi said, "It was fine, but I do not have plans to

go abroad."

"If you're worried about money, there's no need—"

Cheng Feichi didn't let his mother finish. "Didn't you say that I could decide how to deal with everything that man gave me?"

Cheng Xin was a bit startled, but she resumed after a short while. "Don't do anything ridiculous. Not taking your own future seriously is the silliest thing to do."

Cheng Feichi couldn't even speak when he heard the word "silliest." When he was very young, Cheng Xin started to use the kids they knew as examples to tell him which kind of behaviors were foolish and irresponsible. He always tried his best to meet her demands, though she had never appreciated his efforts or even cared to give him a smile.

In the end, she just never took his feelings seriously—as if she regarded him as a compliant puppet that would spend all his life taking her orders and executing them accordingly. She had never, ever asked what he wanted, or what he liked.

Even so, Cheng Feichi still kept persuading himself over and over again that Cheng Xin put all these burdens on him only because of love and expectation. He should never complain about it.

Still, he didn't manage to ask the question that he wanted to ask the whole time. He finished the meal, stood up, and clearly stated, "I will not go abroad." Then he returned to his bedroom.

The next day was a Sunday. In the morning Cheng Feichi worked as a tutor at Wei Jiaqi's house, and went to the fast-food restaurant on Times Square.

At sunset, the whole restaurant was reserved for a birthday party. Several workers cleaned the venue and decorated it with balloons.

Cheng Feichi blew a pink balloon and hung it on the wall. Suddenly he was reminded of the pretty boy who liked wearing pink clothes.

And that soul-stirring confession yesterday.

Cheng Feichi was surprised at the word he unconsciously chose to describe it. But on second thought, it was the most appropriate adjective to use. His heart had been racing when Ye Qin gave his answers. He was afraid that Ye Qin would unveil all his affection in front of so many people and make things extremely tricky.

Many people had claimed in person that they liked or adored him. Some of them seemed more honest and sincere than others. But Ye Qin was the only one who caught him off guard. He didn't know how to deal with this boy. He couldn't say yes, but he couldn't bear to say no either.

He always believed that it was impossible for a youthful crush to last for long. But the boy had already sneaked into his heart, and he couldn't get rid of him anymore.

Cheng Feichi's mind was wandering as he hung the balloons. All of a sudden, he heard Wu Rui shouting to him, "Handsome! Is that your didi?" He immediately jumped off the ladders and ran out of the restaurant.

It was only when he was already standing on the street, amidst the crowd, when he came to realize how excited he was, how fast his heart had been beating.

It turned out that yesterday his heart pounded so hard not merely for fear of facing the unknown.

Right now Ye Qin was gasping for breath, hiding himself in the corner.

He had just fled from the boring family gathering and drove his car around aimlessly in this city. When his fuel was running out, he happened to stop the car near Times Square.

He had intended to keep himself warm in the shopping center and have a bite in the dessert shop that he saw last time. He went upstairs and saw the shop was crowded, its queue reaching as far as the elevator entrance. Having lost all appetite, Ye Qin bought himself a cup of milk tea and idled around in the center.

It was all because the center was not large enough. After a short while, Ye Qin walked across the fast-food restaurant and was caught by a female employee there.

Now he pressed his chest to steady his breath and gradually calmed down. He peeped out at Cheng Feichi from behind the wall and found the latter had already returned to the restaurant. What he caught was a view of Cheng Feichi's back.

He was suddenly relieved. Yet at the same time, he felt so disappointed that he became annoyed. *Can't you just go two steps forward for me?*

Several days later, Ye Qin started to wonder if he was having bad luck recently. What was the very mysterious term that Sun Yiran had always been using? *Mercury Retrograde.* Otherwise, how else could everything go wrong these days?

He spent a whole Chemistry class looking back at the days since he had known Cheng Feichi, and found that he didn't seem to have experienced even one good thing from then on. Now he was sent to the police station, now he had a time-out, now he wrote self-criticism essays...Even when he was playing games, he fell into the trap his friends built for him.

The bad luck didn't end here. It even spread to Ye Qin's friends.

As a generous and good-looking boy, Ye Qin was quite popular in High School No. 6. After the briefing, the whole school was talking about who Ye Qin had a crush on.

On the school forum, someone even created a post for the sake of discussing this. An online vote was at the top of the post, where the names of all the students who went to the briefing were listed. The poser encouraged viewers to vote according to their own knowledge and speculation.

Ye Qin once checked the real-time update on the voting result. A girl from Class No. 1 ranked first, but he had hardly ever talked to her. Sun Yiran got second place.

Zhou Feng was very annoyed. "Are they nuts? I said it was me. Why are they dragging Yiran into this?"

He then asked several junior students to register with multiple accounts and therefore to manipulate the result, making sure that Sun Yiran dropped to the bottom of the ranking.

During the evening sessions, Ye Qin checked the update again. Cheng Feichi ranked first this time.

"I told them to bring Yiran to the bottom, but I didn't say that I wanted that guy to be the top one!" Zhou Feng became so nervous that he started registering new accounts himself.

Ye Qin was even more anxious. After Zhou Feng left, he kept working on the votes for another thirty minutes. He only left the classroom after he made sure that Cheng Feichi's name was lying at the bottom of the ranking.

When Ye Qin got to the bike parking area, he cursed himself for being such a fool. No one would ever think that Cheng Feichi could be the correct answer. Wasn't Cheng Feichi the one who was afraid that people would know? He should have just let Cheng Feichi stay on the top and be tortured by shame and fear.

At this moment, Ye Qin, still daring to have wicked ideas, had completely forgotten what he went through last time when he played a trick on Cheng Feichi. This time, when he'd just pushed his bicycle out of the parking area, he had a flat tire.

Ye Qin rolled his eyes and nearly fainted because of the un-

expected accident. If he hadn't formed a habit of riding bikes in the last semester, would he have gone for his bike this morning instead of driving to school?

It was all Cheng Feichi's fault.

Ye Qin wasn't satisfied with secretly cursing Cheng Feichi, so he kicked the flat tires very hard to vent his fury.

Ye Qin went to the bike garage with frustration. The owner was about to close, but he yawned and left him a few tools. "Do it yourself."

Ye Qin tried his best to recall that night when he first came here and saw that guy repairing his bike. He removed the damaged inner tube and put it in water. It took him a lot of time to pinpoint the puncture. Then he started grinding the tube in extremely low spirits.

A few moments later, someone entered the room.

Ye Qin turned his eyes away from his work to see who it was, but got his thumb hurt consequently. He gasped in pain, yet he still made sure that he adjusted his position to avoid facing Cheng Feichi.

Recently, whenever Ye Qin saw Cheng Feichi, he would definitely give him the cold shoulder. Cheng Feichi didn't really mind it, since Ye Qin was only giving payback for how he had avoided him before. So as long as Ye Qin felt like it, he could treat him in whatever way he wanted.

Ye Qin remained silent. He focused on his own work, failing to realize that the smart boy always learned fast.

"Is the owner asleep already?" Cheng Feichi asked.

The door of the inner room was closed, so obviously Cheng Feichi was talking to Ye Qin. The latter was condemning how shameless Cheng Feichi was. *How dare he still be talking to me?* But Ye Qin didn't reveal a bit about his thoughts. He merely moved two steps away from Cheng Feichi to suggest that he

didn't want to talk to him.

Cheng Feichi searched around in the station. "Did you see the tool kit?"

Ye Qin gritted his teeth to forbid himself from making any response.

Cheng Feichi didn't get any answer for the two questions, but he didn't seem annoyed. He searched the shelves and finally got what he needed—a bike bell.

He went out of the station with the bell and quickly installed it on his bike. Hearing the tinkling sound from the outside, Ye Qin thought Cheng Feichi was leaving. He gritted his teeth even harder. *I'm gonna report you to the owner! I'll write a note to tell him that you stole a bell tonight!*

However, Cheng Feichi returned after he tested the bell. For a while he watched how Ye Qin was grinding the tube with his clumsy fingers, then rolled up his sleeves and squatted down beside him. "Let me do it."

Ye Qin tried to dodge him, but accidentally sat on the ground as a result. He even knocked over the basket full of water. The dirty water splashed, making his sleeve completely wet.

"What the heck are you doing?" Ye Qin finally exploded in extreme frustration. He raised his foot as if he was going to kick Cheng Feichi. "You've been avoiding me forever! Why did you start talking to me now?"

Cheng Feichi reached out to him. "I'm not avoiding you."

Ye Qin kicked his hand away and answered coldly, "Huh, right, you taught me how to do math exercises. That of course was talking to me! I didn't pay you though. I haven't thanked you for that."

Ye Qin didn't know how hard he kicked Cheng Feichi, whose arm went numb because of it. Still, he forced his arm to move to alleviate the numbness, and then bent down again to

pull Ye Qin up. "Let me pull you up first."

Ye Qin swung his hand away and held on to the wall to stand up. He picked up a piece of rag to wipe the water on his arm and hands. He became more and more angry at Cheng Feichi. *How could I be so cursed? Why am I always making a fool of myself in front of him? I've decided not to talk to him anymore, but why am I talking to him again right now?*

...Anyway, I've broken my promise to myself. I might as well talk the shit out with him and get it all done!

Ye Qin threw the rag away and turned to Cheng Feichi in a rage. "How could you be such a dick? You took my gift and suddenly stopped talking to me. Now you're in a good mood, so you come back to me. But if you lose interest, you'll get rid of me again. Do you see me as a fool?" He raised his head to glare at him, as if he had nothing to lose anymore. "Even schoolboys know they need to take responsibility for what they've done. That's what you said. But you don't even measure up to schoolboys!"

Cheng Feichi was caught off guard by his accusation, but soon, slightly dropping his head, he grinned and gave a series of low chuckles.

What a boy! How unwilling he was to be taken advantage of! Otherwise, he couldn't have still remembered what Cheng Feichi had said to him in front of the police station and repeat it to him word for word.

Ye Qin was furious at Cheng Feichi's reaction. His eyes slightly bulged because of anger, just like an angry cat. "What's so funny?!"

He was willing to see Cheng Feichi smile before, because he wanted to pursue him. Now things were different. Cheng Feichi's laugh completely humiliated him.

He was breathing heavily and looking around to find an appropriate weapon. He wanted to beat the shit out of Cheng

Feichi.

Cheng Feichi controlled his arm before he could even move. "Don't."

"Let me go!" Ye Qin, though nothing in his hand, tried to warn him.

Cheng Feichi didn't listen to him. He unbuttoned Ye Qin's soaked sleeve and started rolling it up very slowly. His warm fingers touched the inner side of Ye Qin's forearm, pushing a slight quiver out of him.

"You're taking advantage of me again. If you want to settle this properly, let's go out and have a fight!"

When Ye Qin was about to warn him again, Cheng Feichi held his thin wrist regardless of how he struggled. He gently released his clenched fist, put something in his hand and spoke in a whisper. "Responsibility? I'll take it."

Ye Qin's anger was muffled by this unexpected line. He looked down and saw a paper star quietly lying in the palm of his hand.

He was stunned by the familiar little thing. Too agitated to process Cheng Feichi's words, he resumed screaming to Cheng Feichi. "If you're gonna return my gift, give me the whole jar! What's the point of giving me only one fucking star?!"

Ye Qin couldn't take the fury anymore. He felt dizzy and completely broken. He didn't want justice from Cheng Feichi anymore. He just wanted to hide somewhere and cry his eyes out to release the complicated emotions stuck in his body.

His well-prepared gift had gotten returned. How could there be anyone more pathetic than him?

Cheng Feichi let Ye Qin vent his frustration and anger on him, swallowing all his curses and accusations. It seemed that he wanted to say something, but couldn't.

In the end, he shook his head and sighed. Picking up the

star from Ye Qin's hand, he carefully undid it, returning it to a long stripe of paper.

He held it up to let Ye Qin see it more clearly.

With the help of the incandescent lamp over their heads, Ye Qin recognized the scribbles on it. His mind went blank.

Sun Yiran told him that all the wishes written down inside a paper star could come true. So he wrote down his most urgent wish inside every star. Inside most of the paper stars he gave Cheng Feichi, he wrote: *Will you be my boyfriend?*

After the question mark, he always drew a chubby heart.

Cheng Feichi put the strip of paper back into Ye Qin's hand and held his dirty hands tenderly. Looking directly in Ye Qin's teary but bright eyes, he answered in a deep voice, "Yes."

CHAPTER 07

YE Qin was dumbfounded. It took him a long time to recover from it.

What Cheng Feichi just said was too much like a bombshell for him to believe that he was not imagining things. Only the warmth he felt on his hands removed some of his doubts, reminding him of the fulfillment of what he had wished for.

The pounding sound of Ye Qin's heart was disturbed by a loud noise, when the owner of the station, who had been sleeping in the backroom banged the door with something and yelled, "Boys! Shut up or piss off! I need to sleep!"

Ye Qin struggled to get his hands out, but Cheng Feichi didn't let him go until several seconds later. They both bent down again to resume working on the bicycle, cooperating tacitly. Ye Qin stretched the tube, while Cheng Feichi ground the rubber.

The grinding sound prevailed in this silent night. Ye Qin stared at Cheng Feichi's hands, watching how he quickly got everything fixed. Somehow, he blushed, so he fixed his eyes on the floor instead, as if a magical flower was to grow out of it.

The tire was fixed soon. Ye Qin took out a pen and a piece of paper to leave a note to the owner. He wrote a line and thought for quite a while before poking Cheng Feichi's lower back with his pen. "The bell you took...do I need to put it down?"

Cheng Feichi was rearranging the tools on the shelves. He paused and looked back, giving Ye Qin the positive answer with an "mm."

The early spring evening was still cool. Having left the bike station, the two boys were welcomed by a blowing wind. Ye Qin struggled to hold in a sneeze by pinching his nose, but when Cheng Feichi took off his own jacket to cover him, it exploded from his nose.

The street lamp lit Cheng Feichi's back. A secret smile appeared on his face, which escaped Ye Qin's notice. He closed the jacket for Ye Qin, took over his backpack, and hung it on the bike handlebar. Then he pushed the two bikes forward.

Ye Qin rubbed his reddened nose and kept up with Cheng Feichi. "Aren't you feeling cold?"

According to the school regulations, students could only wear their own clothes on Wednesdays and Fridays. Without the uniform jacket, Cheng Feichi only had a long-sleeve shirt on his upper body. Once the wind blew, the thin shirt clung to his skin, making Ye Qin feel cold for him.

Yet Cheng Feichi said that he wasn't cold at all. Ye Qin doubted, "Don't pretend to be cool. If you catch a cold, I wouldn't be able to take care of you."

Then he buried his head even deeper inside the high collar of Cheng Feichi's jacket.

Considering that Ye Qin was the one who always wore less clothing than necessary to make sure that he looked good, the statement sounded funny. Cheng Feichi answered after thinking for a few seconds. "If you don't believe me, why don't you feel it

for yourself?"

Ye Qin blinked his eyes and suddenly realized that Cheng Feichi was referring to them holding hands earlier. His face started burning again. He wanted to defend himself by claiming "It was you who started it," but that would only make things more embarrassing. He covered his face with the collar of Cheng Feichi's jacket, merely revealing a pair of bright eyes.

When they arrived at the compound where Ye Qin lived, Ye Qin began to slowly and unwillingly take off the uniform. Cheng Feichi parked Ye Qin's bike and stopped him. "Keep it. Your shirt is wet. It's easy to catch a cold at night if you don't keep warm."

The jacket was warm when Ye Qin put it on, and now it just became warmer. Ye Qin could hardly take it off, so he gathered the cheek and accepted Cheng Feichi's kindness. He sniffed and asked hesitantly, "What about you? It's Thursday tomorrow."

"I have another uniform jacket at home," Cheng Feichi said. "Remember to wrap up warm tomorrow and bring it back to me."

Ye Qin started to feel dizzy again. He was not sure whether "wrap up warm" or "bring it back to me" affected him more, but thinking of either made him abashed.

This new kind of bashfulness was totally strange to him. He was not yet comfortable with the shift, but he didn't hate it at all.

As soon as he got home, Ye Qin took a bath.

He soaked himself in the warm water for half an hour, and was not thinking clearly when he came out. No sooner had he returned to the refreshed world from that misty space than his eyes suddenly widened. What just happened? He dashed to where Cheng Feichi's jacket was hanging and took out the strip of paper that had been crumpled into a small ball. He opened

and flattened it, and then read it for many times to make sure that he wasn't in a dream.

It wasn't enough. He picked up his cellphone and sent a short text message to Cheng Feichi.

After one minute or so, Cheng Feichi replied with the same words, "Good night."

Ye Qin pinched his own cheeks, totally flushed due to the steam. No wonder that even a slight touch of Cheng Feichi's hand today could fill him with shyness, when the only thing he felt in the past was the simple warmth.

Things were completely different when Cheng Feichi said "yes."

Uh-huh, this was how "being in a relationship" felt like.

"No way! He said yes?!"

The next morning, Zhou Feng filled the whole classroom with a shout in complete disbelief.

Even students sitting in the front rows looked back at him. He quickly covered his own mouth, sat down and hid himself behind an English textbook. "So he was indeed gay..."

He digested the breaking news for a while and then woke his cellphone to report it to his friends.

Zhou Feng: A-Qin did a brilliant job! He got that guy!

Liu Yangfan: *Really???*

Zhao Yue: Congrats lol

Zhou Feng: Why am I feeling sad as if I'm giving my own daughter away to a man?

Liu Yangfan: No worries. You are going to have a live-in son-in-law.

Zhao Yue: Hahahahahahahahahaha...

Seeing the chat history, Ye Qin made a threat. "Liu Yangfan, watch your mouth!"

Then he kicked Zhou Feng behind the desk, who didn't see

this coming and yelled in pain.

Liao Yifang turned around to ask what happened. Zhou Feng grinned at him. "I was too excited."

But he soon started to worry. He nudged Ye Qin and warned him, "Love is blind. Don't get yourself trapped in it."

Ye Qin thought he was being ridiculous. He was not as blind as the typical heroine in an idol drama, and he never really took this relationship with Cheng Feichi seriously. It was just a show.

But he still remembered the conversation he overheard that day at the International High School. He could sense there was something weird about it, but just couldn't pin a name to it.

Ye Qin was bored in English class, so he texted Cheng Feichi, "Your jacket's been laundered. Do you have time during break?"

A good student like Cheng Feichi wouldn't reply to messages during class.

When the second class was over, the longest break in the day began. It was raining outside, so the students didn't need to leave the classroom and do morning exercises. Ye Qin snatched the PSV from Zhou Feng's hand and started playing *Revelations: Persona*, skipping the boring dialogues when someone called his name.

"Ye Qin, you got a visitor."

He left the classroom with his eyes fixed on the PSV and nearly bumped into someone. The person held out a hand in protection. "Careful."

He raised his head and saw Cheng Feichi.

He looked at him blankly and asked, "Why are you here?"

Cheng Feichi answered, "To get my jacket."

Ye Qin gave his own head a smack. He returned to his seat and picked up a bag hanging behind his chair. Running back to Cheng Feichi, he handed it over while complaining, somewhat

awkwardly, "I asked if you had the time, why don't you replay my message first? I was not saying that you had to come. I could go to your classroom too."

Cheng Feichi smiled and nodded, looking at Ye Qin tenderly.

Ye Qin was shorter than him by half a head. Today he had put on an extra shirt, its white square collar stretching out from a pastel yellow sweater, both covered by the baggy uniform jacket. Ye Qin's neck seemed thinner and lengthier in this outfit, and his face was turning red again.

Conscious of Cheng Feichi's close examination, Ye Qin's ears started burning too. He raised a hand to rub one of his earlobes and tried to continue the conversation. "What's your next class?"

"Chemistry."

Ye Qin frowned because it was his least favorite subject. This topic reached a dead end, so he changed to another one. "Are you hungry? I've got some snacks."

Cheng Feichi shook his head. He picked something out from his pocket and nimbly dropped it into the pocket of Ye Qin's jacket, without revealing what it was.

Zhou Feng had been watching the whole process from the classroom window. When Ye Qin returned to his seat, he kept battering Ye Qin with questions about what Cheng Feichi had said to him. Ye Qin patted Zhou Feng on his face with the Chemistry textbook and answered, "None of your business."

Ye Qin waited until the teacher arrived and the class began. He slowly reached for the mysterious item in his pocket. Hearing the gentle crinkling of plastic, he looked down and saw a milk-flavored lollipop in his hand. It was from the corner shop.

With slightly more than a year before the College Entrance Examination, students in Class No. 2 were still not as busy as

those in Class No. 1. Class No. 2 was always dismissed on time. However, on this particular day, for some mysterious reason, Mr. Sun decided to give a lecture when the evening session was about to end in 45 minutes. He explained the common problems seen in a recent exam, and then handed out new exam sheets to the students who failed this exam to reattempt it. They were expected to at least finish all the gap-filling exercises before they left school today.

Ye Qin was only one point shy of reaching the passing mark, so he was compelled to stay. Seeing that the evening session was going to end in a couple of minutes, when he was out of the teacher's sight, he speedily sent a text message under the desk to Cheng Feichi, telling the latter not to wait for him after school.

The message sent, he came to think that he had taken unnecessary action. Cheng Feichi never promised that he wouldn't leave until Ye Qin came.

Of course, he got no response.

So he stopped worrying and focused on his assignment. He paid unnecessary attention to every number and each operator in the equation. Even the equal sign he wrote was composed of two strictly parallel lines of the same length.

When he was home for lunch today, he heard that Ye Jinxiang had finished his business trip and that he was expected at home today. Ye Qin was avoiding him intentionally. Last time when Ye Jinxiang was home for lunch, he spent most of his time nagging his son about the necessity to study hard. Though he changed his expressions and wording, his lengthy speech was centered around the same thing—his business car had been scratched by an unreasonable concierge. He took the "obviously uneducated" concierge as the perfect example to prove how important it was to read more and learn more.

His arrogance and condescension were disgusting.

When Ye Qin finally stepped out of the empty classroom, it was already 10 p.m. He left the exam sheet on the podium, locked the door, and left. When he arrived at the back gate, he was already yawning nonstop. He even had the idea of leaving the bike at school and calling a cab.

This was when he saw someone standing under the street lamp, in the parking area especially saved for Class No. 2.

Cheng Feichi closed the book in his hand, casually put it in the basket of his bicycle, and patted the seat. "Come on."

When they were already on the street, something finally crossed Ye Qin's mind. "You don't have to work tonight?"

Cheng Feichi answered, "Not tonight. I need to prepare for the Olympiad next week."

Ye Qin couldn't understand the world of top students. After all, he himself couldn't even understand everything in the textbooks.

"What about you? Why did you get held up?" Cheng Feichi asked.

Ye Qin was too ashamed to tell Cheng Feichi that it was because he failed the recent exam, so he just made up something. "Well...I was busy with my homework."

The statement held minimal credibility from someone who always depended on others' homework to get by, but Cheng Feichi didn't make that explicit. He just nodded. "I'll help you if you have any problems."

The excellent tutor had hardly offered to help anyone with his schoolwork in the past. At this moment, Ye Qin finally began to feel that they were in a relationship. He became bolder and raised his first question. "Didn't you receive my text message just now?"

"I did."

"Why didn't you reply?"

Cheng Feichi was pushing two bikes forward while walking. He turned his head to look at Ye Qin. "I was already waiting for you downstairs then."

"But I asked you not to wait for me!"

Cheng Feichi turned his head back, staring at the road ahead. "I wanted to wait for you."

Ye Qin blinked his eyes. He couldn't understand why Cheng Feichi insisted on doing it. Yet he did make up his mind to leave as soon as possible after school in the future, since someone would be there waiting for him.

A peaceful week witnessed the start of a budding relationship. Nothing special happened, but Ye Qin was obviously more and more willing to go to school. He complied to the school's timetable, which totally stunned Zhou Feng. One day, he came to Ye Qin right after the class. "Where were you and that straight-A student?"

Ye Qin was holding a lollipop in his mouth. He answered vaguely, "What?"

Zhou Feng didn't have any experience at all, so he started listing things based on his limited knowledge. "Dating, holding hands, kissing, getting la—"

Ye Qin nearly let the lollipop slip from his mouth. His whole face reddened at once. *"Shut up!"*

The volume made Liao Yifang shudder. He stopped reading English texts and turned around, zipping his mouth in fear.

Zhou Feng patted him on his shoulder to comfort him. "It's not about you, Yuanyuan. Don't take it personally. Calm down."

When Liao Yifang finally turned back, Ye Qin sensed something different in Zhou Feng's words. "Yuanyuan?"

Zhou Feng raised his eyes from his PSV and grinned. "My

nickname for the class monitor."

"Why did you choose Yuanyuan?"

Zhou Feng scratched his head. "Otherwise...should I call him Fangfang?"

Ye Qin was getting goose bumps because of this even weirder alternative. He started to think that perhaps he should give Cheng Feichi a nickname as well. It was not appropriate anymore to just call him by "Hey."

He seldom hesitated, so he was texting Cheng Feichi again during a class. "How do you want me to call you?"

When there was only five minutes before the class ended, Ye Qin got a new message. "Anything will do."

It was no different from giving no response. Cheng Feichi never wore his heart on his sleeve, making it harder for Ye Qin to guess his likes and dislikes. He gave him some options, including "Cheng Feichi," "Mr. Cheng," "Cheng-tongxue," but none of these texts received a reply from Cheng Feichi. It seemed that he liked none of them.

Well, it was always hard to understand what a straight-A student had in his mind. Ye Qin gave up soon. He decided to start by asking Cheng Feichi out. As for the nicknames, he'd just go with the flow. He would come up with one when the right time came.

Ye Qin didn't expect that his first date with Cheng Feichi would be to send him to attend the Olympiad.

Well...it wasn't really a date. A day earlier, Ye Qin had heard that the preliminary of the Physics Olympiad would take place on the coming Saturday, so he offered to drive him to the venue. Yet when the next morning came, Ye Qin himself got up late. Too nervous and hurried to button his shirt, he put on a random pair of shoes and left home.

Cheng Feichi, the person due to attend the contest, was surprisingly calm. He told Ye Qin not to drive so fast, because the candidates would be allowed to enter the venue within fifteen minutes after the exam began.

Ye Qin didn't dare to slow down. Thanks to the freely flowing traffic and the good road conditions, they arrived nearly twenty minutes before the exam began.

Ye Qin leaned over the steering wheel to catch his breath, feebly waving goodbye to Cheng Feichi.

Cheng Feichi got out of the car and approached Ye Qin from outside. He opened the door and bent down to tie Ye Qin's shoelaces. "Promise me you'll never drive that fast in the future, even when time's running out."

Ye Qin looked at Cheng Feichi's hands, pouted his lips and started complaining. "It's all your fault! You didn't answer my calls or my text messages. Why don't you just leave without me? You could've taken a taxi!"

"I muted my phone, so I didn't notice your calls or messages. Plus," Cheng Feichi tied a neat bowknot for Ye Qin and then straightened up, "you came after all, didn't you?"

Ye Qin was again trapped by his unreasonable reasoning, but he just wouldn't admit defeat. "Well...still, you should always reply to my messages! Really, you need to fix that bad habit."

Ye Qin was still unhappy about all the text messages that got no response from Cheng Feichi.

Looking at Ye Qin's sullen face, Cheng Feichi couldn't help but smile. "Indeed. It's a bad habit. I'll never do it again."

Seeing that Cheng Feichi had entered the examination hall, Ye Qin adjusted the driver's seat so he could lay back and kill time with his cellphone.

A few minutes later, he glanced at the time displayed at the

upper right corner of the screen. There were still ten minutes before the exam started.

Thinking of what Cheng Feichi had just said, Ye Qin grew restless, so he sent him a message. "Are you free after the exam? Let's watch a movie together."

This would be an official date. Ye Qin pressed the "send" button and held the cellphone a little bit nervously, secretly counting the seconds.

When he counted to 30, the phone rang just as he expected.

Cheng Feichi didn't go back on his word, though he replied with only one: "OK."

Satisfied, Ye Qin fell asleep in the car. He was busy fighting the little dream monsters when he heard someone tapping on his window.

He unlocked the doors to let Cheng Feichi in, and then checked the time with his still sleepy eyes. It was just after ten.

He was immediately woken up by surprise. Wide-eyed, he asked Cheng Feichi, "You handed in the paper so much earlier than the end time?"

Cheng Feichi sat on the front passenger seat, tossing his backpack on the back seat. "Yes."

Having never attended any academic competitions, Ye Qin took it more seriously than a final exam. He grew anxious. "Why did you do that? With so much time left, you could check your answers more carefully. What if you made careless mistakes?"

Amused by Ye Qin's face befitting a worry parent, Cheng Feichi took a paper napkin and wiped the corner of Ye Qin's mouth. "The exam was easy. Don't worry."

Ye Qin didn't realize that he had drooled all over one of his cheeks until this moment. He suddenly became so embarrassed that he took the napkin in Cheng Feichi's hand and wiped his

face himself. A few moments later, he finally said, "Emm...good."

When they reached Times Square, it was not yet 11 o'clock. Ye Qin was complaining about how hungry he was without a proper breakfast, so he took Cheng Feichi to a KFC restaurant and bought a burger combo. He picked out his favorite parts— the burger and wings—and then set the drumsticks and fries to the side.

It was only after he'd been eating for two or three minutes that he realized the presence of another person. He asked, a bit awkwardly, "Do you want some? I'll buy you another combo."

Cheng Feichi declined and finished everything that Ye Qin didn't like eating.

For the lunch today, they had Japanese food. Ye Qin really liked sashimi, so he ordered several fancy platters.

Ye Qin picked up a slice of salmon preserved in ice, dipped it in the cold sauce, and then directly swallowed it down. Seeing the whole process, Cheng Feichi's face froze. He poured a glass of warm water and pushed it in front of Ye Qin, advising him to neutralize the coldness, lest his stomach be unable to bear the low temperature.

Ye Qin burst out laughing. "I've never heard of anyone having water and sashimi together! Only wine is a good complement." Then he pounded the table and shouted to the waiters, "Hey, do you have any good white wine? I'd like one bottle."

He didn't actually get that bottle of wine. He knew very well how scary it would be if Cheng Feichi put on that stern look, so he would always make sure that he had not been pushed too far.

They were about to finish lunch, and Ye Qin was busy searching online for the interesting movies available these days. Before he'd realized it, Cheng Feichi had already left the table

and paid the bill. When they were on the escalator to the cinema, Ye Qin was still complaining that Cheng Feichi had made him feel so embarrassed by seizing the opportunity of paying for lunch from him.

But when they were buying the film tickets, Cheng Feichi still didn't let Ye Qin spend his money. Ye Qin was furious. "Are you a secret billionaire or what? You would have to work for days for that single meal!"

He took out several 100-yuan notes and tried to stuff them into Cheng Feichi's pockets.

Cheng Feichi raised his own arm to avoid Ye Qin's hands, his face blank. "It's what I should do."

It was after they were seated when Ye Qin suddenly realized that Cheng Feichi was treating him as his girlfriend. He was outraged. But he had to keep silent in the cinema, so he put the large bowl of popcorn between himself and Cheng Feichi and leaned on the right handle of his, so that he could keep himself as far as possible from Cheng Feichi.

They had chosen an action comedy. Twenty minutes later, Ye Qin was so absorbed into the movie that he burst out laughing and nearly choked himself with popcorn. He took the bottle of soda water handed over by someone when he couldn't stop coughing.

When the cool water was flowing down, his nerves soothed, Ye Qin suddenly realized that he was still on the outs with Cheng Feichi. His face grew sullen again. Pursing his lips, he stuffed the bottle of water in the cup holder and continued to watch the movie.

When the second half of this movie began, Ye Qin had digested all the uncomfortable feelings he had. He started secretly glancing at Cheng Feichi from time to time.

Cheng Feichi's posture hadn't changed a bit. He kept his

neck and back straight, his eyes reflecting the changing light from the big screen. He hardly made any facial expressions, not even when everyone else was laughing as crazy. He looked like a sculpture, perfectly cut and polished.

Ye Qin found it very strange. Cheng Feichi smiled often when they were together. *Does it mean that I'm even more amusing than a comedy to him?*

Reaching this conclusion, Ye Qin didn't know whether he should feel flattered or punch Cheng Feichi in the face.

Ye Qin heard that there would be a post-credit scene, so he stayed when other people were standing up and leaving the room.

There was no one around but the two boys. The lights came back on. Ye Qin handed two popcorn kernels to Cheng Feichi. "Do you want some?"

It seemed that he was wrapping up the disagreement they had, but in fact he was just unable to finish the popcorn and wanted Cheng Feichi to take care of it.

Cheng Feichi was not angry with him at all. He slightly tilted his head and took the kernels directly with his mouth.

His dry lips touched the tips of Ye Qin's fingers, making Ye Qin's hand retreat as if suffering from an electric shock. Ye Qin felt the temperature start to rise in his fingers, then in his hand, then in his arm, and then in all parts of his body. Within less than five seconds, his face was all red.

Thank God the lighting was not bright enough to show it. Exiting the cinema, Ye Qin, whose face had returned to normal by then, made himself busy posting his review on WeChat Moments. Cheng Feichi, walking one step ahead at his side, led him through the crowds to a place less crowded. There, Cheng Feichi waited for him patiently.

Ye Qin typed a lot of words, but when he was about to

post it, he felt the words somewhat inadequate. Per his request, Cheng Feichi held out the two tickets in front of him, and Ye Qin took a dozen of photos from different angles before spending as much as five whole minutes selecting a perfect one.

Once he sent the post, he asked Cheng Feichi to "like" his post. But it wasn't until Cheng Feichi asked what that meant that Ye Qin suddenly realized that Cheng Feichi's cellphone was such an outdated model.

Ye Qin took the opportunity to propose his idea. "Why don't you get a new cellphone? No one's using text messages anymore. I couldn't even send you photos!"

He wanted to add "let me buy you one," but the unpleasant memories of how Cheng Feichi used to turn him down flew into his mind. He knew that Cheng Feichi wouldn't take such an expensive gift, so he might as well keep his mouth shut.

Cheng Feichi didn't say yes, but he didn't reject it directly either.

Smart phones had just hit the market, and even the least expensive ones would cost him thousands of yuan. Plus, he didn't really need an amazing smart phone for himself. He was so used to the thrifty lifestyle that weighing out benefits and costs before spending a large sum of money had become instinct.

Seeing his hesitation, Ye Qin pouted his lips unhappily and waved his hands. "Forget it. I'll just book another monthly text plan."

To attend the Physics Olympiad, Cheng Feichi had arranged in advance to postpone all his tutoring classes to this Sunday. While he was preparing the books needed for tomorrow's classes, his phone rang in the corner of his desk. It was, again, a text message from Ye Qin.

It seemed to be a brain teaser. "What would a doctor say to

his patient when his heart transplant surgery went wrong?"

Cheng Feichi thought for a while and answered, "I'm sorry."

Ye Qin laughed. "Ha ha ha ha ha ha ha, nope."

Then another message came in. "He would say: 'In such a lonely night, where should your heart be saved?'"

Cheng Feichi asked, "It was a lyric line?"

Ye Qin said, "Yep. Never heard of it?"

"I might have, but I'm not sure."

"Did you laugh?"

Cheng Feichi asked, "About what?"

Ye Qin said, "...Fine. If only you could use WeChat! Then I could sing it for you! You'd definitely laugh!"

Cheng Feichi didn't know what Ye Qin was planning to do. But the thought of buying a new cellphone reappeared.

He opened the drawer to check the balance recorded on the bankbook. Having calculated his income in the first half of year, he was certain that spending an extra two- or three-thousand yuan wouldn't take a toll on the life of his family. He put the bankbook into his backpack along with books needed for tomorrow.

I am not buying a phone just to listen him sing. There's always something that cannot be measured by currency and so-called "value."

The next Monday morning, Zhou Feng pointed to the pictures Ye Qin posted, questioning him about who he went out with. Ye Qin answered naturally, "Well, that guy, of course."

"You asked him out? Not bad!" Zhou Feng changed his attitude, patting Ye Qin on his shoulder. "Considering how fast your relationship is developing, you guys can get to do some real stuff, huh?"

Ye Qin winced, because this idea made him uncomfortable,

but Zhou Feng dragged him closer and started nagging. "You really need to be less sensitive about physical intimacy. According to Shakespeare, physical intimacy is the key to a deeper relationship. If you keep hiding yourself, how can you really win his heart?"

Ye Qin rolled his eyes. "You're such a pervert."

Zhou Feng was indignant. "Hey, I'm trying to help you! You're both men. What's the big deal about holding hands? It's just like holding your own hands together." Word unfinished, he dragged Liao Yifang backwards and kissed him right on the cheek. "See? How easy that was! I feel like I just kissed myself."

Someone laughed at the flush of embarrassment on Liao Yifang's face. Zhou Feng grasped Liao Yifang's chin and turned his face around to check. "Why are you embarrassed? I didn't kiss you on the lips."

Liao Yifang tried a bit harder to get control of his own head. He adjusted his glasses in the hope of hiding his reddened face behind his hand and glasses while stammering, "William Shakespeare ne...ne...ver s...said that..."

Ye Qin acted as if he hated Zhou Feng's idea, but he actually started thinking about its practicality. *After all, I'm a man. I don't have anything to lose if I touch Cheng Feichi or lean on him. If I can get closer to him by doing so, then it'd be a very good idea.*

But how can I get an opportunity to do that? I can't just grab and kiss him like Zhou Feng did! That's for sure!

During the first two classes in the morning, Ye Qin sent seven or eight messages to Cheng Feichi, telling him lame jokes. Cheng Feichi replied to each of them, but told him to pay attention to the class instead, lest the teacher found out what he was doing.

Ye Qin didn't care about it at all. When all the students

were standing in the recreational yard, listening to the weekly speech, he was still sending messages, using Zhou Feng as a cover to avoid being spotted by the teachers. He asked Cheng Feichi what he would have for lunch. Cheng Feichi told him that he would stay in the classroom. Thus, as soon as the last morning class was over, Ye Qin dashed out of the classroom to where Cheng Feichi's was. Having run all the way through the winding corridors between the two buildings, he walked into the classroom of Class No. 1 without any concern, where there sat only one person.

Ye Qin sat down backwards on the chair in front of Cheng Feichi. He couldn't bear seeing Cheng Feichi heating up the cold dishes with hot water, so he closed the lunch box which had just been opened. "Let's have take-out food instead. I want pork ribs."

Cheng Feichi looked at Ye Qin's hand, which was covering his own. "I made the lunch for two. And I made ribs."

Having a good notion of Cheng Feichi's cooking skills, Ye Qin immediately changed his mind. He took the two lunch boxes, ran to the teachers' office, and begged for the teachers' permission to use the office microwave.

Mr. Sun, Ye Qin's head teacher, was gratified. "I wouldn't have thought that you'd be this frugal—taking your own lunch to school in order to save money for your parents!"

Ye Qin held the spoon in his mouth, smiling at Mr. Sun's comment. He didn't tell the teacher that the lunch was actually made by his "boyfriend" rather than his mother.

Since the rice and other dishes were stored in three different layers of the lunch boxes, they were not equally and fully heated up. But nor were they too cold for this time of the year; plus, the boxes had been kept in an insulation bag all this morning, so the food was fine for Ye Qin.

As carnivorous person, Ye Qin was constantly reaching for the ribs. Each time Cheng Feichi put some green beans in his box, the frown on his forehead grew so evident it was as if he was feuding with the beans.

Finally, Ye Qin finished nearly all the ribs. He kept stroking his belly and started to slightly belch. "Next time, use smaller ribs. I hate eating the large ribs. Hard to chew."

This was typical of him; taking things for granted and asking for more.

But Cheng Feichi was not angry at all. He immediately agreed and added, "I only have the time for cooking on weekends, so from Tuesday to Friday, it'd be better if you go home for dinner."

This arrangement upset Ye Qin. He drowsily watched Cheng Feichi getting everything cleaned and packed, when a thought suddenly came to him. "If I hadn't come today, were you going to invite someone else to have lunch with you?"

Cheng Feichi didn't see this coming, but then he smiled. "Perhaps."

Ye Qin grew even more upset, kicking Cheng Feichi's desk to show his dissatisfaction.

Receiving no comfort, Ye Qin took out his cellphone and leaned against the desk. After a while, Cheng Feichi asked him, "What's your WeChat ID?"

"Why...you don't have WeChat on your pho..."

He stopped before he could finish the sentence.

He saw Cheng Feichi holding a new black cellphone in his hand.

When Cheng Feichi reached home that night, the WeChat account he just registered received a long voice message from Ye Qin.

"The more I think about it, the angrier I get—that model came on the market last year! It couldn't worth more than three thousand yuan! Return it tomorrow! Think about it—you can buy a same cellphone as mine with just a bit more money. If we use cellphones powered by the same system, we can play games together."

Ye Qin was walking to and fro in his bedroom. Cheng Fei-chi could hear his footsteps in the recorded message. In the end, he heard grating and squeaking sounds of someone pulling the chair and then sat down. Then he heard Ye Qin gulping something.

Cheng Feichi replayed the 23-second voice message. He could almost picture how lazy and relaxed Ye Qin was at that moment in his head. He had not gotten used to voice messages yet; even the virtual keyboard was something that he needed to adjust himself to. He typed more slowly than usual. "I find it fine. It's enough for me."

An expected reply. Ye Qin puffed his cheeks and swallowed the words that he nearly sent out down along with the soup: *If you don't have enough money, I can help you out.*

Ye Jinxiang was at home, so Luo Qiuling had gone upstairs after ladling out the soup for her son. Sitting downstairs, Ye Qin could vaguely hear Ye Jinxiang's complaints: the bathwater was too hot; thinner quilts hadn't been put out now that spring had come; the rooms hadn't been properly ventilated, even though Luo Qiuling was staying at home all day...

These harsh comments irritated Ye Qin. He dashed the empty bowl on the desk, along with his cellphone. When voices from upstairs finally died down, Ye Qin got up to go the bathroom.

He only showered in the bathroom downstairs when Ye Jinxiang was at home. When he was finished, he sat down on the

sofa in the living room, drying his hair with a towel—he hated hair dryers, for the noise irritated him.

It was one of the last days in March. The temperature had been going up for quite some time, but thanks to Luo Qiuling's fear that Ye Qin might catch a cold, the floor heating system was still functioning.

The over-heated moist air made Ye Qin more and more drowsy. Too sleepy to keep working on his hair after a while, he gave up and lay down on the sofa.

His head accidentally hit Ye Jinxiang's coat, which had been casually cast down on the sofa. Ye Qin he dragged it out of his way without even opening his eyes—this was when he felt a piece of paper hidden in the pocket of the coat.

It was a receipt. He glanced at the name of the purchased product. Suddenly, his eyes widened.

Ye Jinxiang bought a cellphone. The same brand, type and color as Cheng Feichi's new cellphone.

Ye Qin then checked the date of purchase. The blue print told him it had been bought yesterday.

At the end of Tuesday's P.E. class, Cheng Feichi rushed back to the classroom. Before putting on his jacket, he took out the cellphone to see if there were any unread messages.

A blank screen. Not a word.

His desk-mate, a boy busy wiping his sweat, ridiculed his impatience. "Are you waiting for your girlfriend's message?"

Cheng Feichi smiled, but didn't say anything. Having hesitated for several seconds, he sent an emoji to Ye Qin.

It was not until the end of the last class in the afternoon when he got a sleepy face emoji from Ye Qin.

He must have been too drowsy to reply the message. Cheng Feichi stopped worrying for now.

Having finished all his homework before the start of the night sessions, Cheng Feichi thought of Ye Qin's complaints about the difficulty of understanding the chapter on electrolytes. He then spent two hours writing out a mind map of all the necessary knowledge, copied two chemical word problems from past papers, and provided detailed solutions to them.

The two pieces of paper he used were now covered with a mass of figures and words in red and black. Cheng Feichi did a double check to make sure that everything was comprehensible, then folded the paper and put it in his pocket.

That evening, he waited and waited in the parking area, but Ye Qin did not come.

He went downstairs and saw that the lights in Class No. 2 were already out. Still, he went upstairs to make sure of it. The doors were locked, and the room was indeed empty.

He was leaving through the back gate, when the doorkeeper asked him why he stayed so late. He said that he had been doing homework in the classroom. The middle-aged man smiled knowingly. "Don't think that I know nothing about you guys. You wouldn't stay at school for so long just to get your homework done. Your girlfriend left through the front gate, huh? You need to be more careful next time. I wouldn't mind cutting you loose, but what if you run into one of the patrolling teachers?"

Cheng Feichi had nothing to say in reply. People always said that he was too hot to be single— not that he really saw himself in the same way.

At first, he felt happy being together with Ye Qin, but was still hesitating about whether he should enter a relationship with him. Once he had clearly felt his affection for Ye Qin, he couldn't hesitate anymore. He had surveyed the situation he was in, made sure that he was able to reach a balance with Ye Qin, his own life, and schoolwork, before making the final decision to

accept Ye Qin.

He didn't have any experience with love, so he kept learning along the way.

For example, at this very moment, he had a vague notion that Ye Qin was unhappy with him. He could sense Ye Qin's anger, but he could not think of a reason. Ye Qin behaved just as usual when he sent him home yesterday.

Pushing his bike on his way, Cheng Feichi kept pondering the reason and solution, before sending one more WeChat message to Ye Qin.

Ye Qin skipped the last night session. He went back home, got rid of the backpack, and went to bed directly.

He had spent a whole night thinking about the coincidence between the receipt and Cheng Feichi's new cellphone. In the following morning, he even asked Ye Jinxiang whether he needed a new cellphone.

Ye Jinxiang's calm reaction was unexpected. He praised Ye Qin for his consideration and said that he wouldn't spend the unnecessary money when his old cellphone was still working very well. He meant that Ye Qin should be as frugal as him.

Then the cellphone you bought last Sunday was for whom? Ye Qin tried very hard to keep himself from blurting out the real question. Seeing that his mother was smiling happily serving him and his dad breakfast, he couldn't ruin her rare, beautiful morning.

All in all, if the cellphone was not for Ye Jinxiang himself, then it must be for someone else. After all, why would Cheng Feichi, a poor boy, buy an expensive cellphone from a foreign brand, when there were plenty of cheap domestic brands worth less than one thousand yuan? More importantly, why would he suddenly have the same cellphone that Ye Jinxiang just bought?

When you have eliminated the impossible, whatever remains must be the truth. Ye Qin was so convinced of his conclusion, but he couldn't question his father harshly while his mother was present. All he could do was vent his anger on Cheng Feichi. He deliberately ignored his message and left school early without him.

Though it was hard to keep himself from thinking about Cheng Feichi, the thought of how devastated his mother would be when she found out the truth made Ye Qin more assertive in what he was doing now. Cheng Feichi deserved this.

Half asleep, he heard his cellphone ring. Ye Qin reached for the phone and woke the screen under the covers. It was a new message from Cheng Feichi. "Have you arrived home?"

Not asking him what had happened, or why it took so long for him to reply to his message. He sounded so calm, as if nothing had ever happened.

Such behavior made Ye Qin even more angry. He snorted and threw the cellphone back onto the night stand. Then he covered his head with the quilt, pretending that he hadn't seen anything.

During the major break the next morning, a girl sitting close to the door shouted, "Ye Qin, you've got a visitor!" Ye Qin just pretended that he heard nothing and continued playing games with headphones on.

Shortly afterwards, some well-folded paper was handed to him. He unfolded it and found it was chemistry notes, about one and a half pages long. Having recognized Cheng Feichi's handwriting, Ye Qin crumpled up the paper and threw it into the trash bin at the back of the classroom.

Liao Yifang, who happened to walk by the bin, picked the paper ball up, flattened it and put it back on Ye Qin's desk.

"Why did you throw it away? These are pretty useful!" he said. "It must be Cheng-tongxue's work, right? It turns out that you guys are friends! How nice!" Liao Yifang glanced at the notes again with admiration. "The chapter on electrolytes was quite difficult to understand for most of our classmates. May I copy these notes and send them to everyone?"

Ye Qin swept the paper to the floor impatiently. "They're all yours. Do whatever you want with them. Don't bring them back to me."

Liao Yifang took the crumpled paper and left feeling pleased.

Zhou Feng, who had just returned from the men's room, witnessed everything. He got back to his seat and asked Ye Qin in a low voice, "What happened? Had a fight with your boyfriend?"

Ye Qin frowned. "Who's his boyfriend?"

Zhou Feng thought he was being stubborn again. He put it aside and asked him what he wanted to do on the weekend, either hanging out with them or dating with the straight-A student.

"Screw him," Ye Qin answered with a poker face. "Where do you guys plan to go? The usual spot?"

Friday came very soon.

Not required to attend night sessions on Fridays, the students flocked out of the classrooms at the sunset. Some returned to the dormitories, some headed for the cafeteria, and others went home, arms bending around each other's necks and chatting lively. To them, the following two days were the most beautiful time in the whole week.

But this was not the case for two kinds of students—those who had to attend extracurricular courses and those who had very tight agenda even on weekends, such as Cheng Feichi.

He was starting to tutor a ninth-grade student on each Saturday morning. Attracted by his experience in the Physics Olympiad, the kid's parents wanted him to prepare their kid for the competition as well. Judging from what they said, they were expecting a prize which could be used as a stepping stone to famous universities' independent recruitment tests.

Cheng Feichi couldn't make them understand the difficulty of winning a prize in the Olympiad simply by explaining it, so he decided to let the student have a taste of Calculus during their first class. This was much more straightforward. Many parents were armchair strategists: they wanted their kids to suddenly become geniuses. It was necessary to let them see how harsh the reality was and how much patience and hard work was needed for success.

Cheng Feichi knew too well how to deal with such parents. He learned the tricks all by himself. However, God is always fair in that no one is endowed with two extremes of interpersonal skills. Cheng Feichi was an expert in handling relationships with acquaintances, but handling intimate relationships had always been hard.

For all these years, he had never figured out the right distance between a son and his mother. He couldn't leave her alone, nor did he succeed in being a dear and adorable son to her. Things were never right between them. Having been dependent on each other for almost twenty years, they were more and more like two strangers that knew each other very well. Weird.

As for the relationship with Ye Qin—weird, too. He didn't know whether he should wait for Ye Qin to came back, or if he should approach Ye Qin and try to work things out.

Even though he even did not know what he had done to displease Ye Qin.

In their relationship, he always regarded himself as the giv-

er, and Ye Qin the taker.

It was for no other special reason. Ye Qin was younger and richer, brought up in riches and care, so it was unsurprising for him to have some willfulness. Now that he decided to enter this relationship and took on the responsibility of a boyfriend, he definitely wanted things to work out for as long as possible.

Maybe it was still a bit early for them to think about "stable" and "forever," but Ye Qin came to him with all his heart first and brought so many bright colors to his boring life. He had given in and accepted Ye Qin's love, so now it was his duty to put up with everything.

He didn't find Ye Qin at the parking area that night either. Cheng Feichi checked where Ye Qin usually parked his bike; the bike was gone.

After all, they never promised each other to meet up every day after night sessions. Cheng Feichi thought that maybe Ye Qin was just too busy with some other stuff to have the time for him. Even lovers need space and distance, right? So they shouldn't be stuck to each other all the time.

Cheng Feichi connected the reality with such theories and managed to stop worrying. He peddled back home.

His pocket was now packed with lollipops, which he had not found the right time to give to Ye Qin. There were four already. When he was changing clothes in his bedroom, he took them out and lined them up on his desk.

At night, he stared at the lollipops for a while and took up his cellphone. He took several pictures, picked out the best one, and posted it as his first WeChat moment ever.

Ye Qin didn't see the picture until the next evening.

He had left school early Friday afternoon, right after the last class. He drove Zhou Feng and Sun Yiran to the club that

belonged to Liu Yangfan's family.

The club was definitely advancing with the times. A brand-new stage was built recently, and so-called holographic projection technology was imported from abroad, which could create a virtual world for them to enjoy in real life.

Zhou Feng had been suggesting Ye Qin come to see this, so Ye Qin came. But he thought the "virtual world" was pretty much the same as the ostentatious fashion show that Ye Jinxiang took him to the last summer vacation. Yet the dazzling lights made him giddy, and the dancing girls on the stage were far less appealing than the models. Ye Qin thought he might as well take a nap here.

So he found a quieter place and fell asleep. After he woke up, he called his mother to report his whereabouts. Dawdling, he had a relaxing bath and then watched a movie. If he hadn't picked up his cellphone to check the time, he wouldn't even have known that night had fallen.

It was not usual for Sun Yiran to stay the night with them. Right now, she was in another room, enjoying a facial massage. Zhou Feng stayed at her side and watched for a while, but the massage was no fun for him. Eventually, he returned to where Ye Qin was. A bowl of cherries in his hand, he pushed the door open while throwing cherries into his mouth.

Liu Yangfan and Zhao Yue were playing billiards, while Ye Qin was lying on the couch, overcome with boredom. Zhou Feng was about to put a cherry in Ye Qin's mouth when Ye Qin turned away from him, his expression showing that he wished to be left alone.

Zhou Feng sat beside him, asking the two billiard players, "That's not very charitable of you. Why don't you play with A-Qin? You only care about yourselves."

Zhao Yue finished a split shot. He straightened up and an-

swered, "He's upset. It's him who doesn't want to join us."

"What happened, darling?" Zhou Feng was always the one to console him. "Is it still about your boyfriend?"

Ye Qin didn't answer him. He was staring at a picture of lollipops on his cellphone. There were four of them—from Tuesday to Friday, one for each day. He couldn't help licking his lips, but soon despised himself for this unconscious response. Hadn't he already tasted them? They were nothing special.

He'd been giving Cheng Feichi the cold shoulder for a few days. To whatever Cheng Feichi sent him, he only replied with emojis. Now he wasn't as angry as several days ago, but he just couldn't get rid of the sick feeling stemming from inability and weakness. What was worse, he couldn't tell anyone about it. The only thing he could do was to bury it in his heart, and it was killing him.

Zhao Yue put down the cue stick, walking back from the table while asking, "What's wrong? That guy's making him upset again? My advice is that you stop wasting time like this. We can just teach him a lesson. We won't stop until you're satisfied."

"Don't." Liu Yangfan came, too. He picked up the cigarette that had been pinned against his ear and blew on it, remarking frivolously, "We've already gone this far. If we give up now, all A-Qin's efforts would be in vain."

Ye Qin didn't agree with anyone. He threw his cellphone on the tea table and said, "Just enjoy yourselves. Leave me alone."

"Have you tried the intimacy trick? It doesn't work?" Zhou Feng was surprised. "How could that be? Aren't the gays just like us straight boys? They like cute boys, just like we like cute girls. How could he resist such a temptation as our A-Qin?"

Liu Yangfan sneered. "It's not 'us.' It's just you, okay? You're the only one who can't move when someone pretty walks by, no matter whether it's a girl or a boy."

Zhou Feng chuckled. "That's true. Recently, I found out that the guy sitting in front of me is really good-looking. He's also got this flawless skin; and that face! Sweet and cute as these cherries. I think if I pinched them, cherry juice would drip non-stop."

Ye Qin was really upset now. He couldn't stand Zhou Feng's lewd talk anymore and threw a pillow at him.

When teenage boys gathered, obscene topics like these were quite unavoidable. Liu Yangfan sat on the other side of Ye Qin and asked about how far had he gone in seducing the straight-A student. "What's wrong? I thought he agreed to be your boyfriend. Was he playing you? Did he say yes just because he was bored of being a nerd?"

In the past, Ye Qin could reply to these comments with a casual laugh, but now he was feeling a bit offended, as if his friends were despising him for failing to handle a pauper.

Not wishing to be looked down upon by his friends, he immediately retorted, "Of course not. He's been very obedient. He wouldn't go against my orders."

"Whoo-hoo! You really got something." Zhao Yue was excited by Ye Qin's answer. He lit a cigarette for Liu Yangfan and then sat on the armrest of the sofa. "Then let's call him. We can screw him around a bit right here, right now."

Ye Qin was reminded of what they did to Cheng Feichi last time in the convenience store and how he himself was brought to the police station after that. He felt nervous and rejected their plan. "No way."

Amused by his sudden serious face, Liu Yangfan joked, "See how afraid A-Qin is now? Let me guess...are you the bottom? Seriously?"

Ye Qin was so suggestive that he could be easily triggered to do something that he didn't intend to do. He was too green to

fully understand what "bottom" meant, but he took it as being submissive to Cheng Feichi. He was furious by this assumption and immediately texted Cheng Feichi. "I'm at the South Manor on the Zhongshan Street. Come and pick me up."

Then he raised his cellphone to show everyone the message. He kept his chin up and announced, "See? You'll soon find out who calls the shots!"

CHAPTER 08

CHENG Feichi's Saturday was even busier than he had expected.

The breakfast diner received new orders for brown sugar buns. Having got the numbers wrong, the owner prepared enough brown sugar for making 100 buns, but the customer actually needed 200. So Cheng Feichi rode to the newly opening market to buy more brown sugar, before returning to the diner and immediately resuming kneading dough, working without a second's stop.

When the last steamer was put on the furnace, the owner was on brink of shedding tears of gratitude. He cleaned his hands and gave Cheng Feichi 100 yuan, saying that since he had not yet awarded bonuses, this was for Cheng Feichi to enjoy some snacks. The owner wouldn't take no for an answer, so Cheng Feichi accepted the money.

After the tutoring classes in the morning, Cheng Feichi didn't go to the library. Instead, he went to the hardware market and spent the recently earned money on a heavy steel rear rack after comparing several offers. He borrowed the necessary tools from the store owner and attached the rack to his bike, which took him a lot of effort. Then he straddled it, making sure that it was of good quality and properly installed.

The proprietress remarked with a smile, "With this installed, you can take your lover girl to school!"

The number plate pinned to the back of his bike was clearly provided by High School No. 6, indicating his identity as a student.

Cheng Feichi shook his head with some uneasiness, and gave her a bashful smile. As they became more familiar to each other, Ye Qin started to show his true colors. He was such a lazy boy that he most often just left his bike to Cheng Feichi instead of riding it or pushing it on his own. Once, sleepy after night sessions, Ye Qin could not stop yawning and asked Cheng Feichi whether he could sit on his frame so that he wouldn't need to walk anymore.

Indeed, Cheng Feichi didn't install the frame for a lover girl. It was for a little sleepyhead.

He had a casual lunch at a street diner before going to another student's home. Wei Jiaqi was so careless that he got two of the most complicated word problems wrong in the monthly exam. Consequently he slipped down the academic rankings. His mother was so furious that she scolded not only her son but also Cheng Feichi, doubting Cheng Feichi's ability as a mere high school student to help her son make real progress. Therefore, she announced, she would dock his pay.

Cheng Feichi, understanding too well how a teenager could be hurt by their parent's rage, took all responsibility upon himself and didn't argue about his salary. He let Mrs. Wei dock his pay for a month and spent an extra hour analyzing the math exam paper.

When Wei Jiaqi walked Cheng Feichi to the door, he was on the brink of bursting into tears. He lowered his voice, telling

Cheng Feichi that he would compensate him with his own pocket money. Cheng Feichi comforted him, "It's okay. Your parents just want to get their money's worth. Surely one day they will see how hardworking you are."

When Cheng Feichi got to the first floor, he took a few deep breaths as usual. It was not until he felt that he had got rid of the tiredness and mixed feelings in the chest that he exited the building and peddled back home.

When he rode by the bank, he withdrew several hundred yuan from the ATM. He spent the whole day working without making a dime, even losing several hundred of yuan, so he needed more money to prepare for a probable date tomorrow.

When he reached home, he was still thinking about how to ask Ye Qin whether he was available tomorrow. Though he was supposed to show more initiative in this relationship, Ye Qin had been the one who always asked him out. Making the invitation was still something new for him.

However, when he unlocked the door with his keys, he was suddenly struck by two pairs of shoes at the entrance.

He hadn't expected his grandparents to visit, nor had his mother. Even the mugs on the table were freshly out of the kitchen cabinet. After all, according to Chinese customs, they were supposed to meet during the Spring Festival.

His grandma still looked as she was the last year. She was in a gray duffle coat made from stiff but smooth wool, and her shoulder-length hair was put behind her ears. Seeing that Cheng Feichi was back, she was the first one standing up and walked towards him, sending warm greetings. "Xiao-Chi's home."

The other two people looked rather serious. Cheng Feichi greeted his grandparents and was soon taken to his bedroom by his grandmother.

"Let's give them some space. Your mother has always been close to her father ever since childhood. They have their own secret talks, which I could hardly get involved in." His grandma smiled and focused on Cheng Feichi. She was pleased. "You've grown. A big boy now."

Cheng Feichi offered his own chair to his grandmother, and he sat by the bedside. His grandmother leafed through his books on the desk while asking, "Now you're in High School No. 6?"

He nodded. "Yes."

"In the twelfth grade?"

"No, the eleventh."

His grandmother was stupefied, but she sighed soon. "Your mother was such a stubborn woman. She just wouldn't tell me about her problems. Even though her dad's still angry at her, he wouldn't disregard the issues that kept you from having a better future."

Cheng Feichi was silent for a while, and then said, "I just took a gap year. It doesn't matter at all. I'm good now."

"How could School No. 6 compare to the university's affiliated high school?" His grandmother shook her head. "When we heard about that, you'd already left. Otherwise, we would've asked someone to uncover the truth."

Cheng Feichi's grandparents used to be teachers at the university's affiliated high school. Cheng Xin herself had graduated from there as well.

Cheng Feichi was moved. His grandparents were the dearest two people in the world to him aside from his mother. Though they usually just met once a year, he was always in their hearts. He had not expected the fact that his grandparents neither questioned nor scolded him for the horrible rumor, but trusted him unconditionally.

Not receiving a response, his grandmother comforted him.

"Though you didn't grow up with us, we always know that you're a good boy. How could we not believe in you?"

Then she looked a bit worried, looking as if she was thinking about the past. "Well, it was the same case for your mother. She's also a good girl, just too stubborn. If she had listened to us..."

They suddenly heard an angry exclamation. "Are you out of your mind? Does it feel so good to be someone's mistress?"

Cheng Feichi's grandmother jumped to her feet, and Cheng Feichi followed her out of the bedroom. He got to the living room, finding that his grandfather was standing with his hands clasped behind his back. Cheng Xin stood in front of him, looking just as angry as him. The grim atmosphere had not eased at all.

His grandmother came forward and grabbed his grandfather's arm. "Calm down. We only meet once a year. We should really cherish the good time together."

"She doesn't think the time should be cherished! She left us without a second thought, and then what? She hasn't shown up in the twenty years since!" Cheng Feichi's grandfather then turned back to Cheng Xin. "Aren't you just so capable? Capable enough to get pregnant before marriage, even leaving your parents behind. What about now? Now you live in such a shabby place, and let your kid suffer with you! This is not the kind of decent lady I taught you to be!"

The elderly man was more than seventy years old. Gone was the strength to yell at his daughter. Cheng Feichi could see that the hand he raised was trembling.

Cheng Feichi stayed silent, but his grandmother couldn't bear the sorrow anymore. Hands covering her mouth, she turned aside and started crying. For quite some time, the only sound in the whole room was her sobbing.

Cheng Feichi handed his grandmother some napkins. His grandfather calmed down and changed to a softer tone, "Anyway, you should stop contacting that man. Even if you don't consider your deeds shameful, you should think about your son."

Hearing the word "shameful," Cheng Xin, who had been making no response, suddenly raised her head. She looked at her father in the eyes and replied very calmly, "I'm not his mistress."

When Cheng Feichi saw his grandparents off, it was getting dark.

He went back and saw his mother making porridge in the kitchen. She heard the door close; she knew that her son had come back, but she didn't so much as turn back to glance at him.

Cheng Feichi had so many questions for his mother. His grandfather's words confirmed some assumptions. Combined with the scattered memories, a relatively compete truth could be pieced out. He wanted to ask Cheng Xin if she was actually doing all this for his future, or just to satisfy her own greed.

However, Cheng Xin didn't even let him begin. When they started dinner, she asked Cheng Feichi very calmly whether he had read the provided materials on the foreign universities, as if the quarrel had ever happened.

Cheng Feichi was still sulking over his mother's attitude. He made it very clear again that he wouldn't study abroad.

Cheng Xin didn't make a fuss. "Well, then save it for the next semester. You can just skip the access courses and begin your freshman year."

Cheng Feichi jumped to his feet. His repressed anger was clearly demonstrated on his face.

He was not counting how many times he had been defying his mother recently. He wasn't sure whether it meant that he was not a dutiful son, but compared to what his mother once did ac-

cording to his grandparents, his so-called "rebellion" was child's play.

The biggest irony was that, but for Cheng Xin's "rebellion," he wouldn't have even be born into this world.

For a moment, Cheng Feichi was at a loss, as if he was watching conflicting thoughts twisting and crashing in his mind, turning into one knot after another, which he could not untie.

He returned to his bedroom and sat there for a while. Having calmed down a bit, when he went across the living room to the bathroom, he saw Cheng Xin standing by the sink in the kitchen. He noticed how skinny his mother had become, and it hurt.

She was his mother after all. She was the one who brought him up all on her own.

This was when he received Ye Qin's message. He happened to need some air now, so he went to the entrance and got his shoes changed.

Cheng Xin asked him where he was going. He answered that he was going to see a friend, and then, having grabbed the keys, he was gone.

Zhongshan Street was in the south of the capital city, a rich and famous neighborhood accentuated by green hills and clean streams. On both sides of the street were beautiful villas. Even the lanes and driveways were broader and cleaner than those in other districts.

Cheng Feichi was unfamiliar with this part of the city. After he got off the bus, he consulted the map in his phone and asked two pedestrians for directions before finally reaching the South Manor that Ye Qin mentioned.

Standing in front of the building, Cheng Feichi could see the shining lights and the luxurious furniture and ornaments in the hall from the extremely clear glass wall. Though he had nev-

er been here before, he could tell that this was a place exclusively for the rich.

The doorman wouldn't let him in, so Cheng Feichi stood at the gate and texted Ye Qin, "I'm here at the gate."

In less than a minute, amid the hubbub of laughter and shouting in a private room, Zhou Feng burst into even louder laughter with Ye Qin's cellphone in his hand. "Hey, come and see this! He actually came here!"

Zhao Yue approached him to make sure of it. "Oops. He really did. That's obedient indeed."

Sun Yiran, just back from the massage, asked unknowingly, "Who came?"

Ye Qin had finished three glasses of wine while waiting for Cheng Feichi's response. Now he was both a little tipsy and blushing heavily. He snatched his cellphone from Zhou Feng's hand and stated proudly, "Told you so. He always does what I say."

Liu Yangfan smirked weirdly and patted himself on the thighs. "How nice! Let's come downstairs and 'welcome' him!"

Ye Qin immediately changed his face and took Liu Yangfan by his arm. "No way."

Zhao Yue sneered. "Whoa! A-Qin's worrying about him! We ain't allowed to put our hands on his boyfriend!"

Ye Qin glared at him and burped. Thoroughly drunk, he wagged his head and said, "Let...let him wait at the gate..."

Sun Yiran still didn't understand what was going on. Ye Qin wouldn't provide her with the answer, so she asked Zhou Feng instead. Zhou Feng, however, drew his thumb and forefinger across his lips to show that he would keep his mouth zipped. Zhao Yue and Liu Yangfan said nothing, but smiled at her. With her curiosity aroused, she began to stand up to find it out herself.

Ye Qin was not thinking properly, but he still remembered that Sun Yiran had pursued Cheng Feichi for quite some time.

Alerted at once, he jumped to his feet and dashed to the door of the room. Blocking the door with his body, he yelled, "None of you will get out of here! If any one of you goes downstairs to see him, then we're not friends anymore."

"Easy, easy. We won't do that, okay? Come and sit down." Liu Yangfan fetched two glasses of juice for Ye Qin and Sun Yiran and explained to the latter, "It's just a servant from A-Qin's home. We were making a bet that he would get lost in this district. It turns out that he made it here. There's nothing to see. He'll leave soon if A-Qin doesn't show up."

Sun Yiran took the juice and looked dubious. She examined the boys and concluded, "You're being very naughty."

Zhou Feng gave a careless laugh, and dragged Ye Qin back to the couch. "Well, that's what a servant is for, right? This is not about being naughty."

Ye Qin sat back on the couch, still struggling with the weirdly mixed feelings. He didn't feel happy at all after he had won the bet. He couldn't drink anymore now; even a few glasses of wine could get him a headache and mess up his brain.

The rest of them were really tired now because they didn't sleep last night. Sun Yiran, as the only girl here, naturally occupied the sole lounge in the room. Liu Yangfan turned down the volume of the movie that was playing by the projector, and then the boys slept on the couch or reclining chairs.

Ye Qin rubbed his temples and held a pillow to make himself more comfortable. He fell into the sleep soon because of the liquor.

When he woke up again, it was already half past nine in the evening.

In an earlier phone call, Ye Qin promised his mother that he would come home tonight. Sitting straight, he exercised his

neck and found himself not dizzy any more.

He picked up the coat on the floor and kicked Zhou Feng, who was sleeping with half of his body hanging off the edge of the couch. Somehow, Zhou Feng was murmuring even in his dreams, "Just call me gege one more time..."

When Ye Qin was walking down the hallway, he checked his cellphone and saw a missed call from Cheng Feichi from an hour ago. *So he only waited for less than an hour...*Ye Qin pouted his mouth and thought that Cheng Feichi was clever enough not to call him twice to disturb his sleep.

When he reached the hall on the first floor, a waiter came to him and asked whether he needed someone to drive his car to the gate, since it was raining outside. Ye Qin gave him the keys and stuffed his hands into his pockets, killing time by strolling down and looking at the master's paintings hanging on the wall, which had been bought by Liu Yangfan's father in order to improve the taste of the decorations. Then, he went to the gate to see how heavy the rain was.

The drizzle in the dark was like a dense fog, further restricting the visibility under the disguise of the night, but Ye Qin still managed to see a man standing next to the stone pillar outside in the long corridor.

That man was also looking towards Ye Qin's direction, and then he began to walk towards him. When he finally reached the gate, Ye Qin saw that his hair was soaking wet, and his coat was drenched as its color got darker from the shoulders to the chest—the clothes under it could be wet, too.

"It's over?" Cheng Feichi broke the silence. "Come on, let's get you a cab."

"Hey." Seeing that Cheng Feichi was about to turn around, Ye Qin stopped him. A hand hanging down at the side of his body accidentally touched Cheng Feichi's coat, and all he could

feel was damp coldness.

Cheng Feichi looked back at him with questioning eyes. Ye Qin swallowed hard and hesitated for a long time. Suddenly, he could not find what to say.

He saw a raindrop falling from Cheng Feichi's forehead, gliding across his eyebrows, along his high nose bridge, reaching the tip of his nose, before finally dripping down on his shoulder, absorbed by the coat.

Eventually, Ye Qin managed to find his own voice. "I drove here. The doorman has gone to fetch my car."

Hearing this, Cheng Feichi turned around and looked at him with hesitation.

Ye Qin thought Cheng Feichi was about to ask why he had insisted on getting picked up when it was totally unnecessary, but Cheng Feichi said, "You have had alcohol today. You can't drive now."

Five minutes later, they got in a taxi together. Cheng Feichi gave Ye Qin's address to the driver. It wasn't until they were well on their way when he wiped his face and combed back the wet hair on his forehead.

Feeling Ye Qin's gaze, Cheng Feichi turned to look at him. "What?"

Ye Qin quickly looked away and shook his head, replying with silence.

When they reached the compound where Ye Qin lived, the rain got lighter. Cheng Feichi led him walking under the curb-side trees, which could serve as a shelter against the rain. Cheng Feichi was so fast that Ye Qin couldn't keep up with him, so the latter shouted, "Hey!"

At the sound of his call, Cheng Feichi stopped, but Ye Qin suddenly lost his courage. He slowly walked up, with his shoulders drooping and his head hung low. "Are...are you angry

at me now?"

He looked like a poor pupil ready to receive criticism from the teacher. Cheng Feichi was amused. "Have you stopped being angry at me?"

It took Ye Qin some time to realize that Cheng Feichi was referring to what happened in the past few days. He had been the one who deliberately stayed away from Cheng Feichi, and the fact made him more embarrassed. His face soon became entirely flushed when he tried to explain. "I'm not...no, I've never been angry at you."

His head was a complete mess now, and what came out of his mouth was no better than a mess. When he thought how Cheng Feichi spent two hours waiting for him in the rain, he felt worse. Something was swelling up in his chest. It tasted like lemon. It made his heart sore and numb. It kept growing as if was about to burst out.

The response he got from Cheng Feichi was still a simple "Okay."

"It's not okay! Don't you know how to call me if you don't see me? You knew it was raining so hard. Can't you just find a shelter to keep yourself dry?" Ye Qin couldn't bear it anymore. He didn't know who he was being mad at, Cheng Feichi or himself.

Cheng Feichi was scolded without real reason, but the smile on his face became more and more evident. Even his eyes started smiling. He answered, "It's okay as long as you're not angry."

He didn't tell Ye Qin that he was not allowed to stand under the roof of the luxurious residence. He had never been to places like this, but he subconsciously didn't wish to cause any trouble for Ye Qin. The rain didn't come until an hour after he arrived; such waiting was not a big deal for him.

Ye Qin, on the other hand, lost his words when Cheng Feichi was being so nice. He would rather Cheng Feichi be less tol-

erant, just like how he had been before. He would rather Cheng Feichi put on a stern look and teach him to "take responsibility for what you did" or even bring him to the police station just to frighten him.

He didn't know the emotions growing inside him was called "feelings of guilt." He only knew that he was feeling terrible about the whole thing and that he couldn't take it anymore. He considered it long and hard, before finally making the decision to blame Cheng Feichi for it. He muttered, "Well, it's all because you treated me so badly before. Now you know how upsetting it'd been for me?"

Cheng Feichi restrained himself from bursting into laughter. In order to make Ye Qin feel better, he cleared his throat and put on his sincere face, answering, "Indeed, it really upset me."

They kept walking for a while. When it was time to go their separate ways, Cheng Feichi took out the four lollipops that had been kept in his pocket. Ye Qin immediately grew much more cheerful, grimness flying from his face. "These are for me?"

He certainly knew that they were for no one else but him, but wanted to hear it confirmed by Cheng Feichi. When he saw the picture of the lollipops posted by Cheng Feichi, he was feeling so depressed.

Naturally, Cheng Feichi gave him a very direct answer. "Yes, these are all yours."

Ye Qin stuffed the lollipops inside the kangaroo pocket on his hoodie, which immediately formed a lump in front of his stomach. The sad pupil became a happy kid content with his favorite snacks.

Packed with the lollipops, Ye Qin set out for home. But having made two steps, he returned to Cheng Feichi. In the silent night where nobody was around, he beckoned Cheng Feichi over with a finger and whispered, "Come a little closer."

Cheng Feichi took one step ahead.

"Nah, even closer! Come to me!"

It was the first time that Ye Qin thought Cheng Feichi was somehow a bit dumb. So he took the lead. Putting his arms around Cheng Feichi's neck, he forced him to lower his head. Then he stood on tiptoe and kissed Cheng Feichi on his face.

It was Ye Qin who felt overwhelmed by the kiss first.

As if someone flung a burning tinder stick into his body and lit the fuse, the unbearable heat permeated his flesh and bone and burned all the way to his skin, setting his whole body on fire.

...Zhou Feng was lying! It was by no means close to holding his own hand or kissing the back of it!

Before Cheng Feichi could say anything, Ye Qin stammered, "Th-thank you for the l-lollipops." And then he fled as if he was running for his life.

For Ye Qin, there was nothing that couldn't be fixed after a good sleep. So he returned home, took a shower and then went to bed without any worries. With a total mess still stuck in his head, he waited for his brain to recover during the long night.

However, things didn't go as he expected. He had been having weird dreams for the whole night, and when he woke up, he still felt hot and uncomfortable as if he was in a stuffy room. He looked at himself in the mirror and found his face still slightly blushing.

Suspecting that it was because of the liquor, he gulped down several glasses of water during breakfast, hoping to dilute the liquor inside his body. Luo Qiuling was concerned that he might have gotten a fever and brought him a thermometer. Ye Qin immediately stood up and fled, telling his mother that he wouldn't come home for dinner and maybe would skip the be-

fore-bed soup as well.

Today he and Cheng Feichi were going to have a date in a new shopping center. Ye Qin arrived first, so he walked around on the first floor and bought two frappuccinos while waiting for Cheng Feichi. When the latter finally made it here, the iced drink had nearly reached room temperature.

"Drink it! If everything melts, it won't taste as good." Ye Qin urged him. Seeing the sweat on Cheng Feichi's forehead, he said, "Don't tell me you came here by bike."

Cheng Feichi nodded. "There's no direct bus service between my home and here. The subway would take a lot of time, too. I was afraid that I'd be caught up in traffic."

The distance between Yulin Compound and this shopping center was at least four miles. Ye Qin was speechless. *My boyfriend has neither a decent outfit nor enough money to get a cab! How would others judge them?*

Therefore, he dragged Cheng Feichi into a menswear store. He picked a baseball jacket that was appropriate for the season, secretly lifting it against Cheng Feichi's body to estimate his size, and paid for it.

To the left of this store was the exclusive store of a sportswear brand. Ye Qin picked two pairs of sneakers. He tried on one and let Cheng Feichi put on the other half of the pair, making up a good reason. "It's really annoying to keep changing shoes. If you wear them for me, I can see how they look better."

Cheng Feichi found it somewhat strange, but still did as he had been told. Ye Qin asked Cheng Feichi to walk around with the new shoes on and see if he felt comfortable. Once Cheng Feichi said yes, Ye Qin went directly to the counter.

They had only visited half of the stores in this section, but Cheng Feichi was already exerting himself to hold so many bags. Yet Ye Qin didn't seem to stop here. He took Cheng Feichi to an

exclusive denim store, where he found a pair of light blue trousers to be particularly cool. He got the same trousers in different sizes for Cheng Feichi, shoving Cheng Feichi into the fitting room, stuffing the baseball jacket and sneakers into Cheng Feichi's hands as well.

"Put on all of them and let me see if they look good on you."

Cheng Feichi would be an idiot if he still didn't realize that Ye Qin was buying clothes for him. He held out his arm against the closing door. "I have clothes to wear."

Having been seen through, Ye Qin didn't panic. He blinked his eyes and looked at Cheng Feichi from between the door and its frame. "Your clothes got wet in the rain last night."

Cheng Feichi was caught off guard. "It doesn't matter. I can still wear them after they're clean."

Ye Qin shook his head. "No, it's not the same thing. You were in the rain because of me, so I gotta make it up for you with a new outfit."

Cheng Feichi knew that he was trying to make amends, but he thought it was unnecessary. He pushed the door open. "The tag's still on. It's not too late to return them all."

Ye Qin leaned his whole body against the door, trying to keep the door closed with his weight. "It doesn't work that way! I will lose face if we return the clothes I just bought! I've bought them for you, why can't you just put them on? I want my boyfriend to be neat and handsome...can you do that for me?"

Cheng Feichi stopped pushing.

Ye Qin finally got Cheng Feichi into the fitting room. He breathed heavily with his hands holding on to the wall and asked, "By the way, you never let me pay the bills. Are you treating me like a girl?"

In the end, Ye Qin made Cheng Feichi put the new clothes on.

Cheng Feichi was tall with perfect body proportions. In their baggy school uniform, he could still shine like a model. The well-designed brand clothes would only make him more handsome. When he left the fitting room, the two female shop assistants were literally staring at him. They gasped with admiration at how the trousers fit Cheng Feichi amazingly and praised Ye Qin for his great taste.

Ye Qin was as proud as a peacock. Condescending to adjust the hem of the coat for Cheng Feichi, he compared their heights and murmured, with nose wrinkled, "How could you be so much taller than me..."

Having heard every word, Cheng Feichi comforted gently, "You're the perfect height."

Their closeness pinged on the shop assistants' radar, and one guessed, "Are you brothers? You're very close."

Cheng Feichi smiled and was about to answer her when Ye Qin pulled a long face. "Not brothers," he dropped these two words before quickly exiting the store.

Ye Qin still looked very upset by the time they had lunch. He kept gulping down juice without taking a look at the delicious steamed pork ribs Cheng Feichi had put into his bowl.

Cheng Feichi thought he was probably still upset about how he declined the new clothes, so he put the jacket back on, which had been taken off earlier because of the powerful heating, demonstrating to Ye Qin that he really liked the clothes.

Ye Qin gave him a side glance, put the glass of juice down, and finally started talking, "What are you doing? Don't you feel hot?"

Ye Qin knew how unreasonable he was being; his rage must seem unaccountable in Cheng Feichi's view. But he just didn't know how to hide his true feelings. The word "brothers" embarrassed him as much as a punch right in his face, radiating pierc-

ing hotness.

Cheng Feichi adjusted the coat and answered, "No." And then he quickly added, "It's really nice."

Ye Qin didn't really care about his comment on the jacket. Considering how much it cost, of course it was nice. On a second thought, Ye Qin was reminded that he was using Ye Jinxiang's money. Cheng Feichi was also Ye Jinxiang's son, so this was the natural and right thing to do. Ye Qin didn't know whether he should continue being upset, or secretly mock his father and feel satisfied.

The mixed feelings only lingered until the end of lunch time. After they finished the meal, Cheng Feichi bought him a milk-flavored ice cream. Ye Qin squinted in satisfaction once he had the first lick. Yet he was also wondering: *I've had the same ice cream before. Why didn't I realize how yummy it is back then?*

There were no interesting movies in the cinema that day. After Ye Qin had had the ice cream, he took Cheng Feichi to a video arcade. He traded money for 300 game coins and planned to spend the whole afternoon here.

Holding the basket full of game coins with both arms, Ye Qin went through the crowd and ran into some people he knew at the side of the basketball shooting machine.

Zhou Feng stuffed the big doll he had just won into Liao Yifang's hands, opening his arms trying to embrace Ye Qin. "It must be serendipity that we meet here!"

Ye Qin dodged his arms so that Zhou Feng didn't get to touch him.

Liao Yifang's head appeared from behind the big bear doll and he exclaimed, "Ye-tongxue! And Cheng-tongxue! You're both here!"

The date became a double date.

Ye Qin danced at the DDR machine with Zhou Feng for a while. Upon returning, they found the two nerds discussing things such as wires and photoelectric sensors. Liao Yifang was afraid that Ye Qin and Zhou Feng couldn't understand the conversation, so he explained, "Well, if we get it through, we can build a DDR machine ourselves at home."

Zhou Feng guarded the egos of academic underachievers. "We dance here because we feel like dancing here. What's the point of dancing alone at home?"

Ye Qin didn't say anything. He accepted the bottled water that Cheng Feichi gave him and took several gulps of it. Zhou Feng invited him to play the shooting machine, but he waved his hands. "I need a rest." And then he shoved Cheng Feichi. "Go ahead. Beat him for me."

Cheng Feichi walked that way. Zhou Feng, however, began to feel a bit embarrassed. Probably because he was reminded of what he did to Cheng Feichi in the convenience store last year, gone was his "little master" air when he explaining the rules and giving tips to Cheng Feichi.

Liao Yifang sat on the only vacant seat beside Ye Qin. He was holding the huge bear like a dear child and let it rest on his lap. The size of the bear made it a little difficult for him to talk. "Do you and Cheng-tongxue often come here?"

His thin frame was totally obstructed by the huge bear. Ye Qin couldn't bear it anymore, pushing the head of the bear aside. "Yep. Why are you two together?"

Liao Yifang let out an "Uh," looking bashful. He licked his lips before answering, "I was resting at home, but he asked me to watch a movie with him all of a sudden."

"He asked you out?"

"Yep."

"Where did you get this doll? Aren't you tired of holding it

after such a long time?"

Liao Yifang became more bashful. "He got it, and then gave it to me as a gift. The lockers near the self-checkout aren't big enough."

Ye Qin had a strange feeling, but he didn't know what to ask next. Thus he switched his eyes to the two boys shooting basketballs.

Following his sight, Liao Yifang's eyes fell on Cheng Feichi as well. Then he turned back to Ye Qin's eyes and posed the question that had been lingering in his mind. "Ye-tongxue, are you and Cheng-tongxue...dating?"

Ye Qin nearly jumped to his feet. He took a few deep breaths to keep himself calm and answered with a proper expression, "No way. We're friends. That's all."

Apart from being the class monitor of Class No. 2, Liao Yifang also took charge of the Division of Student Discipline in the Students' Union. He was the one who wore a red armband from morning to night with a small notebook, taking down names of the students who broke the school rules. He was on the side of the Director of Teaching and Learning, not his schoolmates. Who knew if he would betray them someday just to get his work done?

"Ye-tongxue, don't worry. I won't sell you out to the teachers." Liao Yifang seemed to have sensed his concern. Wrapping his free arm around the bear's neck, he reached for his own face and adjusted his glasses. "Even if you're in a relationship, it doesn't matter. You are sunny and cheerful, while he's hardworking and excellent. You're a good match. I'm sure you can help each other and become better versions of yourselves together."

Ye Qin was speechless. *I didn't know that dating could bring so many benefits.*

In the evening, they enjoyed hot pot together. When Liao

Yifang and Zhou Feng left to choose the condiments they needed, Ye Qin explained to Cheng Feichi, "Well, here's the thing. The reason why Zhou Feng was being so unfriendly was that the girl he likes liked you. Now she's not into you anymore, so...anyways, he's a bit childish. Don't take it personally."

Cheng Feichi didn't care much about it from the beginning. He only took the past farce as child's play, not to mention how much time had passed ever since that night. He nodded to show that he didn't mind, yet as if suddenly reminded of something, he asked, "So...you took shots at me just to avenge him or what?"

Cheng Feichi's question was right to the point. Ye Qin's heart was beating fast and he got agitated. He bit the chopsticks and stammered, "Well...it was not only for him."

Cheng Feichi was in for more. "And for what else?"

Ye Qin was always bolder when there were only the two of them, so he lied very directly. "I did it because you're so handsome and I was interested in you. Is that enough?"

Ye Qin finished the line and thought to himself: *It's not entirely a lie. At least the first half is true.*

"Yes."

Cheng Feichi smiled and fetched a glass of juice for him.

Ye Qin couldn't look straight into his eyes because he felt guilty. He drank the juice and touched his own face. It was burning so hot that could be used to fry an egg.

Perhaps because it wasn't a school day, the boys were feeling quite at ease and had a pleasant meal together.

In the end, with several glasses of beer down his throat, Zhou Feng started to call Cheng Feichi his buddy, saying that their gang was just short of someone as outstanding as him, so Cheng Feichi must come to their parties and have fun with them next time.

On the way back home, Ye Qin was sitting behind Cheng

Feichi on the bike. He didn't have the time to fully enjoy the exclusive VIP seat. Instead, he kept nagging about how ridiculous Zhou Feng could be every time he was drunk and how childish he actually was—he could still be holding a grudge against Cheng Feichi for "stealing" his girlfriend! All in all, Cheng Feichi shouldn't trust Zhou Feng and shouldn't be close to him either.

Ye Qin didn't want Cheng Feichi to be anywhere near his usual gang. He couldn't figure out the exact reasons, but he just didn't feel like it.

Cheng Feichi promised to comply with everything Ye Qin demanded without even asking why.

Somehow Ye Qin was annoyed by this response. When they reached a narrower street and Cheng Feichi peddled a bit slower, Ye Qin pulled on his jacket. "Hey, there must be a lot of girls that are really into you, right?"

Cheng Feichi denied, "No."

At that, Ye Qin turned up his nose. "Don't treat me like a three-year-old. I've already heard about some of them."

He barely finished the sentence when he heard a camera's shutter sound. Turning his head, Ye Qin saw two girls pushing each other to the front to hide themselves instead. They were still holding their cellphones, so clearly, this was a crime scene of someone taking stealthies but forgetting to mute their phones.

What was also clear was that they were not interested in Ye Qin, because his face was covered by the coat.

Ye Qin was furious. He even wanted to grab the coat off Cheng Feichi so that he couldn't attract these girls anymore. Though Cheng Feichi's charm didn't come from the clothes; it was his face that played a crucial role.

Ye Qin found that he was always annoyed at Cheng Feichi whenever he met him. But when they had to part ways, he still

found it hard to leave Cheng Feichi.

When they arrived at Ye Qin's compound, Ye Qin started kicking small pebbles with his toe, bowing his head. "Well...tomorrow...I can stay at the school for lunch, right?"

It took Cheng Feichi a few seconds to realize what Ye Qin was thinking about. He was trying to remind him with subtlety that he should make lunch for the two of them. He smiled and said, "Sure. What would you like to have?"

Ye Qin was yet not cheeky enough to order dishes, so he said, "You...you make the call." He waited for a little while, but finding that Cheng Feichi didn't have anything to say, he turned around. "I'll leave now. Be safe on the way home."

"Wait." Cheng Feichi stopped him.

Ye Qin quickly turned back. "Yes?"

Cheng Feichi stared at him for quite some time. It seemed that he was trying to say something, but at last he merely let out a long breath. "Nothing. Go home."

Ye Qin didn't know what was going on in Cheng Feichi's mind, so he left. When he was having a bath at home, he kept wondering about what Cheng Feichi had wanted. Suddenly he had an idea: *Was he waiting for me to kiss him?!*

At first, the idea made him a bit uneasy, but he soon began to feel so proud of himself, as if his charm was officially proven now.

Therefore, the next evening, at the same spot, Ye Qin generously kissed Cheng Feichi on his cheek again.

It was a hurried kiss. Perhaps Cheng Feichi hadn't seen this coming either, as he unconsciously moved slightly aside when Ye Qin approached him. As a result, Ye Qin missed the right spot, and his lips accidentally brushed on Cheng Feichi's lower lip. It felt dry and warm.

For a short while, the two of them froze, as if someone had

put a spell on them.

Many thoughts flashed across Ye Qin's mind, every one of them telling him to act in a cool, natural and easy way. He'd better put on a wry smile, wrap his arms around Cheng Feichi's neck and say, "Darling, you taste so sweet."

But he couldn't. He still chose the worst option—he ran away.

The next morning, Ye Qin texted Cheng Feichi during the class hour as if nothing had happened. "Have you come up with any ideas? What do you want me to call you?"

Cheng Feichi didn't answer to his question directly. "I know what I want to call you."

Ye Qin at once asked him what it was, but Cheng Feichi didn't tell him, even when Ye Qin threatened that he would stop talking to him.

Several days went by and it was Monday again. Ye Qin became smarter this time. Pushing Cheng Feichi aside to heat up the meal, he checked Cheng Feichi's phone behind his back. Cheng Feichi didn't have a password on his cellphone, and the numbers of all his contacts were saved with their real names, including Ye Qin's.

...Well no, not exactly.

Ye Qin was so surprised that he held the phone a bit closer to his eyes to make 200% sure of it. Cheng Feichi had mistyped the character "钦 (Qin)" as "软 (Ruan)"?

Well, as a straight-A student, Cheng Feichi wouldn't make a stupid mistake like that. Ye Qin was certain that he did it on purpose.

Why would he use the character that means "soft" as a substitute for my name? Which part of me on earth is soft?

Ye Qin rested his chin on his arms and kept thinking. An idea suddenly struck him. It stunned him so much that he wid-

ened his eyes and his chin slipped from his arms. His forehead fell on the desk, making a loud noise.

Ye Qin thought angrily: *Zhou Feng's dirty thoughts must've affected me. Otherwise, how would I ever assume that the word was referring to my lips?*

This was more than Ye Qin could handle. He was not a timorous type of person, but this time he hesitated again and again. Before he managed to ask Cheng Feichi about it, Friday came.

They had a different curriculum in the new semester, thus gone was the opportunity to meet each other at the recreational yard. Zhou Feng was feeling upset about this change, claiming that he planned to play basketball with Cheng Feichi again.

"Again? You only played on the basketball shooting machine with him!" Ye Qin didn't want to get his hands dirty, so he dropped the ball on the ground and kicked it like a football. "Don't get him in trouble. I'll take care of him myself."

Zhou Feng smiled wryly. "You said you didn't care about him. I don't think so. You almost look like a helicopter parent now."

The weird comparison set the veins on his forehead jutting. "Eww...stop it. Don't ever say that again."

Zhou Feng wouldn't stop. "I saw you two going home on the same bike yesterday. You once laughed at Yiran for wanting to 'sit in a van with a guy like that,' but now you sit on the back seat of his bike and smile like a sunflower."

Fully irritated, Ye Qin retorted, "Are you serious? Who smiled? I was pretending to be his boyfriend. Isn't it something that I'm supposed to do? I'm not like you; you stick with the class monitor without making things clear..."

The last few words that came out of Ye Qin's mouth were

vague. Zhou Feng was confused. "What's wrong with me and Yuanyuan?"

The nickname forced Ye Qin to shake off goose bumps again. "You call him 'Yuanyuan.' You kiss him, hug him, and take him out to watch movies. Now you're telling me that nothing's going on between you two?"

Zhou Feng tilted his head. "Movie? Right, you're talking about the time we met at the cinema." He stabilized the basketball that Ye Qin kicked to him and shrugged. "I planned to take Yiran out, but she got caught up. You weren't willing to come, and I didn't want to watch the movie alone, so I could only call him."

This was totally different from what Liao Yifang told Ye Qin. Ye Qin looked doubtful.

Zhou Feng at once realized that there must have been some misunderstanding. He laughed as if he heard an unbelievable joke. "He told you that I asked him out? Ha ha, told you so. He's just the kind of ridiculous person who believes whatever you tell him."

With these words, he whistled at Liao Yifang, who was running at the other end of the recreational yard, and blew a kiss to him. Seeing this, Liao Yifang stumbled and nearly fell down.

Ye Qin considered the matter for a while and found it rather inappropriate, so he warned him as if he himself had some experience in dealing with relationships. "You don't really like him? Then stop flirting with him and giving him false hope. What if he takes it for real?"

Zhou Feng was caught off guard, but he soon burst out laughing. "Why does it sound so funny, especially when it comes from you? Ha ha ha ha ha ha ha ha..."

Ye Qin was speechless. "..."

Well, though he hated to admit it, they were indeed birds of

a feather. Zhou Feng was actually better than him, considering that he didn't have evil plans for Liao Yifang despite the heartless flirting. As for Ye Qin, he was getting close to Cheng Feichi on purpose, and his intention was so inappropriate and disgusting that it had to be kept as a secret.

The last lesson was extended again in Class No. 1. As soon as the teacher left the classroom, Cheng Feichi gathered all his stuff and walked out in a rush.

When he made a turn in the staircase, he heard someone yelling, "Hey—" He turned his head and saw Ye Qin squatting at the corner of the staircase, reaching his hand out. "Help me up."

Since Cheng Feichi had left the classroom early, when they got to the parking area, most of the students in Class No. 1 hadn't come here yet. Ye Qin didn't ride the bike to school today. Taking advantage of no one being around, he sat on the back seat of Cheng Feichi's bike, threw his backpack to the front and urged him to leave as soon as possible.

When they were on the street, Ye Qin pulled the hem of Cheng Feichi's clothes to slow him down. "Your damn bike felt so bouncy! My butt really hurts."

Cheng Feichi tilted his head. "What about walking for a while?"

Ye Qin hesitated between sitting all the way home and spending more time with Cheng Feichi, eventually making the difficult decision to jump off the bike, albeit unwillingly. He slowly walked behind Cheng Feichi, complaining that he must order a sponge cushion for the seat.

Cheng Feichi thought that the bike was officially going to be an exclusive means of transportation for an over-age kid. As if having sensed what was going on in Cheng Feichi's mind, Ye

Qin cast a sidelong glance at him. "Why do you have on that weird smile? Do you think that I was making a fuss about it?"

Cheng Feichi immediately put on a serious look. "Definitely not. My damn bike is honored to have the opportunity to take you home."

These words were indeed soothing for Ye Qin's ego; he was pleased. The remaining bit of unhappiness was left behind immediately.

Today Cheng Feichi was wearing the new clothes that Ye Qin bought for him. Born well proportioned, he looked slim, tall, and straight. Since the night hadn't fallen yet, Ye Qin looked around as if scouting before a battle. Whichever girl expressed her interest with a glance at Cheng Feichi would receive his cold stare.

Though it was a fake relationship, Ye Qin wouldn't allow anyone to covet his boyfriend.

When they finally reached the gate of the compound, Ye Qin's nerves relaxed. He put his hands behind his back as if he was the boss. "Well, I'm not free during the weekends. You can enjoy the free days yourself."

Cheng Feichi asked him what he was going to do, but Ye Qin didn't have the patience to explain things. "Just go out and have fun with my mom."

Cheng Feichi nodded. "Have a good time. Call me if anything happens."

"Nothing will happen." Ye Qin pursed his lips.

Cheng Feichi smiled but said nothing.

This Sunday was the anniversary of Ye Qin's grandfather's death. According to the family traditions, the whole Ye Family should go visit the elderly man's tomb.

It was built on a mountain on the outskirts of the city. The

place was not quite accessible, so Ye Qin and his mother went there by car a day earlier in the morning. They stayed in the villa left by his grandfather, which was also used as a vacation home.

Luo Qiuling had had the villa cleaned and prepared beforehand. Ye Qin had a good sleep upon their arrival: for him, getting up early counted as one of the most tiring things in the world.

When he woke up, lunch time had already passed. He walked downstairs with sleepy eyes. Having only taken two steps down the stairs, he heard his mother's anxious voice. "It might rain in a while, then you won't be able to drive uphill. We have to leave first thing in the next mor...What business meal? Can't you postpone it...But you promised me...Wait, don't hang up yet! Hello?"

She stopped talking. It was clear that the other side hung up on her.

From where Ye Qin was standing, he could only see the lonely and sad view of Luo Qiuling's back. She faced the window and sat there alone, as if waiting for the dark cloud to expand and swallow the last stroke of sunlight.

Maybe because he had slept too much in the afternoon, Ye Qin couldn't lay still at night. He got up and drink half a glass of water, before walking barefoot to the door of his mother's bedroom. He stayed there for a while but heard nothing. Returning to his room, he finished the remaining half glass of water, lay down again and forced himself to close his eyes.

On the next day, unsurprisingly, Ye Jinxiang didn't show up. Ye Qin climbed the mountains with his mother. The trail was slippery because of the rain. Ye Qin kept telling funny stories from school to cheer his mother up. He didn't even summon his tears when accidentally falling on the ground, joking that his grandfather must hate to see his ugly crying face.

In fact, Ye Qin could hardly remember the face of his grandfather. In his vague memory, his grandfather was a serious elderly man who always smelt of traditional herbal medicine. The only thing he could still recall was that grandfather bought a Disney backpack for him right before he entered primary school. However, he preferred Spider Man at that time, so the new backpack had been kept in the closet ever since.

If he knew that grandfather would leave in such a short time, he would definitely have worn the Mickey Mouse backpack and shown it to him on the first Saturday of that semester.

But there were no "if"s in the real world.

They arrived early, and the cemetery was empty and quiet. Ye Qin kowtowed towards the tombstone three times and then left his mother to be alone with her dear father. He himself walked away in order to wait.

After being washed by the rain, the forest was deep and of a vivid emerald green. The hills were shrouded in mist. Ye Qin took a deep breath and savored the earthy smell in the humid air, which flew into every corner of his chest.

Ye Qin took several deep breaths, then stretched his neck and chest backwards. He looked past the forest of tombstones, his sight finally falling upon his mother, who was sitting before the tomb. The tombstones of his grandparents were standing together, while his mother was talking to them. She looked very peaceful.

She was telling her parents about the family affairs, that the family company had grown bigger, that the family wealth had accumulated, with properties brought in recently. Brought up in a wealthy family, she was a real lady in nature. Too kind and gentle, she could not bring herself to make a scene. She had never complained about her fate; even when things got really tough for her, she would only report the good news.

Others might take her as a good, dutiful wife, but Ye Qin could only think that his mother had resigned herself to her fate.

He guessed that his mother might have regretted her choice, feeling sorry for herself for being tricked into marriage by Ye Jinxiang's sweet speeches. She had by no means expected such a greedy snob under his decent cover. Even now, she still didn't dare to tell the truth in front of her parents' tombstones, afraid of setting them into worries and away from peace.

But Ye Qin was not like his mother. He couldn't bite the bullet and tolerate everything that his father had done. If not for the fact that he would rather not cause trouble for Luo Qiuling on such an important day, he would've been calling Ye Jinxiang nonstop by now.

He clung to his cellphone for quite some time. The uncontrollable fury that had been growing in his chest was burning even harder. Even deep breaths didn't have any use now. Ye Qin went for someone also relevant but easier to deal with—he called Cheng Feichi.

His original plan was to vent all his anger on him and just be as unreasonable as he would like. After all, Cheng Feichi wouldn't ask questions. However, Cheng Feichi had hardly picked up when he asked Ye Qin why he didn't sleep for a bit longer. This tender greeting magically exterminated all his anger.

Ye Qin was like a balloon blowing up because of unexpected heat. Hanging his head, he leant against the trunk of a nearby tree and tried to come up with something. He asked Cheng Feichi whether he had had breakfast.

"Yes, I had three-dice buns. What about you?"

"Me too." Ye Qin was indeed the sort of sleepyhead who forgot what he had for breakfast when he didn't have enough sleep, so he just went with the flow in conversation. "Well, what

are the three dices?"

Cheng Feichi was very patient. "Ground chicken, ground pork, and diced bamboo shoots."

"Ah." That sounded delicious. Ye Qin unconsciously licked his lips. "Where are you heading?"

"Times Square."

"For work?"

"Yep."

"So your mom...is home alone?"

"Yes, what about her? Are you going to spend time with her for me?"

Ye Qin only wanted to know whether his father was with Cheng Feichi's mother, but he didn't expect that Cheng Feichi would invite him to his home. Thinking about where they were in this relationship, Ye Qin started to stammer, "Wha...wha... what c...can...I do with your mom? I'm not a pupil who needs tutoring."

Cheng Feichi chuckled in a low voice, which instantly made Ye Qin blush. When he was eager to hang up, Cheng Feichi asked, "Why do you call me?"

Ye Qin stopped and answered with perfect assurance, "Do I always have to come up with a reason before I call you?"

"Not at all."

Cheng Feichi was saving his face by not mentioning their conversation last Friday night, but Ye Qin was already getting unhappy. Insatiable, he continued complaining, "If I don't call you, you'll never contact me." And then he added in a very natural way, "You don't care about me at all."

However, the second he finished the sentence, Ye Qin was shocked by his own words. He must be crazy at that moment.

Cheng Feichi was apparently surprised as well, because he didn't reply until a few moments later. "Didn't you say that you

needed to be with your mom during the weekend? I was afraid that I might interrupt something." And then he added, "Of course I care."

He wasn't speaking in a loud voice, especially the final two words, but Ye Qin still heard what he said, quite clearly. He used his nail to peel off a small piece of bark and squeezed it in his fist. The small piece broke into even more tiny pieces, just like his pride and principles. He asked in a nasal voice, "What do you care so much about?"

Cheng Feichi didn't think as much about these things as he did, so he answered very bluntly, "You."

On Monday, on the recreational yard at High School No. 6, the sweet young couple that had been separated for as many as 64 hours finally saw each other. However, all they had were a few seconds to exchange a friendly look under the guise of two people acquainted.

For the whole duration of the ceremony and the morning exercise that followed, Ye Qin kept staring at the back of Cheng Feichi's head. The students between the two of them didn't exist in his gaze.

They didn't manage to have lunch together, as because Cheng Feichi texted Ye Qin that he was needed at the teacher's office to help print exam papers. He told Ye Qin to go home for lunch or take the lunch box on his desk and have the meal alone. What was the point of having lunch without Cheng Feichi? Ye Qin chose to go home and secretly cursed the lazy teacher who unfairly took advantage of a student a thousand times.

Compared to the meals that Cheng Feichi made for him, the dishes at home were horrible. Seeing how little he had eaten, the maid was worried that he might be sick. Receiving the terrifying news, Luo Qiuling forced Ye Qin to take his temperature

several times to make sure that he was physically okay.

In the afternoon, even Zhou Feng could tell that Ye Qin was unhappy. "What's up? You guys had too much fun on the weekend and you're feeling exhausted now?"

Ye Qin stomped on Zhou Feng's toes. "I didn't spend the weekend with him."

Zhou Feng gave a grimace of pain, retorting, "Oh...I see. For lovers, one day spent in separation is like three years."

Ye Qin would never admit that he was missing Cheng Feichi, but now he was thinking to himself: *He said that he cared about me so much, but he never came to me! What a liar!*

They had been together for no more than two months. How dare Cheng Feichi start lying to him at such an early stage? Ye Qin was furious. If chemistry class hadn't been about to start, he would leave the classroom at once.

During the first of the night sessions, teachers responsible for the senior grades of the school had a meeting together. Only several middle school teachers were left patrolling to and from the teaching building, checking up on the students. Ye Qin seized the opportunity to put his hoodie up, leave his own classroom, and sneak into Cheng Feichi's.

The students rarely had the chance to spend a night without the teachers watching over them, thus even the straight-A students were feeling more at ease. After the first class began, the classroom of Class No. 1 was still not full, and the students were chatting and laughing.

The boy sitting next to Cheng Feichi wasn't there as well. Ye Qin sat down at his deskmate's seat and picked up a book to cover his face. Skipping the step of announcing his arrival, he asked Cheng Feichi in a low voice, "Why are you sitting in the back row? Your teacher arranged the seats?"

Cheng Feichi was stunned, his eyes fixed on him for quite a while. Then he dropped the pen in his hand. Following Ye Qin's example, he picked up another book to cover his own face and shrank his neck, so that his eyes were at the same level as Ye Qin's. "The students sitting behind me couldn't see the blackboard."

Ye Qin thumped the desk. "That's their fault! They're too short!" Then he revealed his eyes from behind the book to look around. "Who are those students? I'm gonna have a talk with them."

Ye Qin's eyes bulged like a hooligan about to defend his best buddy. Amused while slightly annoyed, Cheng Feichi tried to calm him. "It's okay. I can see the board very clearly from here."

Ye Qin was about to roll up his sleeves and stand up. "No way. If you don't tell me who they are, I'll ask the head teacher of your class."

Cheng Feichi couldn't stop him. In a moment of desperation, took hold of Ye Qin's hand.

It only took one minute for Ye Qin to go completely silent. He rested his head on his arm behind the standing book and let Cheng Feichi attach a band-aid to his other wrist.

Cheng Feichi's hand was dry and warm, while Ye Qin's hand was cold, its inner part covered with cold sweat that was soon vaporized once their hands held together.

The back row was a good place for secret stuff. Only two or three students turned around to check what they were up to and quickly went back to their own business, since they had seen nothing.

The wound was on one side of Ye Qin's palm and very close to his wrist. Cheng Feichi asked him how he got it. Ye Qin

pouted his lips and complained, "I fell down when climbing the mountain. The trail was too slippery." Meanwhile, he moved the other hand behind his back. "My butt was worse. I couldn't see it myself, but the cheeks could be swelling because of the pain."

Cheng Feichi didn't stop working on Ye Qin's wound, but raised his head to look at Ye Qin in a strange way. Ye Qin suddenly realized how inappropriate his talk was. He moved himself a bit farther from Cheng Feichi and explained in embarrassment, "I...I wasn't inviting you to help me check them out for me..."

Cheng Feichi didn't respond. He got the wound well covered with two band-aids stuck together, then slightly pressed them and helped Ye Qin move his wrist around. "Do you feel any pain?"

Ye Qin shook his head like a pellet drum. A scab was already forming on it; how would he feel the pain anymore? Having made sure that everything was fine, Cheng Feichi let go of his hand and returned to his schoolwork.

Ye Qin curled his fingers to feel the lingering heat on his palm and started to regret the answer he had just given. Sluggishly, he took out a crumpled exercise book from the pocket of the school uniform and started leafing through it with much noise.

While doing this, he asked Cheng Feichi, "Where's your deskmate?"

"He went home."

Having made sure that no one would come to disturb them, Ye Qin got a pen from Cheng Feichi's pencil box and started to do his homework as if he had all the reason to stay.

But he was just pretending. The truth was that he didn't pay any attention to the lines before his eyes. Having been busy with other stuff since his arrival, he was suddenly reminded of why he

came here today in the first place. He began drawing and scribbling on the book, writing two nearly unrecognizable characters "想" (want) between two formulas, and then adding a small and light character "不" (not) between the two.

He sneaked a peek at the one sitting beside him. Cheng Feichi was fully concentrating on his book. He was reading the words on it very carefully, his lips tightly compressed and his jawline very defined. *Apparently, he isn't thinking about me.*

Ye Qin thought to himself what a smooth talker Cheng Feichi was, but he didn't plan to disturb Cheng Feichi. Putting down the pen, he rested his head and arms on the desk in order to take a nap. After all, the teachers wouldn't be back so soon.

In the pleasant spring evening, Ye Qin fell asleep very fast in the warm weather.

He dreamed of a maidenhair tree, under which someone stood.

It was late autumn, and the cold wind kept blowing and roaring. The person under the tree was as cold and serious as when Ye Qin met him for the first time. His mouth was moving, but Ye Qin couldn't hear what he was talking about.

Ye Qin was afraid, but he couldn't control the desire to get closer. But when he was finally standing in front of him, Ye Qin saw the frost in his eyes and heard his question, "Why did you lie to me?"

It is natural for people to dream about things that they think about all the time. But it was quite unusual that Ye Qin would wake up from a nightmare. It was even more rare that, all of a sudden, he couldn't see anything after he woke up.

Extreme fear set him jumping to his feet. He was tripped by something he couldn't see. His body askew, he fell backwards.

Someone caught him before he actually fell onto the

ground. In the overwhelming darkness, Ye Qin felt that with one hand seizing his arm, the other holding his waist, the person was helping him settle straight. He heard him whispering, "It's a blackout. Sit still."

The same voice in the nightmare. The only difference was that in reality, it was far from being cold or scary.

Ye Qin's eyes were gradually adapting to the darkness, and he heard the noises surrounding him. The students in the class-room were moving restlessly. Several students turned on flash-lights and, with the help of the light, looked out of the windows. The teaching building where Class No. 2 was at was in complete darkness, too. Looking to the other side of the teaching build-ing, only in the high-rise buildings across the street did they see some lights.

The whole school was going through a power outage.

When Ye Qin sat down, his body was still stiff, either because of the nightmare or of nearly falling down. He breathed heavily a few times, but couldn't speak.

Cheng Feichi was still grabbing his arm and he slightly squeezed his wrist. "Ye Qin?"

Hearing such a soothing voice calling his name, Ye Qin immediately embraced him, like a drowning man that had just found a swim ring.

Cheng Feichi hesitated only for a second before putting his arms around Ye Qin and asking tentatively, "Are you afraid of the dark?"

Ye Qin clung to Cheng Feichi, shaking his head, then nod-ding, before shaking his head again.

Cheng Feichi gave a laugh because of his self-contradicting response. He patted Ye Qin's back to comfort him. "Relax. Ev-erything's fine."

Ye Qin couldn't bring himself to tell him that he was actu-

ally terrified, nor to say what kind of dream he had had.

As soon as he had calmed down, he pushed Cheng Feichi away and asked, "What did you call me?"

The classroom was filled with noise now. The quiet, calm, and obedient students in Class No. 1 finally revealed their true selves in the darkness. They were chatting with each other happily or singing freely. Some boys pointed the flashlights at the classrooms in the nearby teaching building and shouted to the students there, asking them whether they had finished homework. The other side responded, "No! Are you gonna let me copy yours?" Then the boys all burst into laughter.

Amidst such noise, Cheng Feichi hadn't hear Ye Qin's question clearly. He tilted his head to Ye Qin, he ear fully revealed. "What?"

Ye Qin couldn't see his expression. He just thought that Cheng Feichi's body posture was asking for a kiss.

Endowed with enormous courage in the dark, Ye Qin took a deep breath, approached Cheng Feichi, and suddenly kissed him on his cheek. Then, relying on impulse, he raised the real question that had been keeping him wondering for so many days.

"Your nickname for me was Ye Ruan. I'm asking you, which part of me is soft?"

He couldn't figure out the answer. He had to get to the bottom of this question.

Cheng Feichi wouldn't be stunned by cheek kissing a second time. This time, he wasn't stupefied for too long. He looked straight at Ye Qin through the darkness, raised his arm a little bit, and caught Ye Qin's left hand that was hanging at his side.

He first squeezed Ye Qin's fingertips that were slightly colder than his own fingers, and then, with thumb pressing the center of Ye Qin's had, he wrapped the latter's palm with his own

hand and said, "This is soft."

He then moved raised the other hand upwards, travelled all the way past Ye Qin's shoulder and slightly squeezed Ye Qin's cheek. "This is soft, too."

Ye Qin thought that he should draw himself back from Cheng Feichi's touch, but his body froze. He didn't move an inch.

The light coming from the cellphone of the boy sitting in front of them was dim, but bright enough to let them see each other. Ye Qin's eyes were very big, his pupils sheer black. Two slightly flickering lights danced in his eyes, as if they were the reflection of two people in the rippling water under the moonlight.

When Cheng Feichi approached him again, Ye Qin swallowed hard. Though he was feeling nervous, he still managed to retort, "I'm not soft! I could be harder than you could ever imagine!"

He immediately realized that what embarrassing connotations the word "hard" could have, and his whole face turned red.

He couldn't hide his head in a hole on the ground, but he could still run away. He was ready to jump to his feet and flee, but he forgot that his hand was still in Cheng Feichi's grip. Struggling several times, he didn't manage to get away. Raising his head, he was about to ask Cheng Feichi what he wanted, when Cheng Feichi's face suddenly moved so much closer to him that he didn't have the opportunity to pose the question anymore. His mouth was sealed with a pair of lips.

Ye Qin wasn't into physical intimacy. Even his dear mother needed to knock three times before entering his bedroom. When he was still an infant, any relatives who adored him enough to want to either hug or kiss him would be rewarded with whipping arms, maddening screams, and a lot of tears. Since then, all relatives knew that they should keep away from Ye Qin no matter how much they adored him.

So this was Ye Qin's first kiss, in every sense. One that he

didn't have a plan for and couldn't get away from.

Cheng Feichi's lips were as dry as his hands, albeit much warmer. He gently kissed the corner of Ye Qin's lips, sometimes parting his own lips to cover Ye Qin's upper lip with them.

But Ye Qin's upper lip was not as plump as the lower one. Cheng Feichi gave several pecks on it, but it was unable to find a good spot. Thus he moved towards Ye Qin's lower lip again, and caught the second when Ye Qin breathed in to slowly wipe his lips across Ye Qin's.

Their breaths were squeezed and heated up in the narrow space between their faces. Cheng Feichi was apparently a rookie at kissing as well. Ye Qin could feel that he was just moving his lips around as if he was doing an experiment. Therefore, the kisses weren't so intense, but they were mind-blowing enough for Ye Qin. Weakness came to his limbs, while fire was burning in his chest. His hands were again covered with sweat because of the unbearable heat.

Teenagers had infinite passion for love. Neither of them wanted to wait any longer. They were on the same page, but didn't choose to express their feelings in the same way. The kissing worked perfectly well in the moment. Cheng Feichi's eagerness to comfort him, Cheng Feichi's unspeakable tenderness towards him—Ye Qin got them all figured out.

A whole century seemed to have passed them by, but they also felt as if only a few seconds had passed. Cheng Feichi pulled away from Ye Qin's lips, which had already turned moist and red.

"Nothing's softer than these," he whispered.

Glossary

- *A-, Xiao-*: friendly prefixes attached to a person's name to show closeness.
- *-tongxue*: "classmate", added as a suffix to a school peer's name.
- *Ge, gege*: literally "older brother", but also used between people as a friendly nickname, or occasionally flirtatiously between romantic partners.
- *Di, didi*: literally "younger brother", but also used between people as a friendly nickname, or occasionally flirtatiously between romantic partners.
- *Jie, jiejie*: literally "older sister", but also used between people as a friendly nickname, or occasionally flirtatiously between romantic partners.
- *Mei, meimei*: literally "younger sister", but also used between people as a friendly nickname, or occasionally flirtatiously between romantic partners.
- *Da-ge, lao-ge*: literally "eldest brother" and "older brother, but also used as a friendly nickname between peers.
- *Laogong*: a term used to refer to one's husband.

Cheng Feichi x Ye Qin

Falling
Volume 01
An imprint of Via Lactea Ltd.

Copyright © Yu Cheng